RANSON'S FOLLY
AND OTHERS

BY

RICHARD HARDING DAVIS

British Library Cataloguing-in-Publication Data
A catalogue record for this book is available from the
British Library

Contents

Richard Harding Davis

Richard Harding Davis was born on 18th April 1864, in Philadelphia, Pennsylvania. He was the son of two writers, Rebecca Harding Davis (a prominent author), and Lemuel Clarke Davis (a journalist and editor of the Philadelphia Public Ledger).

Davis attended Lehigh University and Johns Hopkins University, but was asked to leave both due to neglecting his studies in favour socialising. With some help from his father, Davis was able to find a position as a journalist at the Philadelphia Record, but was soon fired from the post. He then spent a short time at the Philadelphia Press before moving to the New York Evening Sun, where he became a controversial figure, writing on subjects such as execution, abortion, and suicide. He went on to edit Harper's Weekly and write for the New York Herald, The Times, and Scribner's Magazine.

During the Second Boer War in South Africa, Davis was a leading correspondent of the conflict. He saw the war first-hand from both parties perspectives and documented it in his publication With Both Armies (1900). Later in his career he wrote a story about his experience on a United States Navy ship that shelled Cuba as part of the Battle of Santiago de Cuba. His article made the headlines and prompted the

Navy to refuse to allow reporters aboard their vessels for the remainder of the war.

He wrote widely from locations such as the Caribbean, Central America, and even from the perspective of the Japanese forces during the Russo-Japanese War. He also covered the Salonika Front in the First World War, where he spent a time detained by the Germans on suspicion of being a spy.

Davis married twice, first to Cecil Clark in 1899, and then to Bessie McCoy in 1912, with whom he had one daughter. Davis died following a heart attack on 11th April, 1916, at the age of 51.

RANSON'S FOLLY

PART I

The junior officers of Fort Crockett had organized a mess at the post-trader's. "And a mess it certainly is," said Lieutenant Ranson. The dining-table stood between hogsheads of molasses and a blazing log-fire, the counter of the store was their buffet, a pool-table with a cloth, blotted like a map of the Great Lakes, their sideboard, and Indian Pete acted as butler. But none of these things counted against the great fact that each evening Mary Cahill, the daughter of the post-trader, presided over the evening meal, and turned it into a banquet. From her high chair behind the counter, with the cash- register on her one side and the weighing-scales on the other, she gave her little Senate laws, and smiled upon each and all with the kind impartiality of a comrade.

At least, at one time she had been impartial. But of late she smiled upon all save Lieutenant Ranson. When he talked, she now looked at the blazing log-fire, and her cheeks glowed and her eyes seemed to reflect the lifting flame.

For five years, ever since her father brought her from the convent at St. Louis, Mary Cahill had watched officers come and officers go. Her knowledge concerning them, and their public and private affairs, was vast and miscellaneous. She was acquainted with the traditions of every regiment, with its war record, with its peace-time politics, its nicknames, its scandals, even with the earnings of each company-canteen. At Fort Crockett, which lay under her immediate observation, she knew more of what was going forward than did the regimental adjutant, more even than did the colonel's wife. If Trumpeter Tyler flatted on church call, if Mrs. Stickney applied to the quartermaster for three feet of stovepipe, if Lieutenant Curtis were granted two days' leave for quail-shooting, Mary Cahill knew it; and if Mrs. "Captain" Stairs obtained the post-ambulance for a drive to Kiowa City, when Mrs. "Captain" Ross wanted it for a picnic, she knew what words passed between those ladies, and which of the two wept. She knew all of these things, for each evening they were retailed to her by her "boarders." Her boarders were very loyal to Mary Cahill. Her position was a difficult one, and had it not been that the boy- officers were so understanding, it would have been much more difficult. For the life of a regimental post is as circumscribed as the life on a ship-of-war, and it would no more be possible for the ship's barber to rub shoulders with the admiral's epaulets than that a post-trader's child should visit the ladies on the "line," or that the wives of the enlisted men should dine with the young girl from whom they "took in" washing.

So, between the upper and the nether grindstones, Mary Cahill was left without the society of her own sex, and was of necessity forced to content herself with the society of the officers. And the officers played fair. Loyalty to Mary Cahill was a tradition at Fort Crockett, which it was the duty of each succeeding regiment to sustain. Moreover, her father, a dark, sinister man, alive only to money-making, was known to handle a revolver with the alertness of a town-marshal.

Since the day she left the convent Mary Cahill had held but two affections: one for this grim, taciturn parent, who brooded over her as jealously as a lover, and the other for the entire United States Army. The Army returned her affection without the jealousy of the father, and with much more than his effusiveness. But when Lieutenant Ranson arrived from the Philippines, the affections of Mary Cahill became less generously distributed, and her heart fluttered hourly between trouble and joy.

There were two rooms on the first floor of the post-trader's—this big one, which only officers and their women-folk might enter, and the other, the exchange of the enlisted men. The two were separated by a partition of logs and hung with shelves on which were displayed calicoes, tinned meats, and patent medicines. A door, cut in one end of the partition, with buffalo-robes for portieres, permitted Cahill to pass from behind the counter of one store to behind the counter of the other. On one side Mary Cahill served the Colonel's wife with many yards of silk ribbons to be converted into german favors, on the other her father weighed out bears' claws (manufactured in Hartford, Conn., from turkey-bones) to make a necklace for Red Wing, the squaw of the Arrephao chieftain. He waited upon everyone with gravity, and in obstinate silence. No one had ever seen Cahill smile. He himself occasionally joked with others in a grim and embarrassed manner. But no one had ever joked with him. It was reported that he came from New York, where, it was whispered, he had once kept bar on the Bowery for McTurk.

Sergeant Clancey, of G Troop, was the authority for this. But when, presuming on that supposition, he claimed acquaintanceship with Cahill, the post-trader spread out his hands on the counter and stared at the sergeant with cold and disconcerting eyes. "I never kept bar nowhere," he said. "I never been on the Bowery, never been in New York, never been east of Denver in my life. What was it you ordered?"

"Well, mebbe I'm wrong," growled the sergeant.

But a month later, when a coyote howled down near the Indian village, the sergeant said insinuatingly, "Sounds just like the cry of the Whyos, don't it?" And Cahill, who was listening to the wolf, unthinkingly nodded his head.

The sergeant snorted in triumph. "Yah, I told you so!" he cried, "a man that's never been on the Bowery, and knows the call of the Whyo gang! The drinks are on you, Cahill."

The post-trader did not raise his eyes, but drew a damp cloth up and down the counter, slowly and heavily, as a man sharpens a knife on a whetstone.

That night, as the sergeant went up the path to the post, a bullet passed through his hat. Clancey was a forceful man, and forceful men, unknown to themselves, make enemies, so he was uncertain as to whether this came from a trooper he had borne upon too harshly, or whether, In the darkness, he had been picked off for someone else. The next night, as he passed in the full light of the post-trader's windows, a shot came from among the dark shadows of the corral, and when he immediately sought safety in numbers among the Indians, cowboys, and troopers in the exchange, he was in time to see Cahill enter it from the other store, wrapping up a bottle of pain-killer for Mrs. Stickney's cook. But Clancey was not deceived. He observed with satisfaction that the soles and the heels of Cahill's boots were wet with the black mud of the corral.

The next morning, when the exchange was empty, the post-trader turned from arranging cans of condensed milk upon an upper shelf to face the sergeant's revolver. He threw up his hands to the level of his ears as though expressing sharp unbelief, and waited in silence. The sergeant advanced until the gun rested on the counter, Its muzzle pointing at the pit of Cahill's stomach. "You or me has got to leave this post," said the sergeant, "and I can't desert, so I guess it's up to you."

"What did you talk for?" asked Cahill. His attitude was still that of shocked disbelief, but his tone expressed a full acceptance of the situation and a desire to temporize.

"At first I thought it might be that new 'cruity' in F Troop," explained the sergeant "You came near making me kill the wrong man. What harm did I do you by saying you kept bar for McTurk? What's there in that to get hot about?"

"You said I run with the Whyos."

"What the h—l do I care what you've done!" roared the sergeant. "I don't kmow nothing about you, but I don't mean you should shoot me in the back. I'm going to tell this to my bunky, an' if I get shot up, the Troop'll know who done it, and you'll hang for it. Now, what are you going to do?"

Cahill did not tell what he would do; for, from the other store, the low voice of Mary Cahill called, "Father! Oh, father!"

The two men dodged, and eyed each other guiltily. The sergeant gazed at the buffalo-robe portieres with wide-opened eyes. Cahill's hands dropped from the region of his ears, and fell flat upon the counter.

When Miss Mary Cahill pushed aside the portieres Sergeant Clancey, of G Troop, was showing her father the mechanism of the new regulation- revolver. He apparently was having some difficulty with the cylinder, for his face was red. Her father was eying the gun with the critical approval of an expert.

"Father," said Miss Cahill petulantly, "why didn't you answer? Where is the blue stationery—the sort Major Ogden always buys? He's waiting."

The eyes of the post-trader did not wander from the gun before him. "Next to the blank books, Mame," he said. "On the second shelf."

Miss Cahill flashed a dazzling smile at the big sergeant, and whispered, so that the officer in the room behind her might not overhear, "Is he trying to sell you Government property, dad? Don't you touch it. Sergeant, I'm surprised at you tempting my poor father." She pulled the two buffalo-robes close around her neck so that her face only showed between them. It was a sweet, lovely face, with frank, boyish eyes.

"When the major's gone, sergeant," she whispered, "bring your gun around my side of the store and I'll buy it from you."

The sergeant nodded in violent assent, laughing noiselessly and slapping his knee in a perfect ecstasy of delight.

The curtains dropped and the face disappeared.

The sergeant fingered the gun and Cahill folded his arms defiantly.

9

"Well?" he said.

"Well?" asked the sergeant.

"I should think you could see how it is," said Cahill, "without my having to tell you."

"You mean you don't want she should know?"

"My God, no! Not even that I kept a bar."

"Well, I don't know nothing. I don't mean to tell nothing, anyway, so if you'll promise to be good I'll call this off."

For the first time in the history of Fort Crockett, Cahill was seen to smile. "May I reach under the counter NOW?" he asked.

The sergeant grinned appreciatively, and shifted his gun. "Yes, but I'll keep this out until I'm sure it's a bottle," he said, and laughed boisterously.

For an instant, under the cover of the counter, Cahill's hand touched longingly upon the gun that lay there, and then passed on to the bottle beside it. He drew it forth, and there was the clink of glasses.

In the other room Mary Cahill winked at the major, but that officer pretended to be both deaf to the clink of the glasses and blind to the wink. And so the incident was closed. Had it not been for the folly of Lieutenant Ranson it would have remained closed.

A week before this happened a fire had started in the Willow Bottoms among the tepees of some Kiowas, and the prairie, as far as one could see, was bruised and black. From the post it looked as though the sky had been raining ink. At the time all of the regiment but G and H Troops was out on a practice-march, experimenting with a new-fangled tabloid-ration. As soon as it turned the buttes it saw from where the light in the heavens came and the practice-march became a race.

At the post the men had doubled out under Lieutenant Ranson with wet horse-blankets, and while he led G Troop to fight the flames, H Troop, under old Major Stickney, burned a space around the post, across which the men of G Troop retreated, stumbling, with their ears and shoulders wrapped in the smoking blankets. The sparks beat upon them and the flames followed so fast that, as they ran, the blazing grass burned their lacings, and they kicked their gaiters ahead of them.

When the regiment arrived it found everybody at Fort Crockett talking enthusiastically of Ranson's conduct and resentfully of the fact that he had regarded the fire as one which had been started for his especial amusement.

"I assure you," said Mrs. Bolland to the colonel, "if it hadn't been for young Ranson we would have been burned in our beds; but he was most aggravating. He treated it as though it were Fourth of July fireworks. It is the only entertainment we have been able to offer him since he joined in which he has shown the slightest interest." Nevertheless, it was generally admitted that Ranson had saved the post. He had been ubiquitous. He had been seen galloping into the advancing flames like a stampeded colt, he had reappeared like a wraith in columns of black, whirling smoke, at the same moment his voice issued orders from twenty places. One instant he was visible beating back the fire with a wet blanket, waving it above him jubilantly, like a substitute at the Army-Navy game when his side scores, and the next staggering from out of the furnace dragging an asphyxiated trooper by the collar, and shrieking, "Hospital-steward, hospital-steward! here's a man on fire. Put him out, and send him back to me, quick!"

Those who met him in the whirlwind of smoke and billowing flame related that he chuckled continuously. "Isn't this fun?" he yelled at them. "Say, isn't this the best ever? I wouldn't have missed this for a trip to New York!"

When the colonel, having visited the hospital and spoken cheering words to those who were sans hair, sans eyebrows and with bandaged hands, complimented Lieutenant Ranson on the parade-ground before the assembled regiment, Ranson ran to his hut muttering strange and fearful oaths.

That night at mess he appealed to Mary Cahill for sympathy. "Goodness, mighty me!" he cried, "did you hear him? Wasn't it awful? If I'd thought he was going to hand me that I'd have deserted. What's the use of spoiling the only fun we've had that way? Why, if I'd known you could get that much excitement out of this rank prairie I'd have put a match to it myself three months ago. It's the only fun I've had, and he goes and preaches a funeral oration at me."

Ranson came into the army at the time of the Spanish war because it promised a new form of excitement, and because everybody else he knew had gone into it too. As the son of his father he was made an adjutant-general of volunteers with the rank of captain, and unloaded on the staff of a Southern brigadier, who was slated never to leave Charleston. But Ranson suspected this, and, after telegraphing his father for three days, was attached to the Philippines contingent and sailed from San Francisco in time to carry messages through the surf when the volunteers moved upon Manila. More cabling at the cost of many Mexican dollars caused him to be removed from the staff, and given a second lieutenancy in a volunteer regiment, and for two years he pursued the little brown men over the paddy sluices, burned villages, looted churches, and collected bolos and altar-cloths with that irresponsibility and contempt for regulations which is found chiefly in the appointment from civil life. Incidentally, he enjoyed himself so much that he believed in the army he had found the one place where excitement is always in the air, and as excitement was the breath of his nostrils he applied for a commission in the regular army. On his record he was appointed a second lieutenant in the Twentieth Cavalry, and on the return of that regiment to the States— was buried alive at Fort Crockett.

After six months of this exile, one night at the mess-table Ranson broke forth in open rebellion. "I tell you I can't stand it a day longer," he cried. "I'm going to resign!"

From behind the counter Mary Cahill heard him in horror. Second Lieutenants Crosby and Curtis shuddered. They were sons of officers of the regular army. Only six months before they themselves had been forwarded from West Point, done up in neat new uniforms. The traditions of the Academy of loyalty and discipline had been kneaded into their vertebrae. In Ranson they saw only the horrible result of giving commissions to civilians.

"Maybe the post will be gayer now that spring has come," said Curtis hopefully, but with a doubtful look at the open fire.

"I wouldn't do anything rash," urged Crosby.

Miss Cahill shook her head. "Why, I like it at the post," she said, "and I've been here five years—ever since I left the convent—and I- —"

Ranson interrupted, bowing gallantly. "Yes, I know, Miss Cahill," he said, "but I didn't come here from a convent. I came here from the blood-stained fields of war. Now, out in the Philippines there's always something doing. They give you half a troop, and so long as you bring back enough Mausers and don't get your men cut up, you can fight all over the shop and no questions asked. But all I do here is take care of sick horses. Any vet. in the States has seen as much fighting as I have in the last half-year. I might as well have had charge of horse-car stables."

"There is some truth in that," said Curtis cautiously. "If you do resign, certainly no one can accuse you of resigning in the face of the enemy."

"Enemy, ye gods!" roared Ranson. "Why, if I were to see a Moro entering that door with a bolo in each fist I'd fall on his neck and kiss him. I'm not trained to this garrison business. You fellows are. They took all the sporting blood out of you at West Point; one bad mark for smoking a cigarette, two bad marks for failing to salute the instructor in botany, and all the excitement you ever knew were charades and a cadet-hop a t Cullum Hall. But, you see, before I went to the Philippines with Merritt, I'd been there twice on a fellow's yacht, and we'd tucked the Spanish governor in his bed with his spurs on. Now, I have to sit around and hear old Bolland tell how he put down a car-strike in St. Louis, and Stickney's long-winded yarns of Table Mountain and the Bloody Angle. He doesn't know the Civil War's over. I tell you, if I can't get excitement on tap I've got to make it, and if I make it out here they'll court-martial me. So there's nothing for it but to resign."

"You'd better wait till the end of the week," said Crosby, grinning. "It's going to be full of gayety. Thursday, paymaster's coming out with our cash, and to-night that Miss Post from New York arrives in the up stage. She's to visit the colonel, so everybody will have to give her a good time."

"Yes, I certainly must wait for that," growled Ranson; "there probably will be progressive euchre parties all along the line, and we'll sit up as late as ten o'clock and stick little gilt stars on ourselves."

Crosby laughed tolerantly.

"I see your point of view," he said. "I remember when my father took me to Monte Carlo I saw you at the tables with enough money in front of you to start a bank. I remember my father asked the croupiers why they allowed a child of your age to gamble. I was just a kid then, and so were you, too. I remember I thought you were the devil of a fellow."

Ranson looked sheepishly at Miss Cahill and laughed. "Well, so I was- -then," he said. "Anybody would be a devil of a fellow who'd been brought up as I was, with a doting parent who owns a trust and doesn't know the proper value of money. And yet you expect me to be happy with a fifty-cent limit game, and twenty miles of burned prairie. I tell you I've never been broken to it. I don't know what not having your own way means. And discipline! Why, every time I have to report one of my men to the colonel I send for him afterward and give him a drink and apologize to him. I tell you the army doesn't mean anything to me unless there's something doing, and as there is no fighting out here I'm for the back room of the Holland House and a rubber-tired automobile. Little old New York is good enough for me!"

As he spoke these fateful words of mutiny Lieutenant Ranson raised his black eyes and snatched a swift side-glance at the face of Mary Cahill. It was almost as though it were from her he sought his answer. He could not himself have told what it was he would have her say. But ever since the idea of leaving the army had come to him, Mary Cahill and the army had become interchangeable and had grown to mean one and the same thing. He fought against this condition of mind fiercely. He had determined that without active service the army was intolerable; but that without Mary Cahill civil life would also prove intolerable, he assured himself did not at all follow. He had laughed at the idea. He had even argued it out sensibly. Was it reasonable to suppose, he asked himself, that after circling the great globe three times he should find the one girl on it who alone could make him happy, sitting behind a post-trader's counter on the open prairie? His interest in Miss Cahill was the result of propinquity, that was all. It was due to the fact that there was no one else at hand, because he was sorry for her loneliness, because her absurd social ostracism had touched his sympathy. How long after he reached New York would he remember the little comrade with the brave, boyish eyes set in the delicate, feminine head, with its great waves of gorgeous hair? It would not be long, he guessed. He might remember the way she rode her pony, how she swung from her Mexican saddle and caught up a gauntlet from the ground. Yes, he certainly would remember that, and he would remember the day he had galloped after her and ridden with her through the Indian village, and again that day when they rode to the water-fall and the Lover's Leap. And he would remember her face at night as it bent over the books he borrowed for her, which she read while they were at mess, sitting in her high chair with her chin resting in her palms, staring down at the book before her. And the trick she had, whenever he spoke, of raising her head and looking into the fire, her eyes lighting and her lips smiling. They would be pleasant memories, he was sure. But once back again in the whirl and rush of the great world outside of Fort Crockett, even as memories they would pass away.

Mary Cahill made no outward answer to the rebellious utterance of Lieutenant Ranson. She only bent her eyes on her book and tried to think what the post would hold for her when he had carried out his threat and betaken himself into the world and out of her life forever. Night after night she had sat enthroned behind her barrier and listened to his talk, wondering deeply. He had talked of a world she knew only in novels, in history, and in books of travel. His view of it was not an educational one: he was no philosopher, nor trained observer. He remembered London—to her the capital of the world— chiefly by its restaurants, Cairo on account of its execrable golf- links. He lived only to enjoy himself. His view was that of a boy, hearty and healthy and seeking only excitement and mischief. She had heard his tales of his brief career at Harvard, of the reunions at Henry's American bar, of the Futurity, the Suburban, the Grand Prix, of a yachting cruise which apparently had encountered every form of adventure, from the rescuing of a stranded opera-company to the ramming of a slaver's dhow. The regret with which he spoke of these free days, which was the regret of an exile marooned upon a desert island, excited all her sympathy for an ill she had never known. His discourteous scorn of the social pleasures of the post, from which she herself was excluded, rilled her with speculation. If he could forego these functions, how full and gay she argued his former life must have been. His attitude helped her to bear the deprivations more easily. And she, as a loyal child of the army, liked him also because he was no "cracker-box" captain, but a fighter, who had fought with no morbid ideas as to the rights or wrongs of the cause, but for the fun of fighting.

And one night, after he had been telling the mess of a Filipino officer who alone had held back his men and himself, and who at last died in his arms cursing him, she went to sleep declaring to herself that Lieutenant Ranson was becoming too like the man she had pictured for her husband than was good for her peace of mind. He had told the story as his tribute to a brave man fighting for his independence and with such regret that such a one should have died so miserably, that, to the embarrassment of the mess, the tears rolled down his cheeks. But he wiped them away with his napkin as unconcernedly as though they were caused by the pepper-box, and said simply, "He had sporting blood, he had. I've never felt so bad about anything as I did about that chap. Whenever I think of him standing up there with his back to the cathedral all shot to pieces, but giving us what for until he died, it makes me cry. So," he added, blowing his nose vigorously, "I won't think of it any more."

Tears are properly a woman's weapon, and when a man makes use of them, even in spite of himself, he is taking an advantage over the other sex which is unfair and outrageous. Lieutenant Ranson never knew the mischief the sympathy he had shown for his enemy caused in the heart of Mary Cahill, nor that from that moment she loved him deeply.

The West Point graduates before they answered Ranson's ultimatum smoked their cigarettes for some time in silence.

"Oh, there's been fighting even at Fort Crockett," said Crosby. "In the last two years the men have been ordered out seven times, haven't they, Miss Cahill? When the Indians got out of hand, and twice after cowboys, and twice after the Red Rider."

"The Red Rider!" protested Ranson; "I don't see anything exciting in rounding up one miserable horse thief."

"Only they don't round him up," returned Curtis crossly. "That's why it's exciting. He's the best in his business. He's held up the stage six times now in a year. Whoever the fellow is, if he's one man or a gang of men, he's the nerviest road-agent since the days of Abe Case."

Ranson in his then present mood was inclined toward pessimism. "It doesn't take any nerve to hold up a coach," he contradicted.

Curtis and Crosby snorted in chorus. "That's what you say," mocked Curtis.

"Well, it doesn't," repeated Ranson. "It's all a game of bluff. The etiquette is that the driver mustn't shoot the road-agent, and that the road-agent mustn't hurt the driver, and the passengers are too scared to move. The moment they see a man rise out of the night they throw up their hands. Why, even when a passenger does try to pull his gun the others won't let him. Each thinks sure that if there's any firing he will be the one to get hurt. And, besides, they don't know how many more men the road agent may have behind him. I don't—-"

A movement on the part of Miss Cahill caused him to pause abruptly. Miss Cahill had descended from her throne and was advancing to meet the post-trader, who came toward her from the exchange.

"Lightfoot's squaw," he said. "Her baby's worse. She's sent for you."

Miss Cahill gave a gasp of sympathy, snatched up her hat from the counter, and the buffalo robes closed behind her.

Ranson stooped and reached for his sombrero. With the flight of Miss Cahill his interest in the courage of the Red Rider had departed also.

But Crosby appealed to the new-comer, "Cahill, YOU know," he said. "We've been talking of the man they call the Red Rider, the chap that wears a red bandanna over his face. Ranson says he hasn't any nerve. That's not so, is it?"

"I said it didn't take any nerve to hold up a stage," said Ranson; "and it doesn't."

The post-trader halted on his way back to the exchange and rubbed one hand meditatively over the other arm. With him speech was golden and difficult. After a pause he said: "Oh, he takes his chances."

"Of course he does," cried Crosby, encouragingly. "He takes the chance of being shot by the passengers, and of being caught by the posse and lynched, but this man's got away with it now six times in the last year. And I say that takes nerve."

"Why, for fifty dollars——" laughed Ranson.

He checked himself, and glanced over his shoulder at the retreating figure of Cahill. The buffalo robes fell again, and the spurs of the post-trader could be heard jangling over the earth-floor of the exchange.

"For fifty dollars," repeated Ranson, in brisk, businesslike tones, "I'll rob the up stage to-night myself!"

Previous knowledge of his moods, the sudden look of mischief in his eyes and a certain vibration in his voice caused the two lieutenants to jump simultaneously to their feet. "Ranson!" they shouted.

Ranson laughed mockingly. "Oh, I'm bored to death," he cried. "What will you bet I don't?"

He had risen with them, but, without waiting for their answer, ran to where his horse stood at the open door. He sank on his knees and began tugging violently at the stirrup-straps. The two officers, their eyes filled with concern, pursued him across the room. With Cahill twenty feet away, they dared not raise their voices, but in pantomime they beckoned him vigorously to return. Ranson came at once, flushed and smiling, holding a hooded army-stirrup in each hand. "Never do to have them see these!" he said. He threw the stirrups from him, behind the row of hogsheads. "I'll ride in the stirrup-straps!" He still spoke in the same low, brisk tone.

Crosby seized him savagely by the arm. "No, you won't!" he hissed. "Look here, Ranson. Listen to me; for Heaven's sake don't be an ass! They'll shoot you, you'll be killed——"

——"And court-martialed," panted Curtis.

"You'll go to Leavenworth for the rest of your life!"

Ranson threw off the detaining hand, and ran behind the counter. From a lower shelf he snatched a red bandanna kerchief. From another he dragged a rubber poncho, and buttoned it high about his throat. He picked up the steel shears which lay upon the counter, and snipping two holes in the red kerchief, stuck it under the brim of his sombrero. It fell before his face like a curtain. From his neck to his knees the poncho concealed his figure. All that was visible of him was his eyes, laughing through the holes in the red mask.

"Behold the Red Rider!" he groaned. "Hold up your hands!"

He pulled the kerchief from his face and threw the poncho over his arm. "Do you see these shears?" he whispered. "I'm going to hold up the stage with 'em. No one ever fires at a road agent. They just shout, 'Don't shoot, colonel, and I'll come down.' I'm going to bring 'em down with these shears."

Crosby caught Curtis by the arm, laughing eagerly. "Come to the stables, quick," he cried. "We'll get twenty troopers after him before he can go a half mile." He turned on Ranson with a triumphant chuckle. "You'll not be dismissed this regiment, if I can help it," he cried.

Ranson gave an ugly laugh, like the snarl of a puppy over his bone. "If you try to follow me, or interfere with me, Lieutenant Crosby," he said, "I'll shoot you and your troopers!"

"With a pair of shears?" jeered Crosby.

"No, with the gun I've got in my pocket. Now you listen to me. I'm not going to use that gun on any stage filled with women, driven by a man seventy years old, but—and I mean it—if you try to stop me, I'll use it on you. I'm going to show you how anyone can bluff a stage full with a pair of tin shears and a red mask for a kicker. And I'll shoot the man that tries to stop me."

Ranson sprang to his horse's side, and stuck his toe into the empty stirrup-strap; there was a scattering of pebbles, a scurry of hoofs, and the horse and rider became a gray blot in the moonlight.

The two lieutenants stood irresolute. Under his breath Crosby was swearing fiercely. Curtis stood staring out of the open door.

"Will he do it?" he asked.

"Of course he'll do it."

Curtis crossed the room and dropped into a chair. "And what—what had we better do?" he asked. For some time the other made no answer. His brows were knit, and he tramped the room, scowling at the floor. Then with an exclamation of alarm he stepped lightly to the door of the exchange and threw back the curtain. In the other room, Cahill stood at its furthest corner, scooping sugar from a hogshead.

Crosby's scowl relaxed, and, reseating himself at the table, he rolled a cigarette. "Now, if he pulls it off," he whispered, "and gets back to quarters, then—it's a case of all's well. But, if he's shot, or caught, and it all comes out, then it's up to us to prove he meant it as a practical joke."

"It isn't our duty to report it now, is it?" asked Curtis, nervously.

"Certainly not! If he chooses to make an ass of himself, that's none of our business. Unless he's found out, we have heard nothing and seen nothing. If he's caught, then we've got to stick by him, and testify that he did it on a bet. He'll probably win out all right. There is nobody expected on the stage but that Miss Post and her aunt. And the driver's an old hand. He knows better than to fight."

"There may be some cowboys coming up."

"That's Ranson's lookout. As Cahill says, the Red Rider takes his chances."

"I wish there was something we could do now," Curtis protested, petulantly. "I suppose we've just got to sit still and wait for him?"

"That's all," answered Crosby, and then leaped to his feet. "What's that?" he asked. Out on the parade ground, a bugle-call broke suddenly on the soft spring air. It rang like an alarm. The noise of a man running swiftly sounded on the path, and before the officers reached the doorway Sergeant Clancey entered it, and halted at attention.

26

"The colonel's orders," panted the sergeant, "and the lieutenant's are to take twenty men from G and H Troops, and ride to Kiowa to escort the paymaster."

"The paymaster!" Crosby cried. "He's not coming till Thursday."

"He's just telegraphed from Kiowa City, lieutenant. He's ahead of his schedule. He wants an escort for the money. He left Kiowa a few minutes ago in the up stage."

The two lieutenants sprang forward, and shouted in chorus: "The stage? He is in the stage!"

Sergeant Clancey stared dubiously from one officer to the other. He misunderstood their alarm, and with the privilege of long service attempted to allay it. "The lieutenant knows nothing can happen to the stage till it reaches the buttes," he said. "There has never been a hold-up in the open, and the escort can reach the buttes long before the stage gets here." He coughed consciously. "Colonel's orders are to gallop, lieutenant."

As the two officers rode knee to knee through the night, the pay escort pounding the trail behind them, Crosby leaned from his saddle. "He has only ten minutes' start of us," he whispered. "We are certain to overtake him. We can't help but do it. We must do it. We MUST! If we don't, and he tries to stop Colonel Patten and the pay-roll, he'll die. Two women and a deaf driver, that—that's a joke. But an Indian fighter like old Patten, and Uncle Sam's money, that

27

means a finish fight-and his death and disgrace." He turned savagely in his saddle. "Close up there!" he commanded. "Stop that talking. You keep your breath till I want it—and ride hard."

After the officers had galloped away from the messroom, and Sergeant Clancey had hurried after them to the stables, the post-trader entered it from the exchange and barred the door, which they in their haste had left open. As he did this, the close observer, had one been present, might have noted that though his movements were now alert and eager, they no longer were betrayed by any sound, and that his spurs had ceased to jangle. Yet that he purposed to ride abroad was evident from the fact that from a far corner he dragged out a heavy saddle. He flung this upon the counter, and swiftly stripped it of its stirrups. These, with more than necessary care, he hid away upon the highest shelf of the shop, while from the lower shelves he snatched a rubber poncho and a red kerchief. For a moment, as he unbarred the door, the post-trader paused and cast a quick glance before and behind him, and then the door closed and there was silence. A minute later it was broken by the hoofs of a horse galloping swiftly along the trail to Kiowa City.

PART II

That winter Miss Post had been going out a great deal more than was good for her, and when the spring came she broke down. The family doctor recommended Aiken, but an aunt of Miss Post's, Mrs. Truesdall, had been at Farmington with Mrs. "Colonel" Bolland, and urged visiting her instead. The doctor agreed that the climatic conditions existing at Fort Crockett were quite as health-giving as those at Aiken, and of the two the invalid decided that the regimental post would be more of a novelty.

So she and her aunt and the maid changed cars twice after leaving St. Louis and then staged it to Kiowa City, where, while waiting for "Pop" Henderson's coach to Fort Crockett, they dined with him on bacon, fried bread, and alkali water tinged with coffee.

It was at Kiowa City, a city of four hundred houses on blue-print paper and six on earth, that Miss Post first felt certain that she was going to enjoy her visit. It was there she first saw, at large and on his native heath, a blanket Indian. He was a tall, beautiful youth, with yellow ochre on his thin, brown arms and blue ochre on his cheekbones, who sat on "Pop's" steps, gazing impassively at the stars. Miss Post came out with her maid and fell over him. The maid screamed. Miss Post said: "I beg your pardon"; and the brave expressed his contempt by gutteral mutterings and by moving haughtily away. Miss Post was then glad that she had not gone to Aiken. For the twelve-mile drive through the moonlit buttes to Fort Crockett there was, besides the women, one other passenger. He was a travelling salesman of the Hancock Uniform Company, and was visiting Fort Crockett to measure the officers for their summer tunics. At dinner he passed Miss Post the condensed milk-can, and in other ways made himself agreeable. He informed her aunt that he was in the Military Equipment Department of the Army, but, much to that young woman's distress, addressed most of his remarks to the maid, who, to his taste, was the most attractive of the three.

"I take it," he said genially to Miss Post, "that you and the young lady are sisters."

"No," said Miss Post, "we are not related."

It was eight o'clock, and the moon was full in the heavens when "Pop" Henderson hoisted them into the stage and burdened his driver, Hunk Smith, with words of advice which were intended solely for the ears of the passengers.

"You want to be careful of that near wheeler, Hunk," he said, "or he'll upset you into a gully. An' in crossing the second ford, bear to the right; the water's running high, and it may carry youse all down stream. I don't want that these ladies should be drowned in any stage of mine. An' if the Red Rider jumps you don't put up no bluff, but sit still. The paymaster's due in a night or two, an' I've no doubt at all but that the Rider's laying for him. But if you tell him that there's no one inside but womenfolk and a tailor, mebbe he won't hurt youse. Now, ladies," he added, putting his head under the leather flap, as though unconscious that all he had said had already reached them, "without wishing to make you uneasy, I would advise your having your cash and jewelry ready in your hands. With road- agents it's mostly wisest to do what they say, an' to do it quick. Ef you give 'em all you've got, they sometimes go away without spilling blood, though, such being their habits, naturally disappointed." He turned his face toward the shrinking figure of the military tailor. "You, being an army man," he said, "will of course want to protect the ladies, but you mustn't do it. You must keep cool. Ef you pull your gun, like as not you'll all get killed. But I'm hoping for the best. Good-night all, an' a pleasant journey."

The stage moved off with many creaks and many cracks of the whip, which in part smothered Hunk Smith's laughter. But after the first mile, he, being a man with feelings and a family, pulled the mules to a halt.

The voice of the drummer could instantly be heard calling loudly from the darkness of the stage: "Don't open those flaps. If they see us, they'll fire!"

"I wanted you folks to know," said Hunk Smith, leaning from the box- seat, "that that talk of Pop's was all foolishness. You're as safe on this trail as in a Pullman palace-car. That was just his way. Pop will have his joke. You just go to sleep now, if you can, and trust to me. I'll get you there by eleven o'clock or break a trace. Breakin' a trace is all the danger there is, anyway," he added, cheerfully, "so don't fret."

Miss Post could not resist saying to Mrs. Truesdall: "I told you he was joking."

The stage had proceeded for two hours. Sometimes it dropped with locked wheels down sheer walls of clay, again it was dragged, careening drunkenly, out of fathomless pits. It pitched and tossed, slid and galloped, danced grotesquely from one wheel to another, from one stone to another, recoiled out of ruts, butted against rocks, and swept down and out of swollen streams that gurgled between the spokes.

"If ever I leave Fort Crockett," gasped Mrs. Truesdall between jolts, "I shall either wait until they build a railroad or walk."

They had all but left the hills, and were approaching the level prairie. That they might see the better the flaps had been rolled up, and the soft dry air came freely through the open sides. The mules were straining over the last hill. On either side only a few of the buttes were still visible. They stood out in the moonlight as cleanly cut as the bows of great battleships. The trail at last was level. Mrs. Truesdall's eyes closed. Her head fell forward. But Miss Post, weary as she was in body, could not sleep. To her the night-ride was full of strange and wonderful mysteries. Gratefully she drank in the dry scent of the prairie-grass, and, holding by the frame of the window, leaned far out over the wheel. As she did so, a man sprang into the trail from behind a wall of rock, and shouted hoarsely. He was covered to his knees with a black mantle. His face was hidden by a blood-red mask.

"Throw up your hands!" he commanded. There was a sharp creaking as the brakes locked, and from the driver's seat an amazed oath. The stage stopped with a violent jerk, and Mrs. Truesdall pitched gently forward toward her niece.

"I really believe I was asleep, Helen," she murmured. "What are we waiting for?"

"I think we are held up," said Miss Post.

The stage had halted beyond the wall of rock, and Miss Post looked behind it, but no other men were visible, only a horse with his bridle drawn around a stone. The man in the mask advanced upon the stage, holding a weapon at arm's-length. In the moonlight it flashed and glittered evilly. The man was but a few feet from Miss Post, and the light fell full upon her. Of him she could see only two black eyes that flashed as evilly as his weapon. For a period of suspense, which seemed cruelly prolonged, the man stood motionless, then he lowered his weapon. When he opened his lips the mask stuck to them, and his words came from behind it, broken and smothered. "Sorry to trouble you, miss," the mask said, "but I want that man beside you to get out."

Miss Post turned to the travelling salesman. "He wants you to get out," she said.

"Wants me!" exclaimed the drummer. "I'm not armed, you know." In a louder voice he protested, faintly: "I say, I'm not armed."

"Come out!" demanded the mask.

The drummer precipitated himself violently over the knees of the ladies into the road below, and held his hands high above him. "I'm not armed," he said; "indeed I'm not."

"Stand over there, with your back to that rock," the mask ordered. For a moment the road agent regarded him darkly, pointing his weapon meditatively at different parts of the salesman's person. He suggested a butcher designating certain choice cuts. The drummer's muscles jerked under the torture as though his anatomy were being prodded with an awl.

"I want your watch," said the mask. The drummer reached eagerly for his waistcoat.

"Hold up your hands!" roared the road agent. "By the eternal, if you play any rough-house tricks on me I'll—" He flourished his weapon until it flashed luminously.

An exclamation from Hunk Smith, opportunely uttered, saved the drummer from what was apparently instant annihilation. "Say, Rider," cried the driver, "I can't hold my arms up no longer. I'm going to put 'em down. But

34

you leave me alone, an' I'll leave you alone. Is that a bargain?" The shrouded figure whirled his weapon upon the speaker. "Have I ever stopped you before, Hunk?" he demanded.

Hunk, at this recognition of himself as a public character, softened instantly. "I dunno whether 'twas you or one of your gang, but—"

"Well, you've still got your health, haven't you?"

"Yes."

"Then keep quiet," snarled the mask.

In retort Hunk Smith muttered audible threatenings, but sank obediently into an inert heap. Only his eyes, under cover of his sombrero, roamed restlessly. They noted the McClellan saddle on the Red Rider's horse, the white patch on its near fore-foot, the empty stirrup-straps, and at a great distance, so great that the eyes only of a plainsman could have detected it, a cloud of dust, or smoke, or mist, that rode above the trail and seemed to be moving swiftly down upon them.

At the sight, Hunk shifted the tobacco in his cheek and nervously crossed his knees, while a grin of ineffable cunning passed across his face.

With his sombrero in his hand, the Red Rider stepped to the wheel of the stage. As he did so, Miss Post observed that above the line of his kerchief his hair was evenly and carefully parted in the middle.

"I'm afraid, ladies," said the road agent, "that I have delayed you unnecessarily. It seems that I have called up the wrong number." He emitted a reassuring chuckle, and, fanning himself with his sombrero, continued speaking in a tone of polite irony: "The Wells, Fargo messenger is the party I am laying for. He's coming over this trail with a package of diamonds. That's what I'm after. At first I thought 'Fighting Bob' over there by the rock might have it on him; but he doesn't act like any Wells, Fargo Express agent I have ever tackled before, and I guess the laugh's on me. I seem to have been weeping over the wrong grave." He replaced his sombrero on his head at a rakish angle, and waved his hand. "Ladies, you are at liberty to proceed."

But instantly he stepped forward again, and brought his face so close to the window that they could see the whites of his eyes. "Before we part," he murmured, persuasively, "you wouldn't mind leaving me something as a souvenir, would you?" He turned the skull-like openings of the mask full upon Miss Post.

Mrs. Truesdall exclaimed, hysterically: "Why, certainly not!" she cried. "Here's everything I have, except what's sewn inside my waist, where I can't possibly get at it. I assure you I cannot. The proprietor of that hotel told us we'd probably— meet you, and so I have everything ready." She thrust her two hands through the window. They held a roll of bills, a watch, and her rings

Miss Post laughed in an ecstasy of merriment "Oh, no, aunt," she protested, "don't. No, not at all. The gentleman only wants a keepsake. Something to remember us by. Isn't that it?" she asked. She regarded the blood-red mask steadily with a brilliant smile.

The road agent did not at once answer. At her words he had started back with such sharp suspicion that one might have thought he meditated instant flight. Through the holes in his mask he now glared searchingly at Miss Post, but still in silence.

"I think this will satisfy him," said Miss Post.

Out of the collection in her aunt's hands she picked a silver coin and held it forward. "Something to keep as a pocket-piece," she said, mockingly, "to remind you of your kindness to three lone females in distress."

Still silent, the road agent reached for the money, and then growled at her in a tone which had suddenly become gruff and overbearing. It suggested to Miss Post the voice of the head of the family playing Santa Claus for the children. "And now you, miss," he demanded.

Miss Post took another coin from the heap, studied its inscription, and passed it through the window. "This one is from me," she said. "Mine is dated 1901. The moonlight," she added, leaning far forward and smiling out at him, "makes it quite easy to see the date; as easy," she went on, picking her words, "as it is to see your peculiar revolver and

the coat-of-arms on your ring." She drew her head back."
Good-night," she cooed, sweetly.

The Red Rider jumped from the door. An exclamation
which might have been a laugh or an oath was smothered
by his mask. He turned swiftly upon the salesman. "Get
back into the coach," he commanded. "And you, Hunk," he
called, "if you send a posse after me, next night I ketch you
out here alone you'll lose the top of your head."

The salesman scrambled into the stage through the door
opposite the one at which the Red Rider was standing, and
the road agent again raised his sombrero with a sweeping
gesture worthy of D'Artagnan. "Good-night, ladies," he
said.

"Good-night, sir," Mrs. Truesdall answered, grimly, but
exuding a relieved sigh. Then, her indignation giving her
courage, she leaned from the window and hurled a Parthian
arrow. "I must say," she protested, "I think you might be in
a better business."

The road agent waved his hand to the young lady.
"Good-by," he said.

"Au revoir," said Miss Post, pleasantly.

"Good-by, miss," stammered the road agent,

"I said 'Au revoir,'" repeated Miss Post.

The road agent, apparently routed by these simple
words, fled muttering toward his horse.

Hunk Smith was having trouble with his brake. He kicked at it and, stooping, pulled at it, but the wheels did not move.

Mrs. Truesdall fell into a fresh panic. "What is it now?" she called, miserably.

Before he answered, Hunk Smith threw a quick glance toward the column of moving dust. He was apparently reassured.

"The brake," he grunted. "The darned thing's stuck!"

The road agent was tugging at the stone beneath which he had slipped his bridle. "Can I help?" he asked, politely. But before he reached the stage, he suddenly stopped with an imperative sweep of his arm for silence. He stood motionless, his body bent to the ground, leaning forward and staring down the trail. Then he sprang upright. "You old fox!" he roared, "you're gaining time, are you?"

With a laugh he tore free his bridle and threw himself across his horse. His legs locked under it, his hands clasped its mane, and with a cowboy yell he dashed past the stage in the direction of Kiowa City, his voice floating back in shouts of jeering laughter. From behind him he heard Hunk Smith's voice answering his own in a cry for "Help!" and from a rapidly decreasing distance the throb of many hoofs. For an instant he drew upon his rein, and then, with a defiant chuckle, drove his spurs deep into his horse's side.

Mrs. Truesdall also heard the pounding of many hoofs, as well as Hunk Smith's howls for help, and feared a fresh attack. "Oh, what is it?" she begged

"Soldiers from the fort," Hunk called, excitedly, and again raised his voice in a long, dismal howl.

"Sounds cheery, doesn't it?" said the salesman; "referring to the soldiers," he explained. It was his first coherent remark since the Red Rider had appeared and disappeared.

"Oh, I hope they won't—" began Miss Post, anxiously.

The hoof-beats changed to thunder, and with the pounding on the dry trail came the jangle of stirrups and sling-belts. Then a voice, and the coach was surrounded by dust-covered troopers and horses breathing heavily. Lieutenant Crosby pulled up beside the window of the stage. "Are you there, Colonel Patten?" he panted. He peered forward into the stage, but no one answered him. "Is the paymaster in here?" he demanded.

The voice of Lieutenant Curtis shouted in turn at Hunk Smith. "Is the paymaster in there, driver?"

"Paymaster? No!" Hunk roared. "A drummer and three ladies. We've been held up. The Red Rider—" He rose and waved his whip over the top of the coach. "He went that way. You can ketch him easy."

Sergeant Clancey and half a dozen troopers jerked at their bridles. But Crosby, at the window, shouted "Halt!"

"What's your name?" he demanded of the salesman.

40

"Myers," stammered the drummer. "I'm from the Hancock Uniform—"

Curtis had spurred his horse beside that of his brother officer. "Is Colonel Patten at Kiowa?" he interrupted.

"I can't give you any information as to that," replied Mr. Myers, importantly; "but these ladies and I have just been held up by the Red Rider. If you'll hurry you'll—"

The two officers pulled back their horses from the stage and, leaning from their saddles, consulted in eager whispers. Their men fidgeted with their reins, and stared with amazed eyes at their officers. Lieutenant Crosby was openly smiling, "He's got away with it," he whispered. "Patten missed the stage, thank God, and he's met nothing worse than these women."

"We MUST make a bluff at following him," whispered Curtis.

"Certainly not! Our orders are to report to Colonel Patten, and act as his escort."

"But he's not at Kiowa; that fellow says so."

"He telegraphed the Colonel from Kiowa," returned Crosby. "How could he do that if he wasn't there?" He turned upon Hunk Smith. "When did you leave Henderson's?" he demanded.

"Seven o'clock," answered Hunk Smith, sulkily. "Say, if you young fellows want to catch—"

"And Patten telegraphed at eight," cried Crosby. "That's it. He reached Kiowa after the stage had gone. Sergeant Clancey!" he called.

The Sergeant pushed out from the mass of wondering troopers.

"When did the paymaster say he was leaving Kiowa?"

"Leaving at once, the telegram said," answered Clancey.

"'Meet me with escort before I reach the buttes.' That's the message I was told to give the lieutenant."

Hunk Smith leaned from the box-seat. "Mebbe Pop's driving him over himself in the buckboard," he volunteered. "Pop often takes 'em over that way if they miss the stage."

"That's how it is, of course," cried Crosby. "He's on his way now in the buckboard."

Hunk Smith surveyed the troopers dismally and shook his head. "If he runs up against the Red Rider, it's 'good-by' your pay, boys," he cried.

"Fall in there!" shouted Crosby. "Corporal Tynan, fall out with two men and escort these ladies to the fort." He touched his hat to Miss Post, and, with Curtis at his side, sprang into the trail. "Gallop! March!" he commanded.

"Do you think he'll tackle the buckboard, too?" whispered Curtis.

Crosby laughed joyously and drew a long breath of relief.

"No, he's all right now," he answered. "Don't you see, he doesn't know about Patten or the buckboard. He's probably well on his way to the post now. I delayed the game at the stage there on purpose to give him a good start. He's safe by now."

"It was a close call," laughed the other. "He's got to give us a dinner for helping him out of this."

"We'd have caught him red-handed," said Crosby, "if we'd been five minutes sooner. Lord!" he gasped. "It makes me cold to think of it. The men would have shot him off his horse. But what a story for those women! I hope I'll be there when they tell it. If Ranson can keep his face straight, he's a wonder." For some moments they raced silently neck by neck, and then Curtis again leaned from his saddle. "I hope he HAS turned back to the post," he said. "Look at the men how they're keeping watch for him. They're scouts, all of them."

"What if they are?" returned Crosby, easily. "Ranson's in uniform— out for a moonlight canter. You can bet a million dollars he didn't wear his red mask long after he heard us coming."

"I suppose he'll think we've followed to spoil his fun. You know you said we would."

"Yes, he was going to shoot us," laughed Crosby. "I wonder why he packs a gun. It's a silly thing to do."

The officers fell apart again, and there was silence over the prairie, save for the creaking of leather and the beat of the hoofs. And then, faint and far away, there came the quick crack of a revolver, another, and then a fusillade. "My God!" gasped Crosby. He threw himself forwards digging his spurs into his horse, and rode as though he were trying to escape from his own men.

No one issued an order, no one looked a question; each, officer and enlisted man, bowed his head and raced to be the first.

The trail was barricaded by two struggling horses and an overturned buckboard. The rigid figure of a man lay flat upon his back staring at the moon, another white-haired figure staggered forward from a rock. "Who goes there?" it demanded.

"United States troops. Is that you, Colonel Patten?"

"Yes."

Colonel Patten's right arm was swinging limply at his side. With his left hand he clasped his right shoulder. The blood, black in the moonlight, was oozing between his fingers.

"We were held up," he said. "He shot the driver and the horses. I fired at him, but he broke my arm. He shot the gun out of my hand. When he reached for the satchel I tried to beat him off with my left arm, but he threw me into the road. He went that way—toward Kiowa."

44

Sergeant Clancey, who was kneeling by the figure in the trail, raised his hand in salute. "Pop Henderson, lieutenant," he said. "He's shot through the heart. He's dead."

"He took the money, ten thousand dollars," cried Colonel Patten. "He wore a red mask and a rubber poncho. And I saw that he had no stirrups in his stirrup-straps."

Crosby dodged, as though someone had thrown a knife, and then raised his hand stiffly and heavily.

"Lieutenant Curtis, you will remain here with Colonel Patten," he ordered. His voice was without emotion. It fell flat and dead. "Deploy as skirmishers," he commanded. "G Troop to the fight of the trail, H Troop to the left. Stop anyone you see—anyone. If he tries to escape, cry 'Halt!' twice and then fire—to kill. Forward! Gallop! March! Toward the post."

"No!" shouted Colonel Patten. "He went toward Kiowa."

Crosby replied in the same dead voice: "He doubled after he left you, colonel. He has gone to the post."

Colonel Patten struggled from the supporting arms that held him and leaned eagerly forward. "You know him, then?" he demanded.

"Yes," cried Crosby, "God help him! Spread out there, you, in open order—and ride like hell!"

Just before the officers' club closed for the night Lieutenant Ranson came in and, seating himself at the piano, picked out "The Queen of the Philippine Islands" with one finger. Major Stickney and others who were playing bridge were considerably annoyed. Ranson then demanded that everyone present should drink his health in champagne for the reason that it was his birthday and that he was glad he was alive, and wished everyone else to feel the same way about it. "Or, for any other reason why," he added generously. This frontal attack upon the whist-players upset the game entirely, and Ranson, enthroned upon the piano-stool, addressed the room. He held up a buckskin tobacco-bag decorated with beads.

"I got this down at the Indian village to-night," he said. "That old squaw, Red Wing, makes 'em for two dollars. Crosby paid five dollars for his in New Mexico, and it isn't half as good. What do you think? I got lost coming back, and went all the way round by the buttes before I found the trail, and I've only been here six months. They certainly ought to make me chief of scouts."

There was the polite laugh which is granted to any remark made by the one who is paying for the champagne.

"Oh, that's where you were, was it?" said the post-adjutant, genially. "The colonel sent Clancey after you and Crosby. Clancey reported that he couldn't find you. So we sent Curtis. They went to act as escort for Colonel Patten and the pay. He's coming up to-night in the stage." Ranson was gazing down into his glass. Before he raised his head he picked several pieces of ice out of it and then drained it.

"The paymaster, hey?" he said. "He's in the stage to-night, is he?"

"Yes," said the adjutant; and then as the bugle and stamp of hoofs sounded from the parade outside, "and that's him now, I guess," he added.

Ranson refilled his glass with infinite care, and then, in spite of a smile that twitched at the corners of his mouth, emptied it slowly.

There was the jingle of spurs and a measured tramp on the veranda of the club-house, and for the first time in its history four enlisted men, carrying their Krags, invaded its portals. They were led by Lieutenant Crosby; his face was white under the tan, and full of suffering. The officers in the room received the intrusion in amazed silence. Crosby strode among them, looking neither to the left nor right, and touched Lieutenant Ranson upon the shoulder.

"The colonel's orders, Lieutenant Ranson," he said. "You are under arrest."

Ranson leaned back against the music-rack and placed his glass upon the keyboard. One leg was crossed over the other, and he did not remove it.

"Then you can't take a joke," he said in a low tone. "You had to run and tell." He laughed and raised his voice so that

47

all in the club might hear, "What am I arrested for, Crosby?" he asked.

The lines in Crosby's face deepened, and only those who sat near could hear him. "You are under arrest for attempting to kill a superior officer, for the robbery of the government pay-train—and for murder."

Ranson jumped to his feet. "My God, Crosby!" he cried.

"Silence! Don't talk!" ordered Crosby. "Come along with me."

The four troopers fell in in rear of Lieutenant Crosby and their prisoner. He drew a quick, frightened breath, and then, throwing back his shoulders, fell into step, and the six men tramped from the club and out into the night.

PART III

That night at the post there was little sleep for any one. The feet of hurrying orderlies beat upon the parade-ground, the windows of the Officers' Club blazed defiantly, and from the darkened quarters of the enlisted men came the sound of voices snarling in violent vituperation. At midnight, half of Ranson's troop, having attacked the rest of the regiment with cavalry-boots, were marched under arrest to the guard-house. As they passed Ranson's hut, where he still paced the veranda, a burning cigarette attesting his wakefulness, they cheered him riotously. At two o'clock it was announced from the hospital that both patients were out of danger; for it had developed that, in his hurried diagnosis, Sergeant Clancey had located Henderson's heart six inches from where it should have been.

When one of the men who guarded Ranson reported this good news the prisoner said, "Still, I hope they'll hang whoever did it. They shouldn't hang a man for being a good shot and let him off because he's a bad one."

At the time of the hold-up Mary Cahill had been a half-mile distant from the post at the camp of the Kiowas, where she had gone in answer to the cry of Lightfoot's squaw. When she returned she found Indian Pete in charge of the exchange. Her father, he told her, had ridden to the Indian village in search of her. As he spoke the post-trader appeared. "I'm sorry I missed you," his daughter called to him.

At the sound Cahill pulled his horse sharply toward the corral. "I had a horse-deal on—with the chief," he answered over his shoulder. "When I got to Lightfoot's tent you had gone."

After he had dismounted, and was coming toward her, she noted that his right hand was bound in a handkerchief, and exclaimed with apprehension.

"It is nothing," Cahill protested. "I was foolin' with one of the new regulation revolvers, with my hand over the muzzle. Ball went through the palm."

Miss Cahill gave a tremulous cry and caught the injured hand to her lips.

Her father snatched it from her roughly.

"Let go!" he growled. "It serves me right."

A few minutes later Mary Cahill, bearing liniment for her father's hand, knocked at his bedroom and found it empty. When she peered from the top of the stairs into the shop-window below she saw him busily engaged with his one hand buckling the stirrup-straps of his saddle.

When she called, he sprang upright with an oath. He had faced her so suddenly that it sounded as though he had sworn, not in surprise, but at her.

"You startled me," he murmured. His eyes glanced suspiciously from her to the saddle. "These stirrup-straps—

they're too short," he announced. "Pete or somebody's been using my saddle."

"I came to bring you this 'first-aid' bandage for your hand," said his daughter.

Cahill gave a shrug of impatience.

"My hand's all right," he said; "you go to bed. I've got to begin taking account of stock."

"To-night?"

"There's no time by day. Go to bed."

For nearly an hour Miss Cahill lay awake listening to her father moving about in the shop below. Never before had he spoken roughly to her, and she, knowing how much the thought that he had done so would distress him, was herself distressed.

In his lonely vigil on the veranda, Ranson looked from the post down the hill to where the light still shone from Mary Cahill's window. He wondered if she had heard the news, and if it were any thought of him that kept sleep from her.

"You ass! you idiot!" he muttered. "You've worried and troubled her. She believes one of her precious army is a thief and a murderer." He cursed himself picturesquely, but the thought that she might possibly be concerned on his account, did not, he found, distress him as greatly as it should. On the contrary, as he watched the light his heart glowed warmly. And long after the light went out he still

51

looked toward the home of the post-trader, his brain filled with thoughts of his return to his former life outside the army, the old life to which he vowed he would not return alone.

The next morning Miss Cahill learned the news when the junior officer came to mess and explained why Ranson was not with them. Her only comment was to at once start for his quarters with his breakfast in a basket. She could have sent it by Pete, but, she argued, when one of her officers was in trouble that was not the time to turn him over to the mercies of a servant. No, she assured herself, it was not because the officer happened to be Ranson. She would have done as much, or as little, for any one of them. When Curtis and Haines were ill of the grippe, had she not carried them many good things of her own making?

But it was not an easy sacrifice. As she crossed the parade-ground she recognized that over-night Ranson's hut, where he was a prisoner in his own quarters, had become to the post the storm-centre of interest, and to approach it was to invite the attention of the garrison. At head-quarters a group of officers turned and looked her way, there was a flutter among the frocks on Mrs. Bolland's porch, and the enlisted men, smoking their pipes on the rail of the barracks, whispered together. When she reached Ranson's hut over four hundred pairs of eyes were upon her, and her cheeks were flushing. Ranson came leaping to the gate, and lifted the basket from her arm as though he were removing an opera-cloak. He set it upon the gate- post, and nervously clasped the palings of the gate with both hands. He had not been to bed, but that fact alone could not explain the strangeness of his manner. Never before had she seen him disconcerted or abashed.

"You shouldn't have done it," he stammered. "Indeed, indeed, you are much too good. But you shouldn't have come."

His voice shook slightly.

"Why not?" asked Mary Cahill. "I couldn't let you go hungry."

"You know it isn't that," he said; "it's your coming here at all. Why, only three of the fellows have been near me this morning. And they only came from a sense of duty. I know they did—I could feel it. You shouldn't have come here. I'm not a proper person; I'm an outlaw. You might think this was a pest-house, you might think I was a leper. Why, those Stickney girls have been watching me all morning through a field-glass." He clasped and unclasped his fingers around the palings. "They believe I did it," he protested, with the bewildered accents of a child. "They all believe it."

Miss Cahill laughed. The laugh was quieting and comforting. It brought him nearer to earth, and her next remark brought him still further.

"Have you had any breakfast?" she asked.

"Breakfast!" stammered Ranson. "No. The guard brought some, but I couldn't eat it. This thing has taken the life out of me—to think sane, sensible people—my own people—could believe that I'd steal, that I'd kill a man for money."

"Yes, I know," said Miss Cahill soothingly; "but you've not had any sleep, and you need your coffee." She lifted the lid of the basket. "It's getting cold," she said. "Don't you worry about what people think. You must remember you're a prisoner now under arrest. You can't expect the officers to run over here as freely as they used to. What do you want?" she laughed. "Do you think the colonel should parade the band and give you a serenade?" For a moment Ranson stared at her dully, and then his sense of proportion returned to him. He threw back his head and laughed with her joyfully.

From verandas, barracks, and headquarters, the four hundred pairs of eyes noted this evidence of heartlessness with varied emotions. But, unmindful of them, Ranson now leaned forward, the eager, searching look coming back into his black eyes. They were so close to Mary Cahill's that she drew away. He dropped his voice to a whisper and spoke swiftly.

"Miss Cahill, whatever happens to me I won't forget this. I won't forget your coming here and throwing heart into me. You were the only one who did. I haven't asked you if you believe that I—"

She raised her eyes reproachfully and smiled. "You know you don't have to do that," she said.

The prisoner seized the palings as though he meant to pull apart the barrier between them. He drew a long breath like one inhaling a draught of clean morning air.

"No," he said, his voice ringing, "I don't have to do that."

He cast a swift glance to the left and right. The sentry's bayonet was just disappearing behind the corner of the hut. To the four hundred other eyes around the parade-ground Lieutenant Ranson's attitude suggested that he was explaining to Cahill's daughter what he wanted for his luncheon. His eyes held her as firmly as though the palings he clasped were her two hands.

"Mary," he said, and the speaking of her name seemed to stop the beating of his heart. "Mary," he whispered, as softly as though he were beginning a prayer, "you're the bravest, the sweetest, the dearest girl in all the world. And I've known it for months, and now you must know. And there'll never be any other girl in my life but you."

Mary Cahill drew away from him in doubt and wonder.

"I didn't mean to tell you just yet," he whispered, "but now that I've seen you I can't help it. I knew it last night when I stood back there and watched your windows, and couldn't think of this trouble, nor of anything else, but just

55

you. And you've got to promise me, if I get out of this all right—you must—must promise me—"

Mary Cahill's eyes, as she raised them to his, were moist and glowing. They promised him with a great love and tenderness. But at the sight Ranson protested wildly.

"No," he whispered, "you mustn't promise—anything. I shouldn't have asked it. After I'm out of this, after the court-martial, then you've got to promise that you'll never, never leave me."

Miss Cahill knit her hands together and turned away her head. The happiness in her heart rose to her throat like a great melody and choked her. Before her, exposed in the thin spring sunshine, was the square of ugly brown cottages, the bare parade-ground, in its centre Trumpeter Tyler fingering his bugle, and beyond on every side an ocean of blackened prairie. But she saw nothing of this. She saw instead a beautiful world opening its arms to her, a world smiling with sunshine, glowing with color, singing with love and content.

She turned to him with all that was in her heart showing in her face.

"Don't!" he begged, tremblingly, "don't answer. I couldn't bear it— if you said 'no' to me." He jerked his head toward the men who guarded him. "Wait until I'm tried, and not in disgrace." He shook the gate between them savagely as though it actually held him a prisoner.

Mary Cahill raised her head proudly.

"You have no right. You've hurt me," she whispered. "You hurt me."

"Hurt you?" he cried.

She pressed her hands together. It was impossible to tell him, it was impossible to speak of what she felt; of the pride, of the trust and love, to disclose this new and wonderful thing while the gate was between them, while the sentries paced on either side, while the curious eyes of the garrison were fastened upon her.

"Oh, can't you see?" she whispered. "As though I cared for a court- martial! I KNOW you. You are just the same. You are just what you have always been to me—what you always will be to me."

She thrust her hand toward him and he seized it in both of his, and then released it instantly, and, as though afraid of his own self- control, backed hurriedly from her, and she turned and walked rapidly away.

Captain Carr, who had been Ranson's captain in the Philippines, and who was much his friend, had been appointed to act as his counsel. When later that morning he visited his client to lay out a line of defence he found Ranson inclined to treat the danger which threatened him with the most arrogant flippancy. He had never seen him in a more objectionable mood.

"You can call the charge 'tommy-rot' if you like," Carr protested, sharply. "But, let me tell you that's not the view any one else takes of it, and if you expect the officers of the court-martial and the civil authorities to take that view of it you've got to get down to work and help me prove that it IS 'tommy rot.' That Miss Post, as soon as she got here, when she thought it was only a practical joke, told them that the road agent threatened her with a pair of shears. Now, Crosby and Curtis will testify that you took a pair of shears from Cahill's, and from what Miss Post saw of your ring she can probably identify that, too; so—"

"Oh, we concede the shears," declared Ranson, waving his hand grandly. "We admit the first hold-up."

"The devil we do!" returned Carr. "Now, as your counsel, I advise nothing of the sort."

"You advise me to lie?"

"Sir!" exclaimed Carr. "A plea of not guilty is only a legal form. When you consider that the first hold-up in itself is enough to lose you your commission—"

"Well, it's MY commission," said Ranson. "It was only a silly joke, anyway. And the War Department must have some sense of humor or it wouldn't have given me a commission in the first place. Of course, we'll admit the first hold-up, but we won't stand for the second one. I had no more to do with that than with the Whitechapel murders."

"How are we to prove that?" demanded Carr. "Where's your alibi? Where were you after the first hold-up?"

"I was making for home as fast as I could cut," said Ranson. He suddenly stopped in his walk up and down the room and confronted his counsel sternly. "Captain," he demanded, "I wish you to instruct me on a point of law."

Carr's brow relaxed. He was relieved to find that Ranson had awakened to the seriousness of the charges against him.

"That's what I'm here for," he said, encouragingly.

"Well, captain," said Ranson, "if an officer is under arrest as I am and confined to his quarters, is he or is he not allowed to send to the club for a bottle of champagne?"

"Really, Ranson!" cried the captain, angrily, "you are impossible."

"I only want to celebrate," said Ranson, meekly. "I'm a very happy man; I'm the happiest man on earth. I want to ride across the prairie shooting off both guns and yelling like a cowboy. Instead of which I am locked up indoors and have to talk to you about a highway robbery which does not amuse me, which does not concern me—and of which I know nothing and care less. Now, YOU are detailed to prove me innocent. That's your duty, and you ought to do your duty, But don't drag me in. I've got much more important things to think about."

Bewilderment, rage, and despair were written upon the face of the captain.

"Ranson!" he roared. "Is this a pose, or are you mad? Can't you understand that you came very near to being hanged for murder and that you are in great danger of going to jail for theft? Let me put before you the extremely unpleasant position in which you have been ass enough to place yourself. You don't quite seem to grasp it. You tell two brother-officers that you are going to rob the stage. To do so you disguise yourself in a poncho and a red handkerchief, and you remove the army-stirrups from your stirrup-leathers. You then do rob this coach, or at least hold it up, and you are recognized. A few minutes later, in the same trail and in the same direction you have taken, there is a second hold-up, this time of the paymaster. The man who robs the paymaster wears a poncho and a red kerchief, and he has no stirrups in his stirrup-leathers. The two hold-ups take place within a half-mile of each other, within five minutes of each other. Now, is it reasonable to believe that last night two men were hiding in the buttes intent upon robbery, each in an army poncho, each wearing a red bandanna handkerchief, and each riding without stirrups? Between believing in such a strange coincidence and that you did it, I'll be hanged if I don't believe you did it."

"I don't blame you," said Ranson. "What can I do to set your mind at rest?"

"Well, tell me exactly what persons knew that you meant to hold up the stage."

"Curtis and Crosby; no one else."

"Not even Cahill?"

"No, Cahill came in just before I said I would stop the stage, but I remember particularly that before I spoke I waited for him to get back to the exchange."

"And Crosby tells me," continued Carr, "that the instant you had gone he looked into the exchange and saw Cahill at the farthest corner from the door. He could have heard nothing."

"If you ask me, I think you've begun at the wrong end," said Ranson. "If I were looking for the Red Rider I'd search for him in Kiowa City."

"Why?"

"Because, at this end no one but a few officers knew that the paymaster was coming, while in Kiowa everybody in the town knew it, for they saw him start. It would be very easy for one of those cowboys to ride ahead and lie in wait for him in the buttes. There are several tough specimens in Kiowa. Any one of them would rob a man for twenty dollars—let alone ten thousand. There's 'Abe' Fisher and Foster King, and the Chase boys, and I believe old 'Pop' Henderson himself isn't above holding up one of his own stages."

"He's above shooting himself in the lungs," said Carr. "Nonsense. No, I am convinced that someone followed you from this post, and perhaps Cahill can tell us who that was.

I sent for him this morning, and he's waiting at my quarters now. Suppose I ask him to step over here, so that we can discuss it together."

Before he answered, Ranson hesitated, with his eyes on the ground. He had no way of knowing whether Mary Cahill had told her father anything of what he had said to her that morning. But if she had done so, he did not want to meet Cahill in the presence of a third party for the first time since he had learned the news.

"I'll tell you what I wish you would do," he said. "I wish you'd let me see Cahill first, by myself. What I want to see him about has nothing to do with the hold-up," he added. "It concerns only us two, but I'd like to have it out of the way before we consult him as a witness."

Carr rose doubtfully. "Why, certainly," he said; "I'll send him over, and when you're ready for me step out on the porch and call. I'll be sitting on my veranda. I hope you've had no quarrel with Cahill—I mean I hope this personal matter is nothing that will prejudice him against you."

Ranson smiled. "I hope not, too," he said. "No, we've not quarrelled- -yet," he added.

Carr still lingered. "Cahill is like to be a very important witness for the other side—"

"I doubt it," said Ranson, easily. "Cahill's a close-mouthed chap, but when he does talk he talks to the point and he'll tell the truth. That can't hurt us."

As Cahill crossed the parade-ground from Captain Carr's quarters on his way to Ranson's hut his brain was crowded swiftly with doubts, memories, and resolves. For him the interview held no alarms. He had no misgivings as to its outcome. For his daughter's sake he was determined that he himself must not be disgraced in her eyes and that to that end Ranson must be sacrificed. It was to make a lady of her, as he understood what a lady should be, that on six moonlit raids he had ventured forth in his red mask and robbed the Kiowa stage. That there were others who roamed abroad in the disguise of the Red Rider he was well aware. There were nights the stage was held up when he was innocently busy behind his counter in touch with the whole garrison. Of these nights he made much. They were alibis furnished by his rivals. They served to keep suspicion from himself, and he, working for the same object, was indefatigable in proclaiming that all the depredations of the Red Rider showed the handiwork of one and the same individual.

"He comes from Kiowa of course," he would point out. "Some feller who lives where the stage starts, and knows when the passengers carry money. You don't hear of him holding up a stage full of recruits or cow-punchers. It's always the drummers and the mine directors that the Red Rider lays for. How does he know they're in the stage if he don't see 'em start from Kiowa? Ask 'Pop' Henderson. Ask 'Abe' Fisher. Mebbe they know more than they'd care to tell."

The money which at different times Cahill had taken from the Kiowa stage lay in a New York bank, and the law of limitation made it now possible for him to return to that city and claim it. Already his savings were sufficient in amount to support both his daughter and himself in one of those foreign cities, of which she had so often told him and for which he knew she hungered. And for the last five years he had had no other object in living than to feed her wants. Through some strange trick of the mind he remembered suddenly and vividly a long-forgotten scene in the back room of McTurk's, when he was McTurk's bouncer. The night before a girl had killed herself in this same back room; she made the third who had done so in the month. He recalled the faces of the reporters eyeing McTurk in cold distaste as that terror of the Bowery whimpered before them on his knees. "But my daughters will read it," he had begged. "Suppose they believe I'm what you call me. Don't go and give me a bad name to them, gentlemen. It ain't my fault the girl's died here. You wouldn't have my daughters think I'm to blame for that? They're ladies, my daughters, they're just out of the convent, and they don't know that there is such women in the world as come to this place. And I can't have 'em turned against their old pop. For God's sake, gentlemen, don't let my girls know!"

Cahill remembered the contempt he had felt for his employer as he pulled him to his feet, but now McTurk's appeal seemed just and natural. His point of view was that of the loving and considerate parent. In Cahill's mind there was no moral question involved. If to make his girl rich and a lady, and to lift her out of the life of the Exchange, was a sin the sin was his own and he was willing to "stand for it." And, like McTurk, he would see that the sin of the father was not visited upon the child. Ranson was rich, foolishly, selfishly rich; his father was a United States Senator with influence enough, and money enough, to fight the law—to buy his son out of jail. Sooner than his daughter should know that her father was one of those who sometimes wore the mask of the Red Rider, Ranson, for all he cared, could go to jail, or to hell. With this ultimatum in his mind, Cahill confronted his would-be son-in-law with a calm and assured countenance.

Ranson greeted him with respectful deference, and while Cahill seated himself, Ranson, chatting hospitably, placed cigars and glasses before him. He began upon the subject that touched him the most nearly.

"Miss Cahill was good enough to bring up my breakfast this morning," he said. "Has she told you of what I said to her?"

Cahill shook his head. "No, I haven't seen her. We've been taking account of stock all morning."

"Then—then you've heard nothing from her about me?" said Ranson.

The post trader raised his head in surprise. "No. Captain Carr spoke to me about your arrest, and then said you wanted to see me first about something private." The post trader fixed Ranson with his keen, unwavering eyes. "What might that be?" he asked.

"Well, it doesn't matter now," stammered Ranson; "I'll wait until Miss Cahill tells you."

"Any complaint about the food?" inquired the post trader.

Ranson laughed nervously. "No, it's not that," he said. He rose, and, to protect what Miss Cahill evidently wished to remain a secret, changed the subject. "You see you've lived in these parts so long, Mr. Cahill," he explained, "and you know so many people, I thought maybe you could put me on the track or give me some hint as to which of that Kiowa gang really did rob the paymaster." Ranson was pulling the cork from the whiskey bottle, and when he asked the question Cahill pushed his glass from him and shook his head. Ranson looked up interrogatively and smiled. "You mean you think I did it myself?" he asked.

"I didn't understand from Captain Carr," the post trader began in heavy tones, "that it's my opinion you're after. He said I might be wanted to testify who was present last night in my store."

"Certainly, that's all we want," Ranson answered, genially. "I only thought you might give me a friendly pointer or two on the outside. And, of course, if it's your opinion I did the deed we certainly don't want your opinion. But that needn't prevent your taking a drink with me, need it? Don't be afraid. I'm not trying to corrupt you. And I'm not trying to poison a witness for the other fellows, either. Help yourself."

Cahill stretched out his left hand. His right remained hidden in the side pocket of his coat. "What's the matter with your right hand?" Ranson asked. "Are you holding a gun on me? Really, Mr. Cahill, you're not taking any chances, are you?" Ranson gazed about the room as though seeking an appreciative audience. "He's such an important witness," he cried, delightedly, "that first he's afraid I'll poison him and he won't drink with me, and now he covers me with a gun."

Reluctantly, Cahill drew out his hand. "I was putting the bridle on my pony last night," he said. "He bit me."

Ranson exclaimed sympathetically, "Oh, that's too bad," he said. "Well, you know you want to be careful. A horse's teeth really are poisonous." He examined his own hands complacently. "Now, if I had a bandage like that on my right hand they would hang me sure, no matter whether it was a bite, or a burn, or a bullet."

Cahill raised the glass to his lips and sipped the whiskey critically. "Why?" he asked.

"Why? Why, didn't you know that the paymaster boasted last night to the surgeons that he hit this fellow in the hand? He says—"

Cahill snorted scornfully. "How'd he know that? What makes him think so?"

"Well, never mind, let him think so," Ranson answered, fervently. "Don't discourage him. That's the only evidence I've got on my side. He says he fired to disarm the man, and that he saw him shift his gun to his left hand. It was the shot that the man fired when he held his gun in his left that broke the colonel's arm. Now, everybody knows I can't hit a barn with my left. And as for having any wounds concealed about my person"—Ranson turned his hands like a conjurer to show the front and back—"they can search me. So, if the paymaster will only stick to that story—that he hit the man—it will help me a lot." Ranson seated himself on the table and swung his leg. "And of course it would be a big help, too, if you could remember who was in your Exchange when I was planning to rob the coach. For someone certainly must have overheard me, someone must have copied my disguise, and that someone is the man we must find. Unless he came from Kiowa."

Cahill shoved his glass from him across the table and, placing his hands on his knees, stared at his host coldly and defiantly. His would-be son-in-law observed the aggressiveness of his attitude, but, in his fuller knowledge of their prospective relations, smiled blandly.

"Mr. Ranson," began Cahill, "I've no feelings against you personally. I've a friendly feeling for all of you young gentlemen at my mess. But you're not playing fair with me. I can see what you want, and I can tell you that you and Captain Carr are not helping your case by asking me up here to drink and smoke with you, when you know that I'm the most important witness they've got against you."

Ranson stared at his father-in-law-elect in genuine amazement, and then laughed lightly.

"Why, dear Mr. Cahill," he cried, "I wouldn't think of bribing you with such a bad brand of whiskey as this. And I didn't know you were such an important witness as all that. But, of course, I know whatever you say in this community goes, and if your testimony is against me, I'm sorry for it, very sorry. I suppose you will testify that there was no one in the Exchange who could have heard my plan?"

Cahill nodded.

"And, as it's not likely two men at exactly the same time should have thought of robbing the stage in exactly the same way, I must have robbed it myself."

Cahill nursed his bandaged hand with the other. "That's the court's business," he growled; "I mean to tell the truth."

"And the truth is?" asked Ransom

"The truth is that last night there was no one in the Exchange but you officers and me. If anybody'd come in on the store side you'd have seen him, wouldn't you? and if he'd come into the Exchange I'd have seen him. But no one come in. I was there alone—and certainly I didn't hear your plan, and I didn't rob the stage. When you fellows left I went down to the Indian village. Half the reservation can prove I was there all the evening—so of the four of us, that lets me out. Crosby and Curtis were in command of the pay escort—that's their alibi—and as far as I can see, lieutenant, that puts it up to you."

Ranson laughed and shook his head. "Yes, it certainly looks that way," he said. "Only I can't see why you need be so damned pleased about it." He grinned wickedly. "If you weren't such a respectable member of Fort Crockett society I might say you listened at the door, and rode after me in one of your own ponchos. As for the Indian village, that's no alibi. A Kiowa swear his skin's as white as yours if you give him a drink."

"And is that why I get this one?" Cahill demanded. "Am I a Kiowa?"

Ranson laughed and shoved the bottle toward his father-in-law-elect.

"Oh, can't you take a joke?" he said. "Take another drink, then."

The voice outside the hut was too low to reach the irate Cahill, but Ranson heard it and leaped to his feet.

"Wait," he commanded. He ran to the door, and met Sergeant Clancey at the threshold.

"Miss Cahill, lieutenant," said the sergeant, "wants to see her father."

Cahill had followed Ranson to the door, "You want to see me, Mame? "he asked.

"Yes," Miss Cahill cried; "and Mr. Ransom, too, if I may." She caught her father eagerly by the arm, but her eyes were turned joyfully upon Ranson. They were laughing with excitement. Her voice was trembling and eager.

"It is something I have discovered," she cried; "I found it out just now, and I think—oh, I hope!—it is most important. I believe it will clear Mr. Ranson!" she cried, happily. "At least it will show that last night someone went out to rob the coach and went dressed as he was."

Cahill gave a short laugh. "What's his name?" he asked, mockingly. "Have you seen him?"

"I didn't see him and I don't know his name, but—"

Cahill snorted, and picked up his sombrero from the table. "Then it's not so very important after all," he said. "Is that all that brought you here?"

"The main thing is that she is here," said Ranson; "for which the poor prisoner is grateful—grateful to her and to the man she hasn't seen, in the mask and poncho, whose name she doesn't know. Mr. Cahill, bad as it is, I insist on your finishing your whiskey. Miss Cahill, please sit down."

He moved a chair toward her and, as he did so, looked full into her face with such love and happiness that she turned her eyes away.

"Well?" asked Cahill.

"I must first explain to Lieutenant Ranson, father," said his daughter, "that to-day is the day we take account of stock."

"Speaking of stock," said Ranson, "don't forget that I owe you for a red kerchief and a rubber poncho. You can have them back, if you like. I won't need a rain coat where I am going."

"Don't," said Miss Cahill. "Please let me go on. After I brought you your breakfast here, I couldn't begin to work just at once. I was thinking about—something else. Everyone was talking of you—your arrest, and I couldn't settle down to take account of stock." She threw a look at Ranson which asked for his sympathy. "But when I did start I began with the ponchos and the red kerchiefs, and then I found out something." Cahill was regarding his daughter in strange distress, but Ranson appeared indifferent to her words, and intent only on the light and beauty in her face. But he asked, smiling, "And that was?"

"You see," continued Miss Cahill, eagerly, "I always keep a dozen of each article, and as each one is sold I check it off in my day-book. Yesterday Mrs. Bolland bought a poncho for the colonel. That left eleven ponchos. Then a few minutes later I gave Lightfoot a red kerchief for his squaw. That left eleven kerchiefs."

"Stop!" cried Ranson. "Miss Cahill," he began, severely, "I hope you do not mean to throw suspicion on the wife of my respected colonel, or on Mrs. Lightfoot, 'the Prairie Flower.' Those ladies are my personal friends; I refuse to believe them guilty. And have you ever seen Mrs. Bolland on horseback? You wrong her. It is impossible."

"Please," begged Miss Cahill, "please let me explain. When you went to hold up the stage you took a poncho and a kerchief. That should have left ten of each. But when I counted them this morning there were nine red kerchiefs and nine ponchos."

Ranson slapped his knee sharply. "Good!" he said. "That is interesting."

"What does it prove?" demanded Cahill.

"It proves nothing, or it proves everything," said Miss Cahill. "To my mind it proves without any doubt that someone overheard Mr. Ranson's plan, that he dressed like him to throw suspicion on him, and that this second person was the one who robbed the paymaster. Now, father, this is where you can help us. You were there then. Try to remember. It is so important. Who came into the store after the others had gone away?"

Cahill tossed his head like an angry bull.

"There are fifty places in this post," he protested, roughly, "where a man can get a poncho. Every trooper owns his slicker."

"But, father, we don't know that theirs are missing," cried Miss Cahill, "and we do know that those in our store are. Don't think I am foolish. It seemed such an important fact to me, and I had hoped it would help."

"It does help—immensely!" cried Ranson.

"I think it's a splendid clue. But, unfortunately, I don't think we can prove anything by your father, for he's just been telling me that there was no one in the place but himself. No one came in, and he was quite alone—" Ranson had begun speaking eagerly, but either his own words or the intentness with which Cahill received them caused him to halt and hesitate—"absolutely—alone."

"You see," said Cahill, thickly, "as soon as they had gone I rode to the Indian village."

"Why, no, father," corrected Miss Cahill. "Don't you remember, you told me last night that when you reached Lightfoot's tent I had just gone. That was quite two hours after the others left the store." In her earnestness Miss Cahill had placed her hand upon her father's arm and clutched it eagerly. "And you remember no one coming in before you left?" she asked. "No one?"

Cahill had not replaced the bandaged hand in his pocket, but had shoved it inside the opening of his coat. As Mary Cahill caught his arm her fingers sank into the palm of the hand and he gave a slight grimace of pain.

"Oh, father," Miss Cahill cried, "your hand! I am so sorry. Did I hurt it? Please—let me see."

Cahill drew back with sudden violence.

"No!" he cried. "Leave it alone! Come, we must be going." But Miss Cahill held the wounded hand in both her own. When she turned her eyes to Ranson they were filled with tender concern.

"I hurt him," she said, reproachfully. "He shot himself last night with one of those new cylinder revolvers."

Her father snatched the hand from her. He tried to drown her voice by a sudden movement toward the door. "Come!" he called. "Do you hear me?"

But his daughter in her sympathy continued. "He was holding it so," she said, "and it went off, and the bullet passed through here." She laid the tip of a slim white finger on the palm of her right hand.

"The bullet!" cried Ranson. He repeated, dully, "The bullet!"

There was a sudden, tense silence. Outside they could hear the crunch of the sentry's heel in the gravel, and from the baseball field back of the barracks the soft spring air was rent with the jubilant crack of the bat as it drove the ball. Afterward Ranson remembered that while one half of his brain was terribly acute to the moment, the other was wondering whether the runner had made his base. It seemed an interminable time before Ranson raised his eyes from Miss Cahill's palm to her father's face. What he read in them caused Cahill to drop his hand swiftly to his hip.

Ranson saw the gesture and threw out both his hands. He gave a hysterical laugh, strangely boyish and immature, and ran to place himself between Cahill and the door. "Drop it!" he whispered. "My God, man!" he entreated, "don't make a fool of yourself. Mr. Cahill," he cried aloud, "you can't go till you know. Can he, Mary? Yes, Mary." The tone in which he repeated the name was proprietary and commanding. He took her hand. "Mr. Cahill," he said, joyously, "we've got something to tell you. I want you to understand that in spite of all I'VE done—I say in spite of all I'VE done—I mean getting into this trouble and disgrace, and all that—I've dared to ask your daughter to marry me." He turned and led Miss Cahill swiftly toward the veranda. "Oh, I knew he wouldn't like it," he cried. "You see. I told you so. You've got to let me talk to him alone. You go outside and wait. I can talk better when you are not here. I'll soon bring him around."

"Father," pleaded Miss Cahill, timidly. From behind her back Ranson shook his head at the post-trader in violent pantomime. "She'd better go outside and wait, hadn't she, Mr. Cahill?" he directed.

As he was bidden, the post-trader raised his head and nodded toward the door. The onslaught of sudden and new conditions overwhelmed and paralyzed him.

"Father!" said Miss Cahill, "it isn't just as you think. Mr. Ranson did ask me to marry him—in a way—At least, I knew what he meant. But I did not say—in a way—that I would marry him. I mean it was not settled, or I would have told you. You mustn't think I would have left you out of this—of my happiness, you who have done everything to make me happy."

She reproached her father with her eyes fastened on his face. His own were stern, fixed, and miserable. "You will let it be, won't you, father?" she begged. "It—it means so much. I—can't tell you—" She threw out her hand toward Ranson as though designating a superior being. "Why, I can't tell HIM. But if you are harsh with him or with me it will break my heart. For as I love you, father, I love him—and it has got to be. It must be. For I love him so. I have always loved him. Father," she whispered, "I love him so."

Ranson, humbly, gratefully, took the girl's hand and led her gently to the veranda and closed the door upon her. Then he came down the room and regarded his prospective father-in-law with an expression of amused exasperation. He thrust his hands deep into the pockets of his riding-breeches and nodded his head. "Well," he exclaimed, "you've made a damned pretty mess of it, haven't you?"

Cahill had sunk heavily into a chair and was staring at Ranson with the stupid, wondering gaze of a dumb animal in pain. During the moments in which the two men eyed each other Ranson's smile disappeared. Cahill raised himself slowly as though with a great effort.

"I done it," said Cahill, "for her. I done it to make her happy."

"That's all right," said Ranson, briskly. "She's going to be happy. We're all going to be happy."

"An' all I did," Cahill continued, as though unconscious of the interruption, "was to disgrace her." He rose suddenly to his feet. His mental sufferings were so keen that his huge body trembled. He recognized how truly he had made "a mess of it." He saw that all he had hoped to do for his daughter by crime would have been done for her by this marriage with Ranson, which would have made her a "lady," made her rich, made her happy. Had it not been for his midnight raids she would have been honored, loved, and envied, even by the wife of the colonel herself. But through him disgrace had come upon her, sorrow and trouble. She would not be known as the daughter of Senator Ranson, but of Cahill, an ex-member of the Whyo gang, a highway robber, as the daughter of a thief who was serving his time in State prison. At the thought Cahill stepped backward unsteadily as though he had been struck. He cried suddenly aloud. Then his hand whipped back to his revolver, but before he could use it Ranson had seized his wrist with both hands. The two struggled silently and fiercely. The fact of opposition brought back to Cahill all of his great strength.

"No, you don't!" Ranson muttered. "Think of your daughter, man. Drop it!"

"I shall do it," Cahill panted. "I am thinking of my daughter. It's the only way out. Take your hands off me—I shall!"

With his knuckles Ranson bored cruelly into the wounded hand, and it opened and the gun dropped from it; but as it did so it went off with a report that rang through the building. There was an instant rush of feet upon the steps of the veranda, and at the sound the two men sprang apart, eyeing each other sheepishly like two discovered truants. When Sergeant Clancey and the guard pushed through the door Ranson stood facing it, spinning the revolver in cowboy fashion around his fourth finger. He addressed the sergeant in a tone of bitter irony.

"Oh, you've come at last," he demanded. "Are you deaf? Why didn't you come when I called?" His tone showed he considered he had just cause for annoyance.

"The gun brought me, I—" began Clancey.

"Yes, I hoped it might. That's why I fired it," snapped Ranson. "I want two whiskey-and-sodas. Quick now!"

"Two—" gasped Clancey.

"Whiskey-and-sodas. See how fast one of you can chase over to the club and get 'em. And next time I want a drink don't make me wake the entire garrison."

As the soldiers retreated Ranson discovered Miss Cahill's white face beyond them. He ran and held the door open by a few inches.

"It's all right," he whispered, reassuringly. "He's nearly persuaded. Wait just a minute longer and he'll be giving us his blessing."

"But the pistol-shot?" she asked.

"I was just calling the guard. The electric bell's broken, and your father wanted a drink. That's a good sign, isn't it? Shows he's friendly, What kind did you say you wanted, Mr. Cahill—Scotch was it, or rye?" Ranson glanced back at the sombre, silent figure of Cahill, and then again opened the door sufficiently for him to stick out his head. "Sergeant," he called, "make them both Scotch—long ones."

He shut the door and turned upon the post-trader. "Now, then, father- in-law," he said, briskly, "you've got to cut and run, and you've got to run quick. We'll tell 'em you're going to Fort Worth to buy the engagement ring, because I can't, being under arrest. But you go to Duncan City instead, and from there take the cars, to—"

"Run away!" Cahill repeated, dazedly. "But you'll be court- martialled."

"There won't be any court-martial!"

Cahill glanced around the room quickly. "I see," he cried. In his eagerness he was almost smiling. "I'm to leave a confession and give it to you."

"Confession! What rot!" cried Ranson.

"They can't prove anything against me. Everyone knows by now that there were two men on the trail, but they don't know who the other man was, and no one ever must know—especially Mary."

Cahill struck the table with his fist. "I won't stand for it!" he cried. "I got you into this and I'm goin'—"

"Yes, going to jail," retorted Ranson. "You'll look nice behind the bars, won't you? Your daughter will be proud of you in a striped suit. Don't talk nonsense. You're going to run and hide some place, somewhere, where Mary and I can come and pay you a visit. Say— Canada. No, not Canada. I'd rather visit you in jail than in a Montreal hotel. Say Tangier, or Buenos Ayres, or Paris. Yes, Paris is safe enough—and so amusing."

Cahill seated himself heavily. "I trapped you into this fix, Mr. Ranson," he said, "you know I did, and now I mean to get you out of it. I ain't going to leave the man my Mame wants to marry with a cloud on him. I ain't going to let her husband be jailed."

Ranson had run to his desk and from a drawer drew forth a roll of bills. He advanced with them in his hand.

"Yes, Paris is certainly the place," he said. "Here's three hundred dollars. I'll cable you the rest. You've never been to Paris, have you? It's full of beautiful sights—Henry's American Bar, for instance, and the courtyard of the Grand Hotel, and Maxim's. All good Americans go to Paris when they die and all the bad ones while they are alive. You'll find lots of both kinds, and you'll sit all day on the sidewalk and drink Bock and listen to Hungarian bands. And Mary and I will join you there and take you driving in the Bois. Now, you start at once. I'll tell her you've gone to New York to talk it over with father, and buy the ring. Then I'll say you've gone on to Paris to rent us apartments for the honeymoon. I'll explain it somehow. That's better than going to jail, isn't it, and making us bow our heads in grief?"

Cahill, in his turn, approached the desk and, seating himself before it, began writing rapidly.

"What is it?" asked Ranson.

"A confession," said Cahill, his pen scratching.

"I won't take it," Ranson said, "and I won't use it."

"I ain't going to give it to you," said Cahill, over his shoulder. "I know better than that. But I don't go to Paris unless I leave a confession behind me. Call in the guard," he commanded; "I want two witnesses."

"I'll see you hanged first," said Ranson.

Cahill crossed the room to the door and, throwing it open, called, "Corporal of the guard!"

As he spoke, Captain Carr and Mrs. Bolland, accompanied by Miss Post and her aunt, were crossing the parade-ground. For a moment the post- trader surveyed them doubtfully, and then, stepping out upon the veranda, beckoned to them.

"Here's a paper I've signed, captain," he said; "I wish you'd witness my signature. It's my testimony for the court-martial."

"Then someone else had better sign it," said Carr. "Might look prejudiced if I did." He turned to the ladies. "These ladies are coming in to see Ranson now. They'll witness it."

Miss Cahill, from the other end of the veranda, and the visitors entered the room together.

"Mrs. Truesdale!" cried Ranson. "You are pouring coals of fire upon my head. And Miss Post! Indeed, this is too much honor. After the way I threatened and tried to frighten you last night I expected you to hang me, at least, instead of which you have, I trust, come to tea."

"Nothing of the sort," said Mrs. Bolland, sternly. "These ladies insisted on my bringing them here to say how sorry they are that they talked so much and got you into this trouble. Understand, Mr. Ranson," the colonel's wife added, with dignity, "that I am not here officially as Mrs. Bolland, but as a friend of these ladies."

"You are welcome in whatever form you take, Mrs. Bolland," cried Ranson, "and, believe me, I am in no trouble—no trouble, I assure you. In fact, I am quite the most contented man in the world. Mrs. Bolland, in spite of the cloud, the temporary cloud which rests upon my fair name, I take great pride in announcing to you that this young lady has done me the honor to consent to become my wife. Her father, a very old and dear friend, has given his consent. And I take this occasion to tell you of my good fortune, both in your official capacity and as my friend."

There was a chorus of exclamations and congratulations in which Mrs. Bolland showed herself to be a true wife and a social diplomatist. In the post-trader's daughter she instantly recognized the heiress to the Ranson millions, and the daughter of a Senator who also was the chairman of the Senate Committee on Brevets and Promotions. She fell upon Miss Cahill's shoulder and kissed her on both cheeks. Turning eagerly upon Mrs. Truesdale, she said, "Alice, you can understand how I feel when I tell you that this child has always been to me like one of my own."

Carr took Ranson's hand and wrung it. Sergeant Clancey grew purple with pleasure and stole back to the veranda, where he whispered joyfully to a sentry. In another moment a passing private was seen racing delightedly toward the baseball field.

At the same moment Lieutenants Crosby and Curtis and the regimental adjutant crossed the parade ground from the colonel's quarters and ran up the steps of Ranson's hut. The expressions of good-will, of smiling embarrassment and general satisfaction which Lieutenant Crosby observed on the countenances of those present seemed to give him a momentary check.

"Oh," he exclaimed, disappointedly, "someone has told you!"

Ranson laughed and took the hand which Crosby held doubtfully toward him. "No one has told me," he said. "I've been telling them."

"Then you haven't heard?" Crosby cried, delightedly. "That's good. I begged to be the first to let you know, because I felt so badly at having doubted you. You must let me congratulate you. You are free."

"Free?" smiled Ranson.

"Yes, relieved from arrest," Crosby cried, joyfully. He turned and took Ranson's sword from the hands of the adjutant. "And the colonel's let your troop have the band to give you a serenade."

But Ranson's face showed no sign of satisfaction.

"Wait!" he cried. "Why am I relieved from arrest?"

"Why? Because the other fellow has confessed."

Ranson placed himself suddenly in front of Mary Cahill as though to shield her. His eyes stole stealthily towards

Cahill's confession. Still unread and still unsigned, it lay unopened upon the table. Cahill was gazing upon Ranson in blank bewilderment.

Captain Carr gasped a sigh of relief that was far from complimentary to his client.

"Who confessed?" he cried.

"'Pop' Henderson," said Crosby.

"'Pop' Henderson!" shouted Cahill. Unmindful of his wound, he struck the table savagely with his fist. For the first time in the knowledge of the post he exhibited emotion. "'Pop' Henderson, by the eternal!" he cried. "And I never guessed it!"

"Yes," said Crosby, eagerly. "Abe Fisher was in it. Henderson persuaded the paymaster to make the trip alone with him. Then he dressed up Fisher to represent the Red Rider and sent him on ahead to hold him up. They were to share the money afterward. But Fisher fired on 'Pop' to kill, so as to have it all, and 'Pop's' trying to get even. And what with wanting to hurt Fisher, and thinking he is going to die, and not wishing to see you hanged, he's told the truth. We wired Kiowa early this morning and arrested Fisher. They've found the money, and he has confessed, too."

"But the poncho and the red kerchief?" protested Carr. "And he had no stirrups!"

"Oh, Fisher had the make-up all right," laughed Crosby; "Henderson says Fisher's the 'only, original' Red Rider. And as for the stirrups, I'm afraid that's my fault. I asked the colonel if the man wasn't riding without stirrups, and I guess the wish was father to the fact. He only imagined he hadn't seen any stirrups. The colonel was rattled. So, old man," he added, turning to Ranson, "here's your sword again, and God bless you."

Already the post had learned the news from the band and the verandas of the enlisted men overflowed with delighted troopers. From the stables and the ball field came the sound of hurrying feet, and a tumult of cheers and cowboy yells. Across the parade-ground the regimental band bore down upon Ranson's hut, proclaiming to the garrison that there would be a hot time in the old town that night. But Sergeant Clancey ran to meet the bandmaster, and shouted in his ear. "He's going to marry Mary Cahill," he cried. "I heard him tell the colonel's wife. Play 'Just Because She Made Them Goo-goo Eyes.'"

"Like hell!" cried the bandmaster, indignantly, breaking in on the tune with his baton. "I know my business! Now, then, men," he commanded, "'I'll Leave My Happy Home for You.'"

As Mrs. Bolland dragged Miss Cahill into view of the assembled troopers Ranson pulled his father-in-law into a far corner of the room. He shook the written confession in his face.

"Now, will you kindly tell me what that means?" he demanded. "What sort of a gallery play were you trying to make?"

Cahill shifted his sombrero guiltily. "I was trying to get you out of the hole," he stammered. "I—I thought you done it."

"You thought I done it!"

"Sure. I never thought nothing else."

"Then why do you say here that YOU did it?"

"Oh, because," stammered Cahill, miserably, "'cause of Mary, 'cause she wanted to marry you—'cause you were going to marry her."

"Well—but—what good were you going to do by shooting yourself?"

"Oh, then?" Cahill jerked back his head as though casting out an unpleasant memory. "I thought you'd caught me, you, too—between you!"

"Caught you! Then you did—?"

"No, but I tried to. I heard your plan, and I did follow you in the poncho and kerchief, meaning to hold up the stage first, and leave it to Crosby and Curtis to prove you did it. But when I reached the coach you were there ahead of me, and I rode away and put in my time at the Indian village. I never saw the paymaster's cart, never heard of it till this morning. But what with Mame missing the poncho out of our shop and the wound in my hand I guessed they'd all soon suspect me. I saw you did. So I thought I'd just confess to what I meant to do, even if I didn't do it."

Ranson surveyed his father-in-law with a delighted grin. "How did you get that bullet-hole in your hand?" he asked.

Cahill laughed shamefacedly. "I hate to tell you that," he said. "I got it just as I said I did. My new gun went off while I was fooling with it, with my hand over the muzzle. And me the best shot in the Territory! But when I heard the paymaster claimed he shot the Red Rider through the palm I knew no one would believe me if I told the truth. So I lied."

Ranson glanced down at the written confession, and then tore it slowly into pieces. "And you were sure I robbed the stage, and yet you believed that I'd use this? What sort of a son-in-law do you think you've got?"

"You thought I robbed the stage, didn't you?"

"Yes."

"And you were going to stand for robbing it yourself, weren't you? Well, that's the sort of son-in-law I've got!"

The two men held out their hands at the same instant.

Mary Cahill, her face glowing with pride and besieged with blushes, came toward them from the veranda. She was laughing and radiant, but she turned her eyes on Ranson with a look of tender reproach.

"Why did you desert me?" she said. "It was awful. They are calling you now. They are playing 'The Conquering Hero.'"

"Mr. Cahill," commanded Ranson, "go out there and make a speech." He turned to Mary Cahill and lifted one of her hands in both of his. "Well, I AM the conquering hero," he said. "I've won the only thing worth winning, dearest," he whispered; "we'll run away from them in a minute, and we'll ride to the waterfall and the Lover's Leap." He looked down at her wistfully. "Do you remember?"

Mary Cahill raised her head and smiled. He leaned toward her breathlessly.

"Why, did it mean that to you, too?" he asked.

She smiled up at him in assent.

"But I didn't say anything, did I?" whispered Ranson. "I hardly knew you then. But I knew that day that I—that I would marry you or nobody else. And did you think—that you—"

"Yes," Mary Cahill whispered.

He bent his head and touched her hand with his lips.

"Then we'll go back this morning to the waterfall," he said, "and tell it that it's all come right. And now, we'll bow to those crazy people out there, those make-believe dream-people, who don't know that there is nothing real in this world but just you and me, and that we love each other."

A dishevelled orderly bearing a tray with two glasses confronted Ranson at the door. "Here's the Scotch and sodas, lieutenant," he panted. "I couldn't get 'em any sooner. The men wanted to take 'em off me—to drink Miss Cahill's health."

"So they shall," said Ranson. "Tell them to drink the canteen dry and charge it to me. What's a little thing like the regulations between friends? They have taught me my manners. Mr. Cahill," he called.

The post-trader returned from the veranda.

Ranson solemnly handed him a glass and raised the other in the air. "Here's hoping that the Red Rider rides on his raids no more," he said; "and to the future Mrs. Ranson—to Mary Cahill, God bless her!"

He shattered the empty glass in the grate and took Cahill's hand.

"Father-in-law," said Ranson, "let's promise each other to lead a new and a better life."

THE BAR SINISTER

PART I

The Master was walking most unsteady, his legs tripping each other. After the fifth or sixth round, my legs often go the same way.

But even when the Master's legs bend and twist a bit, you mustn't think he can't reach you. Indeed, that is the time he kicks most frequent. So I kept behind him in the shadow, or ran in the middle of the street. He stopped at many public-houses with swinging doors, those doors that are cut so high from the sidewalk that you can look in under them, and see if the Master is inside. At night when I peep beneath them the man at the counter will see me first and say, "Here's the Kid, Jerry, come to take you home. Get a move on you," and the Master will stumble out and follow me. It's lucky for us I'm so white, for no matter how dark the night, he can always see me ahead, just out of reach of his boot. At night the Master certainly does see most amazing. Sometimes he sees two or four of me, and walks in a circle, so that I have to take him by the leg of his trousers and lead him into the right road. One night, when he was very nasty-tempered and I was coaxing him along, two men passed us and one of them says, "Look at that brute!" and the other asks "Which?" and they both laugh. The Master, he cursed them good and proper.

This night, whenever we stopped at a public-house, the Master's pals left it and went on with us to the next. They spoke quite civil to me, and when the Master tried a flying kick, they gives him a shove. "Do you want we should lose our money?" says the pals.

I had had nothing to eat for a day and a night, and just before we set out the Master gives me a wash under the hydrant. Whenever I am locked up until all the slop-pans in our alley are empty, and made to take a bath, and the Master's pals speak civil, and feel my ribs, I know something is going to happen. And that night, when every time they see a policeman under a lamp-post, they dodged across the street, and when at the last one of them picked me up and hid me under his jacket, I began to tremble; for I knew what it meant. It meant that I was to fight again for the Master.

I don't fight because I like it. I fight because if I didn't the other dog would find my throat, and the Master would lose his stakes, and I would be very sorry for him and ashamed. Dogs can pass me and I can pass dogs, and I'd never pick a fight with none of them. When I see two dogs standing on their hind-legs in the streets, clawing each other's ears, and snapping for each other's windpipes, or howling and swearing and rolling in the mud, I feel sorry they should act so, and pretend not to notice. If he'd let me, I'd like to pass the time of day with every dog I meet. But there's something about me that no nice dog can abide. When I trot up to nice dogs, nodding and grinning, to make friends, they always tell me to be off. "Go to the devil!" they bark at me; "Get out!" and when I walk away they shout "mongrel," and "gutter-dog," and sometimes, after my back is turned, they rush me. I could kill most of them with three shakes, breaking the back-bone of the little ones, and squeezing the throat of the big ones. But what's the good? They are nice dogs; that's why I try to make up to them, and though it's not for them to say it, I am a street-dog, and if I try to push into the company of my betters, I suppose it's their right to teach me my place.

Of course, they don't know I'm the best fighting bull-terrier of my weight in Montreal. That's why it wouldn't be right for me to take no notice of what they shout. They don't know that if I once locked my jaws on them I'd carry away whatever I touched. The night I fought Kelley's White Rat, I wouldn't loosen up until the Master made a noose in my leash and strangled me, and if the handlers hadn't thrown red pepper down my nose, I never would have let go of that Ottawa dog. I don't think the handlers treated me quite right that time, but maybe they didn't know the Ottawa dog was dead. I did.

I learned my fighting from my mother when I was very young. We slept in a lumber-yard on the river-front, and by day hunted for food along the wharves. When we got it, the other tramp-dogs would try to take it off us, and then it was wonderful to see mother fly at them, and drive them away. All I know of fighting I learned from mother, watching her picking the ash-heaps for me when I was too little to fight for myself. No one ever was so good to me as mother. When it snowed and the ice was in the St. Lawrence she used to hunt alone, and bring me back new bones, and she'd sit and laugh to see me trying to swallow 'em whole. I was just a puppy then, my teeth was falling out. When I was able to fight we kept the whole river-range to ourselves, I had the genuine long, "punishing" jaw, so mother said, and there wasn't a man or a dog that dared worry us. Those were happy days, those were; and we lived well, share and share alike, and when we wanted a bit of fun, we chased the fat old wharf-rats. My! how they would squeal!

Then the trouble came. It was no trouble to me. I was too young to care then. But mother took it so to heart that she grew ailing, and wouldn't go abroad with me by day. It was the same old scandal that they're always bringing up against me. I was so young then that I didn't know. I couldn't see any difference between mother—and other mothers.

But one day a pack of curs we drove off snarled back some new names at her, and mother dropped her head and ran, just as though they had whipped us. After that she wouldn't go out with me except in the dark, and one day she went away and never came back, and though I hunted for her in every court and alley and back street of Montreal, I never found her.

One night, a month after mother ran away, I asked Guardian, the old blind mastiff, whose Master is the night-watchman on our slip, what it all meant. And he told me.

"Every dog in Montreal knows," he says, "except you, and every Master knows. So I think it's time you knew."

Then he tells me that my father, who had treated mother so bad, was a great and noble gentleman from London. "Your father had twenty-two registered ancestors, had your father," old Guardian says, "and in him was the best bull-terrier blood of England, the most ancientest, the most royal; the winning 'blue-ribbon' blood, that breeds champions. He had sleepy pink eyes, and thin pink lips, and he was as white all over as his own white teeth, and under his white skin you could see his muscles, hard and smooth, like the links of a steel chain. When your father stood still, and tipped his nose in the air, it was just as though he was saying, 'Oh, yes, you common dogs and men, you may well stare. It must be a rare treat for you Colonials to see a real English royalty.' He certainly was pleased with hisself, was your father. He looked just as proud and haughty as one of them stone dogs in Victoria Park—them as is cut out of white marble. And you're like him," says the old mastiff—"by that, of course, meaning you're white, same as him. That's the only likeness.

But, you see, the trouble is, Kid—well, you see, Kid, the trouble is—your mother- -"

"That will do," I said, for I understood then without his telling me, and I got up and walked away, holding my head and tail high in the air.

But I was, oh, so miserable, and I wanted to see mother that very minute, and tell her that I didn't care.

Mother is what I am, a street-dog; there's no royal blood in mother's veins, nor is she like that father of mine, nor—and that's the worst—she's not even like me. For while I, when I'm washed for a fight, am as white as clean snow, she—and this is our trouble, she— my mother, is a black-and-tan.

When mother hid herself from me, I was twelve months old and able to take care of myself, and, as after mother left me, the wharves were never the same, I moved uptown and met the Master. Before he came, lots of other men-folks had tried to make up to me, and to whistle me home. But they either tried patting me or coaxing me with a piece of meat; so I didn't take to 'em. But one day the Master pulled me out of a street-fight by the hind-legs, and kicked me good.

"You want to fight, do you?" says he. "I'll give you all the FIGHTING you want!" he says, and he kicks me again. So I knew he was my Master, and I followed him home. Since that day I've pulled off many fights for him, and they've brought dogs from all over the province to have a go at me, but up to that night none, under thirty pounds, had ever downed me.

But that night, so soon as they carried me into the ring, I saw the dog was over-weight, and that I was no match for him. It was asking too much of a puppy. The Master should have known I couldn't do it. Not that I mean to blame the Master, for when sober, which he sometimes was, though not, as you might say, his habit, he was most kind to me, and let me out to find food, if I could get it, and only kicked me when I didn't pick him up at night and lead him home.

But kicks will stiffen the muscles, and starving a dog so as to get him ugly-tempered for a fight may make him nasty, but it's weakening to his insides, and it causes the legs to wabble.

The ring was in a hall, back of a public-house. There was a red-hot whitewashed stove in one corner, and the ring in the other. I lay in the Master's lap, wrapped in my blanket, and, spite of the stove, shivering awful; but I always shiver before a fight; I can't help gettin' excited. While the men-folks were a-flashing their money and taking their last drink at the bar, a little Irish groom in gaiters came up to me and give me the back of his hand to smell, and scratched me behind the ears.

"You poor little pup," says he. "You haven't no show," he says. "That brute in the tap-room, he'll eat your heart out."

"That's what you think," says the Master, snarling. "I'll lay you a quid the Kid chews him up."

The groom, he shook his head, but kept looking at me so sorry-like, that I begun to get a bit sad myself. He seemed like he couldn't bear to leave off a-patting of me, and he says, speaking low just like he would to a man-folk, "Well, good-luck to you, little pup," which I thought so civil of him, that I reached up and licked his hand. I don't do that to many men. And the Master, he knew I didn't, and took on dreadful.

"What 'ave you got on the back of your hand?" says he, jumping up.

"Soap!" says the groom, quick as a rat. "That's more than you've got on yours. Do you want to smell of it?" and he sticks his fist under the Master's nose. But the pals pushed in between 'em.

"He tried to poison the Kid!" shouts the Master.

"Oh, one fight at a time," says the referee. "Get into the ring, Jerry. We're waiting." So we went into the ring.

I never could just remember what did happen in that ring. He give me no time to spring. He fell on me like a horse. I couldn't keep my feet against him, and though, as I saw, he could get his hold when he liked, he wanted to chew me over a bit first. I was wondering if they'd be able to pry him off me, when, in the third round, he took his hold; and I began to drown, just as I did when I fell into the river off the Red C slip. He closed deeper and deeper, on my throat, and everything went black and red and bursting; and then, when I were sure I were dead, the handlers pulled him off, and the Master give me a kick that brought me to. But I couldn't move none, or even wink, both eyes being shut with lumps.

"He's a cur!" yells the Master, "a sneaking, cowardly cur. He lost the fight for me," says he, "because he's a———
——-cowardly cur." And he kicks me again in the lower ribs, so that I go sliding across the sawdust. "There's gratitude fer yer," yells the Master. "I've fed that dog, and nussed that dog, and housed him like a prince; and now he puts his tail between his legs, and sells me out, he does. He's a coward; I've done with him, I am. I'd sell him for a pipeful of tobacco." He picked me up by the tail, and swung me for the men-folks to see. "Does any gentleman here want to buy a dog," he says, "to make into sausage-meat?" he says. "That's all he's good for."

Then I heard the little Irish groom say, "I'll give you ten bob for the dog."

And another voice says, "Ah, don't you do it; the dog's same as dead- -mebby he is dead."

"Ten shillings!" says the Master, and his voice sobers a bit; "make it two pounds, and he's yours."

But the pals rushed in again.

"Don't you be a fool, Jerry," they say. "You'll be sorry for this when you're sober. The Kid's worth a fiver."

One of my eyes was not so swelled up as the other, and as I hung by my tail, I opened it, and saw one of the pals take the groom by the shoulder.

"You ought to give 'im five pounds for that dog, mate," he says; "that's no ordinary dog. That dog's got good blood in him, that dog has. Why, his father—that very dog's father—"

I thought he never would go on. He waited like he wanted to be sure the groom was listening.

"That very dog's father," says the pal, "is Regent Royal, son of Champion Regent Monarch, champion bull-terrier of England for four years."

I was sore, and torn, and chewed most awful, but what the pal said sounded so fine that I wanted to wag my tail, only couldn't, owing to my hanging from it.

But the Master calls out, "Yes, his father was Regent Royal; who's saying he wasn't? but the pup's a cowardly cur, that's what his pup is, and why—I'll tell you why—because his mother was a black-and- tan street-dog, that's why!"

I don't see how I get the strength, but some way I threw myself out of the Master's grip and fell at his feet, and turned over and fastened all my teeth in his ankle, just across the bone.

When I woke, after the pals had kicked me off him, I was in the smoking-car of a railroad-train, lying in the lap of the little groom, and he was rubbing my open wounds with a greasy, yellow stuff, exquisite to the smell, and most agreeable to lick off.

PART II

"Well—what's your name—Nolan? Well, Nolan, these references are satisfactory," said the young gentleman my new Master called "Mr. Wyndham, sir." "I'll take you on as second man. You can begin to- day."

My new Master shuffled his feet, and put his finger to his forehead. "Thank you, sir," says he. Then he choked like he had swallowed a fish-bone. "I have a little dawg, sir," says he.

"You can't keep him," says "Mr. Wyndham, sir," very short.

"'Es only a puppy, sir," says my new Master; "'e wouldn't go outside the stables, sir."

"It's not that," says "Mr. Wyndham, sir;" "I have a large kennel of very fine dogs; they're the best of their breed in America. I don't allow strange dogs on the premises."

The Master shakes his head, and motions me with his cap, and I crept out from behind the door. "I'm sorry, sir," says the Master. "Then I can't take the place. I can't get along without the dog, sir."

"Mr. Wyndham, sir," looked at me that fierce that I guessed he was going to whip me, so I turned over on my back and begged with my legs and tail.

"Why, you beat him!" says "Mr. Wyndham, sir," very stern.

103

"No fear!" the Master says, getting very red. "The party I bought him off taught him that. He never learnt that from me!" He picked me up in his arms, and to show "Mr. Wyndham, sir," how well I loved the Master, I bit his chin and hands.

"Mr. Wyndham, sir," turned over the letters the Master had given him. "Well, these references certainly are very strong," he says. "I guess I'll let the dog stay this time. Only see you keep him away from the kennels—or you'll both go."

"Thank you, sir," says the Master, grinning like a cat when she's safe behind the area-railing.

"He's not a bad bull-terrier," says "Mr. Wyndham, sir," feeling my head. "Not that I know much about the smooth-coated breeds. My dogs are St. Bernards." He stopped patting me and held up my nose. "What's the matter with his ears?" he says. "They're chewed to pieces. Is this a fighting dog?" he asks, quick and rough-like.

I could have laughed. If he hadn't been holding my nose, I certainly would have had a good grin at him. Me, the best under thirty pounds in the Province of Quebec, and him asking if I was a fighting dog! I ran to the Master and hung down my head modest-like, waiting for him to tell my list of battles, but the Master he coughs in his cap most painful. "Fightin' dog, sir," he cries. "Lor' bless you, sir, the Kid don't know the word. 'Es just a puppy, sir, same as you see; a pet dog, so to speak. 'Es a regular old lady's lap-dog, the Kid is."

"Well, you keep him away from my St. Bernards," says "Mr. Wyndham, sir," "or they might make a mouthful of him."

"Yes, sir, that they might," says the Master. But when we gets outside he slaps his knee and laughs inside hisself, and winks at me most sociable.

The Master's new home was in the country, in a province they called Long Island. There was a high stone wall about his home with big iron gates to it, same as Godfrey's brewery; and there was a house with five red roofs, and the stables, where I lived, was cleaner than the aerated bakery-shop, and then there was the kennels, but they was like nothing else in this world that ever I see. For the first days I couldn't sleep of nights for fear someone would catch me lying in such a cleaned-up place, and would chase me out of it, and when I did fall to sleep I'd dream I was back in the old Master's attic, shivering under the rusty stove, which never had no coals in it, with the Master flat on his back on the cold floor with his clothes on. And I'd wake up, scared and whimpering, and find myself on the new Master's cot with his hand on the quilt beside me; and I'd see the glow of the big stove, and hear the high-quality horses below-stairs stamping in their straw-lined boxes, and I'd snoop the sweet smell of hay and harness-soap, and go to sleep again.

The stables was my jail, so the Master said, but I don't ask no better home than that jail.

"Now, Kid," says he, sitting on the top of a bucket upside down, "you've got to understand this. When I whistle it means you're not to go out of this 'ere yard. These stables is your jail. And if you leave 'em I'll have to leave 'em, too, and over the seas, in the County Mayo, an old mother will 'ave to leave her bit of a cottage. For two pounds I must be sending her every month, or she'll have naught to eat, nor no thatch over 'er head; so, I can't lose my place, Kid, an' see you don't lose it for me. You must keep away from the kennels," says he; "they're not for the likes of you. The kennels are for the quality. I wouldn't take a litter of them woolly dogs for one wag of your tail, Kid, but for all that they are your betters, same as the gentry up in the big house are my betters. I know my place and keep away from the gentry, and you keep away from the Champions."

So I never goes out of the stables. All day I just lay in the sun on the stone flags, licking my jaws, and watching the grooms wash down the carriages, and the only care I had was to see they didn't get gay and turn the hose on me. There wasn't even a single rat to plague me. Such stables I never did see.

"Nolan," says the head-groom, "some day that dog of yours will give you the slip. You can't keep a street-dog tied up all his life. It's against his natur'." The head-groom is a

nice old gentleman, but he doesn't know everything. Just as
though I'd been a street-dog because I liked it. As if I'd rather
poke for my vittles in ash-heaps than have 'em handed me in
a wash-basin, and would sooner bite and fight than be polite
and sociable. If I'd had mother there I couldn't have asked for
nothing more. But I'd think of her snooping in the gutters,
or freezing of nights under the bridges, or, what's worse of
all, running through the hot streets with her tongue down,
so wild and crazy for a drink, that the people would shout
"mad dog" at her, and stone her. Water's so good, that I don't
blame the men-folks for locking it up inside their houses,
but when the hot days come, I think they might remember
that those are the dog-days and leave a little water outside in
a trough, like they do for the horses. Then we wouldn't go
mad, and the policemen wouldn't shoot us. I had so much of
everything I wanted that it made me think a lot of the days
when I hadn't nothing, and if I could have given what I had
to mother, as she used to share with me, I'd have been the
happiest dog in the land. Not that I wasn't happy then, and
most grateful to the Master, too, and if I'd only minded him,
the trouble wouldn't have come again.

But one day the coachman says that the little lady they
called Miss Dorothy had come back from school, and that
same morning she runs over to the stables to pat her ponies,
and she sees me.

"Oh, what a nice little, white little dog," said she; "whose little dog are you?" says she.

"That's my dog, miss," says the Master. "'Is name is Kid," and I ran up to her most polite, and licks her fingers, for I never see so pretty and kind a lady.

"You must come with me and call on my new puppies," says she, picking me up in her arms and starting off with me.

"Oh, but please, Miss," cries Nolan, "Mr. Wyndham give orders that the Kid's not to go to the kennels."

"That'll be all right," says the little lady; "they're my kennels too. And the puppies will like to play with him."

You wouldn't believe me if I was to tell you of the style of them quality-dogs. If I hadn't seen it myself I wouldn't have believed it neither. The Viceroy of Canada don't live no better. There was forty of them, but each one had his own house and a yard—most exclusive— and a cot and a drinking-basin all to hisself. They had servants standing 'round waiting to feed 'em when they was hungry, and valets to wash 'em; and they had their hair combed and brushed like the grooms must when they go out on the box. Even the puppies had overcoats with their names on 'em in blue letters, and the name of each of those they called champions was painted up fine over his front door just like it was a public-house or a veterinary's. They were the biggest St. Bernards I ever did see. I could have walked under them if they'd have let me. But they were very proud and haughty dogs, and looked only once at me, and then sniffed in the air. The little lady's own dog was an old gentleman bull-dog. He'd come along with us, and when he notices how taken aback I was with all I see, 'e turned quite kind and affable and showed me about.

"Jimmy Jocks," Miss Dorothy called him, but, owing to his weight, he walked most dignified and slow, waddling like a duck as you might say, and looked much too proud and handsome for such a silly name.

"That's the runway, and that's the Trophy House," says he to me, "and that over there is the hospital, where you have to go if you get distemper, and the vet. gives you beastly medicine."

"And which of these is your 'ouse, sir?" asks I, wishing to be respectful. But he looked that hurt and haughty. "I don't live in the kennels," says he, most contemptuous. "I am a house-dog. I sleep in Miss Dorothy's room. And at lunch I'm let in with the family, if the visitors don't mind. They most always do, but they're too polite to say so. Besides," says he, smiling most condescending, "visitors are always afraid of me. It's because I'm so ugly," says he. "I suppose," says he, screwing up his wrinkles and speaking very slow and impressive, "I suppose I'm the ugliest bull-dog in America," and as he seemed to be so pleased to think hisself so, I said,

"Yes, sir, you certainly are the ugliest ever I see," at which he nodded his head most approving.

"But I couldn't hurt 'em, as you say," he goes on, though I hadn't said nothing like that, being too polite. "I'm too old," he says; "I haven't any teeth. The last time one of those grizzly bears," said he, glaring at the big St. Bernards, "took a hold of me, he nearly was my death," says he. I thought his eyes would pop out of his head, he seemed so wrought up about it. "He rolled me around in the dirt, he did," says Jimmy Jocks, "an' I couldn't get up. It was low," says Jimmy Jocks, making a face like he had a bad taste in his mouth. "Low, that's what I call it, bad form, you understand, young man, not done in our circles—and—and low." He growled, way down in his stomach, and puffed hisself out, panting and blowing like he had been on a run.

"I'm not a street-fighter," he says, scowling at a St. Bernard marked "Champion." "And when my rheumatism is not troubling me," he says, "I endeavor to be civil to all dogs, so long as they are gentlemen."

"Yes, sir," said I, for even to me he had been most affable.

At this we had come to a little house off by itself and Jimmy Jocks invites me in. "This is their trophy-room," he says, "where they keep their prizes. Mine," he says, rather grand-like, "are on the sideboard." Not knowing what a sideboard might be, I said, "Indeed, sir, that must be very

gratifying." But he only wrinkled up his chops as much as to
say, "It is my right."

The trophy-room was as wonderful as any public-house
I ever see. On the walls was pictures of nothing but beautiful
St. Bernard dogs, and rows and rows of blue and red and
yellow ribbons; and when I asked Jimmy Jocks why they was
so many more of blue than of the others, he laughs and says,
"Because these kennels always win." And there was many
shining cups on the shelves which Jimmy Jocks told me were
prizes won by the champions.

"Now, sir, might I ask you, sir," says I, "wot is a
champion?"

At that he panted and breathed so hard I thought
he would bust hisself. "My dear young friend!" says he.
"Wherever have you been educated? A champion is a—a
champion," he says. "He must win nine blue ribbons in the
'open' class. You follow me—that is—against all comers. Then
he has the title before his name, and they put his photograph
in the sporting papers. You know, of course, that I am a
champion," says he. "I am Champion Woodstock Wizard
III., and the two other Woodstock Wizards, my father and
uncle, were both champions."

"But I thought your name was Jimmy Jocks," I said.

He laughs right out at that.

"That's my kennel name, not my registered name,"
he says. "Why, you certainly know that every dog has two

111

names. Now, what's your registered name and number, for instance?" says he.

"I've only got one name," I says. "Just Kid."

Woodstock Wizard puffs at that and wrinkles up his forehead and pops out his eyes.

"Who are your people?" says he. "Where is your home?"

"At the stable, sir," I said. "My Master is the second groom."

At that Woodstock Wizard III. looks at me for quite a bit without winking, and stares all around the room over my head.

"Oh, well," says he at last, "you're a very civil young dog," says he, "and I blame no one for what he can't help," which I thought most fair and liberal. "And I have known many bullterriers that were champions," says he, "though as a rule they mostly run with fire- engines, and to fighting. For me, I wouldn't care to run through the streets after a hose-cart, nor to fight," says he; "but each to his taste."

I could not help thinking that if Woodstock Wizard III. tried to follow a fire-engine he would die of apoplexy, and that, seeing he'd lost his teeth, it was lucky he had no taste for fighting, but, after his being so condescending, I didn't say nothing.

"Anyway," says he, "every smooth-coated dog is better than any hairy old camel like those St. Bernards, and if ever you're hungry down at the stables, young man, come up to the house and I'll give you a bone. I can't eat them myself, but I bury them around the garden from force of habit, and in case a friend should drop in. Ah, I see my Mistress coming," he says, "and I bid you good-day. I regret," he says, "that our different social position prevents our meeting frequent, for you're a worthy young dog with a proper respect for your betters, and in this country there's precious few of them have that." Then he waddles off, leaving me alone and very sad, for he was the first dog in many days that had spoken to me. But since he showed, seeing that I was a stable-dog, he didn't want my company, I waited for him to get well away. It was not a cheerful place to wait, the Trophy House. The pictures of the champions seemed to scowl at me, and ask what right had such as I even to admire them, and the blue and gold ribbons and the silver cups made me very miserable. I had never won no blue ribbons or silver cups; only stakes for the old Master to spend in the publics, and I hadn't won them for being a beautiful, high-quality dog, but just for fighting—which, of course, as Woodstock Wizard III. says, is low. So I started for the stables, with my head down and my tail between my legs, feeling sorry I had ever left the Master. But I had more reason to be sorry before I got back to him.

The Trophy House was quite a bit from the kennels, and as I left it I see Miss Dorothy and Woodstock Wizard

III. walking back toward them, and that a fine, big St. Bernard, his name was Champion Red Elfberg, had broke his chain, and was running their way. When he reaches old Jimmy Jocks he lets out a roar like a grain-steamer in a fog, and he makes three leaps for him. Old Jimmy Jocks was about a fourth his size; but he plants his feet and curves his back, and his hair goes up around his neck like a collar. But he never had no show at no time, for the grizzly bear, as Jimmy Jocks had called him, lights on old Jimmy's back and tries to break it, and old Jimmy Jocks snaps his gums and claws the grass, panting and groaning awful. But he can't do nothing, and the grizzly bear just rolls him under him, biting and tearing cruel. The odds was all that Woodstock Wizard III. was going to be killed. I had fought enough to see that, but not knowing the rules of the game among champions, I didn't like to interfere between two gentlemen who might be settling a private affair, and, as it were, take it as presuming of me. So I stood by, though I was shaking terrible, and holding myself in like I was on a leash. But at that Woodstock Wizard III., who was underneath, sees me through the dust, and calls very faint, "Help, you!" he says. "Take him in the hind- leg," he says. "He's murdering me," he says. And then the little Miss Dorothy, who was crying, and calling to the kennel-men, catches at the Red Elfberg's hind-legs to pull him off, and the brute, keeping his front pats well in Jimmy's stomach, turns his big head and snaps at her. So that was all I asked for, thank you. I went up under him. It was really nothing. He stood so high that I had only to take off about three feet from him and come in from the side, and my long, "punishing jaw" as mother was always talking about, locked on his woolly throat, and my back teeth met. I couldn't shake him, but I shook myself, and every time I shook myself there was thirty pounds of weight tore at his windpipes. I couldn't see nothing for his long hair, but I heard Jimmy Jocks puffing and blowing on one side, and munching the brute's leg with his old gums. Jimmy was an old sport that day, was Jimmy, or, Woodstock Wizard III., as I should say. When the Red Elfberg was out and down I had to run, or those kennel-men would have had my life. They chased me right into the stables; and from under the hay I watched the head-groom take down a carriage-whip and order them to the right about. Luckily Master and the young grooms were out, or that day there'd have been fighting for everybody.

Well, it nearly did for me and the Master. "Mr. Wyndham, sir," comes raging to the stables and said I'd half-killed his best prize-winner, and had oughter be shot, and he gives the Master his notice. But Miss Dorothy she follows him, and says it was his Red Elfberg what began the fight, and that I'd saved Jimmy's life, and that old Jimmy Jocks was worth more to her than all the St. Bernards in the Swiss mountains—where-ever they be. And that I was her champion, anyway. Then she cried over me most beautiful, and over Jimmy Jocks, too, who was that tied up in bandages he couldn't even waddle. So when he heard that side of it, "Mr. Wyndham, sir," told us that if Nolan put me on a chain, we could stay. So it came out all right for everybody but me. I was glad the Master kept his place, but I'd never worn a chain before, and it disheartened me—but that was the least of it. For the quality-dogs couldn't forgive my whipping their champion, and they came to the fence between the kennels and the stables, and laughed through the bars, barking most cruel words at me. I couldn't understand how they found it out, but they knew. After the fight Jimmy Jocks was most condescending to me, and he said the grooms had boasted to the kennel-men that I was a son of Regent Royal, and that when the kennel-men asked who was my mother they had had to tell them that too. Perhaps that was the way of it, but, however, the scandal was out, and every one of the quality-dogs knew that I was a street- dog and the son of a black-and-tan.

"These misalliances will occur," said Jimmy Jocks, in his old- fashioned way, "but no well-bred dog," says he, looking most scornful at the St. Bernards, who were howling behind the palings, "would refer to your misfortune before you, certainly not cast it in your face. I, myself, remember your father's father, when he made his debut at the Crystal Palace. He took four blue ribbons and three specials."

But no sooner than Jimmy would leave me, the St. Bernards would take to howling again, insulting mother and insulting me. And when I tore at my chain, they, seeing they were safe, would howl the more. It was never the same after that; the laughs and the jeers cut into my heart, and the chain bore heavy on my spirit. I was so sad that sometimes I wished I was back in the gutter again, where no one was better than me, and some nights I wished I was dead. If it hadn't been for the Master being so kind, and that it would have looked like I was blaming mother, I would have twisted my leash and hanged myself.

About a month after my fight, the word was passed through the kennels that the New York Show was coming, and such goings on as followed I never did see. If each of them had been matched to fight for a thousand pounds and the gate, they couldn't have trained more conscientious. But, perhaps, that's just my envy. The kennel-men rubbed 'em and scrubbed 'em and trims their hair and curls and combs it, and some dogs they fatted, and some they starved. No one talked of nothing but the Show, and the chances "our kennels" had against the other kennels, and if this one of our champions would win over that one, and whether them as hoped to be champions had better show in the "open" or the "limit" class, and whether this dog would beat his own dad, or whether his little puppy sister couldn't beat the two of them. Even the grooms had their money up, and day or night you heard nothing but praises of "our" dogs, until I, being so far out of it, couldn't have felt meaner if I had been running the streets with a can to my tail. I knew shows were not for such as me, and so I lay all day stretched at the end of my chain, pretending I was asleep, and only too glad that they had something so important to think of, that they could leave me alone.

But one day before the Show opened, Miss Dorothy came to the stables with "Mr. Wyndham, sir," and seeing me chained up and so miserable, she takes me in her arms.

"You poor little tyke," says she. "It's cruel to tie him up so; he's eating his heart out, Nolan," she says. "I don't know nothing about bull-terriers," says she, "but I think Kid's got good points," says she, "and you ought to show him. Jimmy Jocks has three legs on the Rensselaer Cup now, and I'm going to show him this time so that he can get the fourth, and if you wish, I'll enter your dog too. How would you like that, Kid?" says she. "How would you like to see the most beautiful dogs in the world? Maybe, you'd meet a pal or two," says she. "It would cheer you up, wouldn't it, Kid?" says she. But I was so upset, I could only wag my tail most violent. "He says it would!" says she, though, being that excited, I hadn't said nothing.

So, "Mr. Wyndham, sir," laughs and takes out a piece of blue paper, and sits down at the head-groom's table.

"What's the name of the father of your dog, Nolan?" says he. And Nolan says, "The man I got him off told me he was a son of Champion Regent Royal, sir. But it don't seem likely, does it?" says Nolan.

"It does not!" says "Mr. Wyndham, sir," short-like.

"Aren't you sure, Nolan?" says Miss Dorothy.

"No, Miss," says the Master.

"Sire unknown," says "Mr. Wyndham, sir," and writes it down.

"Date of birth?" asks "Mr. Wyndham, sir."

"I—I—unknown, sir," says Nolan. And "Mr. Wyndham, sir," writes it down.

"Breeder?" says "Mr. Wyndham, sir."

"Unknown," says Nolan, getting very red around the jaws, and I drops my head and tail. And "Mr. Wyndham, sir," writes that down.

"Mother's name?" says "Mr. Wyndham, sir."

"She was a—unknown," says the Master. And I licks his hand.

"Dam unknown," says "Mr. Wyndham, sir," and writes it down. Then he takes the paper and reads out loud: "Sire unknown, dam unknown, breeder unknown, date of birth unknown. You'd better call him the 'Great Unknown,'" says he. "Who's paying his entrance-fee?"

"I am," says Miss Dorothy.

Two weeks after we all got on a train for New York; Jimmy Jocks and me following Nolan in the smoking-car, and twenty-two of the St. Bernards, in boxes and crates, and on chains and leashes. Such a barking and howling I never did hear, and when they sees me going, too, they laughs fit to kill.

"Wot is this; a circus?" says the railroad-man.

But I had no heart in it. I hated to go. I knew I was no "show" dog, even though Miss Dorothy and the Master did their best to keep me from shaming them. For before we set out Miss Dorothy brings a man from town who scrubbed and rubbed me, and sand-papered my tail, which hurt most awful, and shaved my ears with the Master's razor, so you could most see clear through 'em, and sprinkles me over with pipe- clay, till I shines like a Tommy's cross-belts.

"Upon my word!" says Jimmy Jocks when he first sees me. "What a swell you are! You're the image of your grand-dad when he made his debut at the Crystal Palace. He took four firsts and three specials." But I knew he was only trying to throw heart into me. They might scrub, and they might rub, and they might pipe-clay, but they couldn't pipe-clay the insides of me, and they was black-and-tan.

Then we came to a Garden, which it was not, but the biggest hall in the world. Inside there was lines of benches, a few miles long, and on them sat every dog in the world. If all the dog-snatchers in Montreal had worked night and day for a year, they couldn't have caught so many dogs. And they was all shouting and barking and howling so vicious, that my heart stopped beating. For at first I thought they was all enraged at my presuming to intrude, but after I got in my place, they kept at it just the same, barking at every dog as he come in; daring him to fight, and ordering him out, and asking him what breed of dog he thought he was, anyway. Jimmy Jocks was chained just behind me, and he said he never see so fine a show. "That's a hot class you're in, my lad," he says, looking over into my street, where there were thirty bull-terriers. They was all as white as cream, and each so beautiful that if I could have broke my chain, I would have run all the way home and hid myself under the horse-trough.

All night long they talked and sang, and passed greetings with old pals, and the home-sick puppies howled dismal. Them that couldn't sleep wouldn't let no others sleep, and all the electric lights burned in the roof, and in my eyes. I could hear Jimmy Jocks snoring peaceful, but I could only doze by jerks, and when I dozed I dreamed horrible. All the dogs in the hall seemed coming at me for daring to intrude, with their jaws red and open, and their eyes blazing like the lights in the roof. "You're a street-dog! Get out, you street-dog!" they yells. And as they drives me out, the pipe-clay drops off me, and they laugh and shriek; and when I looks down I see that I have turned into a black-and-tan.

They was most awful dreams, and next morning, when Miss Dorothy comes and gives me water in a pan, I begs and begs her to take me home, but she can't understand. "How well Kid is!" she says. And when I jumps into the Master's arms, and pulls to break my chain, he says, "If he knew all as he had against him, Miss, he wouldn't be so gay." And from a book they reads out the names of the beautiful high-bred terriers which I have got to meet. And I can't make 'em understand that I only want to run away, and hide myself where no one will see me.

Then suddenly men comes hurrying down our street and begins to brush the beautiful bull-terriers, and Nolan rubs me with a towel so excited that his hands trembles awful, and Miss Dorothy tweaks my ears between her gloves, so that the blood runs to 'em, and they turn pink and stand up straight and sharp.

"Now, then, Nolan," says she, her voice shaking just like his fingers, "keep his head up—and never let the Judge lose sight of him." When I hears that my legs breaks under me, for I knows all about judges. Twice, the old Master goes up before the Judge for fighting me with other dogs, and the Judge promises him if he ever does it again, he'll chain him up in jail. I knew he'd find me out. A Judge can't be fooled by no pipe-clay. He can see right through you, and he reads your insides.

The judging-ring, which is where the Judge holds out, was so like a fighting-pit, that when I came in it, and find six other dogs there, I springs into position, so that when they lets us go I can defend myself, But the Master smoothes down my hair and whispers, "Hold 'ard, Kid, hold 'ard. This ain't a fight," says he. "Look your prettiest," he whispers. "Please, Kid, look your prettiest," and he pulls my leash so tight that I can't touch my pats to the sawdust, and my nose goes up in the air. There was millions of people a- watching us from the railings, and three of our kennel-men, too, making fun of Nolan and me, and Miss Dorothy with her chin just reaching to the rail, and her eyes so big that I thought she was a- going to cry. It was awful to think that when the Judge stood up and exposed me, all those people, and Miss Dorothy, would be there to see me driven from the show.

The Judge, he was a fierce-looking man with specs on his nose, and a red beard. When I first come in he didn't see me owing to my being too quick for him and dodging behind the Master. But when the Master drags me round and I pulls at the sawdust to keep back, the Judge looks at us careless-like, and then stops and glares through his specs, and I knew it was all up with me.

"Are there any more?" asks the Judge, to the gentleman at the gate, but never taking his specs from me.

The man at the gate looks in his book. "Seven in the novice-class," says he. "They're all here. You can go ahead," and he shuts the gate.

The Judge, he doesn't hesitate a moment. He just waves his hand toward the corner of the ring. "Take him away," he says to the Master. "Over there and keep him away," and he turns and looks most solemn at the six beautiful bull-terriers. I don't know how I crawled to that corner. I wanted to scratch under the sawdust and dig myself a grave. The kennel-men they slapped the rail with their hands and laughed at the Master like they would fall over. They pointed at me in the corner, and their sides just shaked. But little Miss Dorothy she presses her lips tight against the rail, and I see tears rolling from her eyes. The Master, he hangs his head like he had been whipped. I felt most sorry for him, than all. He was so red, and he was letting on not to see the kennel-men, and blinking his eyes. If the Judge had ordered me right out, it wouldn't have disgraced us so, but it was keeping me there while he was judging the high-bred dogs that hurt so hard. With all those people staring too. And his doing it so quick, without no doubt nor questions. You can't fool the judges. They see insides you.

But he couldn't make up his mind about them high-bred dogs. He scowls at 'em, and he glares at 'em, first with his head on the one side and then on the other. And he feels of 'em, and orders 'em to run about. And Nolan leans against

124

the rails, with his head hung down, and pats me. And Miss Dorothy comes over beside him, but don't say nothing, only wipes her eye with her finger. A man on the other side of the rail he says to the Master, "The Judge don't like your dog?"

"No," says the Master.

"Have you ever shown him before?" says the man.

"No," says the Master, "and I'll never show him again. He's my dog," says the Master, "an' he suits me! And I don't care what no judges think." And when he says them kind words, I licks his hand most grateful.

The Judge had two of the six dogs on a little platform in the middle of the ring, and he had chased the four other dogs into the corners, where they was licking their chops, and letting on they didn't care, same as Nolan was.

The two dogs on the platform was so beautiful that the Judge hisself couldn't tell which was the best of 'em, even when he stoops down and holds their heads together. But at last he gives a sigh, and brushes the sawdust off his knees and goes to the table in the ring, where there was a man keeping score, and heaps and heaps of blue and gold and red and yellow ribbons. And the Judge picks up a bunch of 'em and walks to the two gentlemen who was holding the beautiful dogs, and he says to each "What's his number?" and he hands each gentleman a ribbon. And then he turned sharp, and comes straight at the Master.

"What's his number?" says the Judge. And Master was so scared that he couldn't make no answer.

But Miss Dorothy claps her hands and cries out like she was laughing, "Three twenty-six," and the Judge writes it down, and shoves Master the blue ribbon.

I bit the Master, and I jumps and bit Miss Dorothy, and I waggled so hard that the Master couldn't hold me. When I get to the gate Miss Dorothy snatches me up and kisses me between the ears, right before millions of people, and they both hold me so tight that I didn't know which of them was carrying of me. But one thing I knew, for I listened hard, as it was the Judge hisself as said it.

"Did you see that puppy I gave 'first' to?" says the Judge to the gentleman at the gate.

"I did. He was a bit out of his class," says the gate-gentleman.

"He certainly was!" says the Judge, and they both laughed.

But I didn't care. They couldn't hurt me then, not with Nolan holding the blue ribbon and Miss Dorothy hugging my ears, and the kennel-men sneaking away, each looking like he'd been caught with his nose under the lid of the slop-can.

We sat down together, and we all three just talked as fast as we could. They was so pleased that I couldn't help feeling proud myself, and I barked and jumped and leaped

126

about so gay, that all the bull- terriers in our street stretched on their chains, and howled at me.

"Just look at him!" says one of those I had beat. "What's he giving hisself airs about?"

"Because he's got one blue ribbon!" says another of 'em. "Why, when I was a puppy I used to eat 'em, and if that Judge could ever learn to know a toy from a mastiff, I'd have had this one."

But Jimmy Jocks he leaned over from his bench, and says, "Well done, Kid. Didn't I tell you so!" What he 'ad told me was that I might get a "commended," but I didn't remind him.

"Didn't I tell you," says Jimmy Jocks, "that I saw your grandfather make his debut at the Crystal—"

"Yes, sir, you did, sir," says I, for I have no love for the men of my family.

A gentleman with a showing leash around his neck comes up just then and looks at me very critical. "Nice dog you've got, Miss Wyndham," says he; "would you care to sell him?"

"He's not my dog," says Miss Dorothy, holding me tight. "I wish he were."

"He's not for sale, sir," says the Master, and I was that glad.

"Oh, he's yours, is he?" says the gentleman, looking hard at Nolan. "Well, I'll give you a hundred dollars for him," says he, careless- like.

"Thank you, sir, he's not for sale," says Nolan, but his eyes get very big. The gentleman, he walked away, but I watches him, and he talks to a man in a golf-cap, and by and by the man comes along our street, looking at all the dogs, and stops in front of me.

"This your dog?" says he to Nolan. "Pity he's so leggy," says he. "If he had a good tail, and a longer stop, and his ears were set higher, he'd be a good dog. As he is, I'll give you fifty dollars for him."

But before the Master could speak, Miss Dorothy laughs, and says, "You're Mr. Polk's kennel-man, I believe. Well, you tell Mr. Polk from me that the dog's not for sale now any more than he was five minutes ago, and that when he is, he'll have to bid against me for him." The man looks foolish at that, but he turns to Nolan quick- like. "I'll give you three hundred for him," he says.

"Oh, indeed!" whispers Miss Dorothy, like she was talking to herself. "That's it, is it," and she turns and looks at me just as though she had never seen me before. Nolan, he was a gaping, too, with his mouth open. But he holds me tight.

"He's not for sale," he growls, like he was frightened, and the man looks black and walks away.

"Why, Nolan!" cries Miss Dorothy, "Mr. Polk knows more about bull- terriers than any amateur in America. What can he mean? Why, Kid is no more than a puppy! Three hundred dollars for a puppy!"

"And he ain't no thoroughbred neither!" cries the Master. "He's 'Unknown,' ain't he? Kid can't help it, of course, but his mother, Miss—"

I dropped my head. I couldn't bear he should tell Miss Dorothy. I couldn't bear she should know I had stolen my blue ribbon.

But the Master never told, for at that, a gentleman runs up, calling, "Three Twenty-Six, Three Twenty-Six," and Miss Dorothy says, "Here he is, what is it?"

"The Winner's Class," says the gentleman "Hurry, please. The Judge is waiting for him."

Nolan tries to get me off the chain onto a showing leash, but he shakes so, he only chokes me. "What is it, Miss?" he says. "What is it?"

"The Winner's Class," says Miss Dorothy. "The Judge wants him with the winners of the other classes—to decide which is the best. It's only a form," says she. "He has the champions against him now."

"Yes," says the gentleman, as he hurries us to the ring. "I'm afraid it's only a form for your dog, but the Judge wants all the winners, puppy class even."

We had got to the gate, and the gentleman there was writing down my number.

"Who won the open?" asks Miss Dorothy.

"Oh, who would?" laughs the gentleman. "The old champion, of course. He's won for three years now. There he is. Isn't he wonderful?" says he, and he points to a dog that's standing proud and haughty on the platform in the middle of the ring.

I never see so beautiful a dog, so fine and clean and noble, so white like he had rolled hisself in flour, holding his nose up and his eyes shut, same as though no one was worth looking at. Aside of him, we other dogs, even though we had a blue ribbon apiece, seemed like lumps of mud. He was a royal gentleman, a king, he was. His Master didn't have to hold his head with no leash. He held it hisself, standing as still as an iron dog on a lawn, like he knew all the people was looking at him. And so they was, and no one around the ring pointed at no other dog but him.

"Oh, what a picture," cried Miss Dorothy; "he's like a marble figure by a great artist—one who loved dogs. Who is he?" says she, looking in her book. "I don't keep up with terriers."

"Oh, you know him," says the gentleman. "He is the Champion of champions, Regent Royal."

The Master's face went red.

"And this is Regent Royal's son," cries he, and he pulls me quick into the ring, and plants me on the platform next my father.

I trembled so that I near fall. My legs twisted like a leash. But my father he never looked at me. He only smiled, the same sleepy smile, and he still keep his eyes half-shut, like as no one, no, not even his son, was worth his lookin' at.

The Judge, he didn't let me stay beside my father, but, one by one, he placed the other dogs next to him and measured and felt and pulled at them. And each one he put down, but he never put my father down. And then he comes over and picks up me and sets me back on the platform, shoulder to shoulder with the Champion Regent Royal, and goes down on his knees, and looks into our eyes.

The gentleman with my father, he laughs, and says to the Judge, "Thinking of keeping us here all day. John?" but the Judge, he doesn't hear him, and goes behind us and runs his hand down my side, and holds back my ears, and takes my jaws between his fingers. The crowd around the ring is very deep now, and nobody says nothing. The gentleman at the score-table, he is leaning forward, with his elbows on his knees, and his eyes very wide, and the gentleman at the gate is whispering quick to Miss Dorothy, who has turned white. I stood as stiff as stone. I didn't even breathe. But out of the corner of my eye I could see my father licking his pink chops, and yawning just a little, like he was bored.

The Judge, he had stopped looking fierce, and was looking solemn. Something inside him seemed a troubling him awful. The more he stares at us now, the more solemn he gets, and when he touches us he does it gentle, like he was patting us. For a long time he kneels in the sawdust, looking at my father and at me, and no one around the ring says nothing to nobody.

Then the Judge takes a breath and touches me sudden. "It's his," he says, but he lays his hand just as quick on my father. "I'm sorry," says he.

The gentleman holding my father cries:

"Do you mean to tell me—"

And the Judge, he answers, "I mean the other is the better dog." He takes my father's head between his hands and looks down at him, most sorrowful. "The King is dead," says he, "long live the King. Good-by, Regent," he says.

The crowd around the railings clapped their hands, and some laughed scornful, and everyone talks fast, and I start for the gate so dizzy that I can't see my way. But my father pushes in front of me, walking very daintily, and smiling sleepy, same as he had just been waked, with his head high, and his eyes shut, looking at nobody.

So that is how I "came by my inheritance," as Miss Dorothy calls it, and just for that, though I couldn't feel where I was any different, the crowd follows me to my bench, and pats me, and coos at me, like I was a baby in a baby-carriage. And the handlers have to hold 'em back so that the gentlemen from the papers can make pictures of me, and Nolan walks me up and down so proud, and the men shakes their heads and says, "He certainly is the true type, he is!" And the pretty ladies asks Miss Dorothy, who sits beside me letting me lick her gloves to show the crowd what friends we is, "Aren't you afraid he'll bite you?" and Jimmy Jocks calls to me, "Didn't I tell you so! I always knew you were one of us. Blood will out, Kid, blood will out. I saw your grandfather," says he, "make his debut at the Crystal Palace. But he was never the dog you are!"

After that, if I could have asked for it, there was nothing I couldn't get. You might have thought I was a snow-dog, and they was afeerd I'd melt. If I wet my pats, Nolan gave me a hot bath and chained me to the stove; if I couldn't eat my food, being stuffed full by the cook, for I am a house-dog now, and let in to lunch whether there is visitors or not, Nolan would run to bring the vet. It was all tommy-rot, as Jimmy says, but meant most kind. I couldn't scratch myself comfortable, without Nolan giving me nasty drinks, and rubbing me outside till it burnt awful, and I wasn't let to eat bones for fear of spoiling my "beautiful" mouth, what mother used to call my "punishing jaw," and my food was cooked special on a gas-stove, and Miss Dorothy gives me an overcoat, cut very stylish like the champions', to wear when we goes out carriage-driving.

After the next show, where I takes three blue ribbons, four silver cups, two medals, and brings home forty-five dollars for Nolan, they gives me a "Registered" name, same as Jimmy's. Miss Dorothy wanted to call me "Regent Heir Apparent," but I was THAT glad when Nolan says, "No, Kid don't owe nothing to his father, only to you and hisself. So, if you please, Miss, we'll call him Wyndham Kid." And so they did, and you can see it on my overcoat in blue letters, and painted top of my kennel. It was all too hard to understand. For days I just sat and wondered if I was really me, and how it all come about, and why everybody was so kind. But, oh, it was so good they was, for if they hadn't been, I'd never have got the thing I most wished after. But, because they was kind, and not liking to deny me nothing, they gave it me, and it was more to me than anything in the world.

It came about one day when we was out driving. We was in the cart they calls the dog-cart, because it's the one Miss Dorothy keeps to take Jimmy and me for an airing. Nolan was up behind, and me in my new overcoat was sitting beside Miss Dorothy. I was admiring the view, and thinking how good it was to have a horse pull you about so that you needn't get yourself splashed and have to be washed, when I hears a dog calling loud for help, and I pricks up my ears and looks over the horse's head. And I sees something that makes me tremble down to my toes. In the road before us three big dogs was chasing a little, old lady-dog. She had a string to her tail, where some boys had tied a can, and she was dirty with mud and ashes, and torn most awful. She was too far done up to get away, and too old to help herself, but she was making a fight for her life, snapping her old gums savage, and dying game. All this I see in a wink, and then the three dogs pinned her down, and I can't stand it no longer and clears the wheel and lands in the road on my head. It was my stylish overcoat done that, and I curse it proper, but I gets my pats again quick, and makes a rush for the fighting. Behind me I hear Miss Dorothy cry, "They'll kill that old dog. Wait, take my whip. Beat them off her! The Kid can take care of himself," and I hear Nolan fall into the road, and the horse come to a stop. The old lady-dog was down, and the three was eating her vicious, but as I come up, scattering the pebbles, she hears, and thinking it's one more of them, she lifts her head and my heart breaks open like someone had sunk his teeth in it. For, under the ashes and the dirt and the blood, I can see who it is, and I know that my mother has come back to me.

I gives a yell that throws them three dogs off their legs.

"Mother!" I cries. "I'm the Kid," I cries. "I'm coming to you, mother, I'm coming."

And I shoots over her, at the throat of the big dog, and the other two, they sinks their teeth into that stylish overcoat, and tears it off me, and that sets me free, and I lets them have it. I never had so fine a fight as that! What with mother being there to see, and not having been let to mix up in no fights since I become a prize-winner, it just naturally did me good, and it wasn't three shakes before I had 'em yelping. Quick as a wink, mother, she jumps in to help me, and I just laughed to see her. It was so like old times. And Nolan, he made me laugh too. He was like a hen on a bank, shaking the butt of his whip, but not daring to cut in for fear of hitting me.

"Stop it, Kid," he says, "stop it. Do you want to be all torn up?" says he. "Think of the Boston show next week," says he, "Think of Chicago. Think of Danbury. Don't you never want to be a champion?" How was I to think of all them places when I had three dogs to cut up at the same time. But in a minute two of 'em begs for mercy, and mother and me lets 'em run away. The big one, he ain't able to run away. Then mother and me, we dances and jumps, and barks and laughs, and bites each other and rolls each other in the road. There never was two dogs so happy as we, and Nolan, he whistles and calls and begs me to come to him, but I just laugh and play larks with mother.

"Now, you come with me," says I, "to my new home, and never try to run away again." And I shows her our house with the five red roofs, set on the top of the hill. But mother trembles awful, and says: "They'd never let the likes of me in such a place. Does the Viceroy live there, Kid?" says she. And I laugh at her. "No, I do," I says; "and if they won't let you live there, too, you and me will go back to the streets together, for we must never be parted no more." So we trots up the hill, side by side, with Nolan trying to catch me, and Miss Dorothy laughing at him from the cart.

"The Kid's made friends with the poor old dog," says she. "Maybe he knew her long ago when he ran the streets himself. Put her in here beside me, and see if he doesn't follow."

So, when I hears that, I tells mother to go with Nolan and sit in the cart, but she says no, that she'd soil the pretty lady's frock; but I tells her to do as I say, and so Nolan lifts her, trembling still, into the cart, and I runs alongside, barking joyful.

When we drives into the stables I takes mother to my kennel, and tells her to go inside it and make herself at home. "Oh, but he won't let me!" says she.

"Who won't let you?" says I, keeping my eye on Nolan, and growling a bit nasty, just to show I was meaning to have my way. "Why, Wyndham Kid," says she, looking up at the name on my kennel.

"But I'm Wyndham Kid!" says I.

"You!" cries mother. "You! Is my little Kid the great Wyndham Kid the dogs all talk about?" And at that, she, being very old, and sick, and hungry, and nervous, as mothers are, just drops down in the straw and weeps bitter.

Well, there ain't much more than that to tell. Miss Dorothy, she settled it.

"If the Kid wants the poor old thing in the stables," says she, "let her stay."

"You see," says she, "she's a black-and-tan, and his mother was a black-and-tan, and maybe that's what makes Kid feel so friendly toward her," says she.

"Indeed, for me," says Nolan, "she can have the best there is. I'd never drive out no dog that asks for a crust nor a shelter," he says. "But what will Mr. Wyndham do?"

"He'll do what I say," says Miss Dorothy, "and if I say she's to stay, she will stay, and I say—she's to stay!"

And so mother and Nolan, and me, found a home. Mother was scared at first—not being used to kind people—but she was so gentle and loving, that the grooms got fonder of her than of me, and tried to make me jealous by patting of her, and giving her the pick of the vittles. But that was the wrong way to hurt my feelings. That's all, I think. Mother is so happy here that I tell her we ought to call it the Happy Hunting Grounds, because no one hunts you, and there is nothing to hunt; it just all comes to you. And so we live in peace, mother sleeping all day in the sun, or behind the stove in the head- groom's office, being fed twice a day regular by Nolan, and all the day by the other grooms most irregular, And, as for me, I go hurrying around the country to the bench-shows; winning money and cups for Nolan, and taking the blue ribbons away from father.

A DERELICT

When the war-ships of a navy lie cleared for action outside a harbor, and the war-ships of the country with which they are at war lie cleared for action inside the harbor, there is likely to be trouble. Trouble between war-ships is news, and wherever there is news there is always a representative of the Consolidated Press.

As long as Sampson blockaded Havana and the army beat time back of the Tampa Bay Hotel, the central office for news was at Key West, but when Cervera slipped into Santiago Harbor and Sampson stationed his battle-ships at its mouth, Key West lost her only excuse for existence, and the press-boats burled their bows in the waters of the Florida Straits and raced for the cable-station at Port Antonio. It was then that Keating, the "star" man of the Consolidated Press Syndicate, was forced to abandon his young bride and the rooms he had engaged for her at the Key West Hotel, and accompany his tug to the distant island of Jamaica.

Keating was a good and faithful servant to the Consolidated Press. He was a correspondent after its own making, an industrious collector of facts. The Consolidated Press did not ask him to comment on what it sent him to see; it did not require nor desire his editorial opinions or impressions. It was no part of his work to go into the motives which led to the event of news interest which he was sent to report, nor to point out what there was of it which was dramatic, pathetic, or outrageous.

The Consolidated Press, being a mighty corporation, which daily fed seven hundred different newspapers, could not hope to please the policy of each, so it compromised by giving the facts of the day fairly set down, without heat, prejudice, or enthusiasm. This was an excellent arrangement for the papers that subscribed for the service of the Consolidated Press, but it was death to the literary strivings of the Consolidated Press correspondents.

"We do not want descriptive writing," was the warning which the manager of the great syndicate was always flashing to its correspondents. "We do not pay you to send us pen-pictures or prose poems. We want the facts, all the facts, and nothing but the facts."

And so, when at a presidential convention a theatrical speaker sat down after calling James G. Blaine "a plumed knight," each of the "special" correspondents present wrote two columns in an effort to describe how the people who heard the speech behaved in consequence, but the Consolidated Press man telegraphed, "At the conclusion of these remarks the cheering lasted sixteen minutes."

No event of news value was too insignificant to escape the watchfulness of the Consolidated Press, none so great that it could not handle it from its inception up to the moment when it ceased to be quoted in the news-market of the world. Each night, from thousands of spots all over the surface of the globe, it received thousands of facts, of cold, accomplished facts. It knew that a tidal wave had swept through China, a cabinet had changed in Chili, in Texas an express train had been held up and robbed, "Spike" Kennedy had defeated the "Dutchman" in New Orleans, the Oregon had coaled outside of Rio Janeiro Harbor, the Cape Verde fleet had been seen at anchor off Cadiz; it had been located in the harbor of San Juan, Porto Rico; it had been sighted steaming slowly past Fortress Monroe; and the Navy Department reported that the St. Paul had discovered the lost squadron of Spain in the harbor of Santiago. This last fact was the one which sent Keating to Jamaica. Where he was sent was a matter of indifference to Keating. He had worn the collar of the Consolidated Press for so long a time that he was callous. A board meeting—a mine disaster—an Indian uprising—it was all one to Keating. He collected facts and his salary. He had no enthusiasms, he held no illusions. The prestige of the mammoth syndicate he represented gained him an audience where men who wrote for one paper only were repulsed on the threshold. Senators, governors, the presidents of great trusts and railroad systems, who fled from the reporter of a local paper as from a leper, would send for Keating and dictate to him whatever it was they wanted the people of the United States to believe, for when they talked to Keating they talked to many millions of readers. Keating, in turn, wrote out what they had said to him and transmitted it, without color or bias, to the clearinghouse of the Consolidated Press. His "stories," as all newspaper writings are called by men who write them, were as picturesque reading as the quotations of a stock- ticker. The personal equation appeared no more offensively than it does in a page of typewriting in his work.

Consequently, he was dear to the heart of the Consolidated Press, and, as a "safe" man, was sent to the beautiful harbor of Santiago— to a spot where there were war-ships cleared for action, Cubans in ambush, naked marines fighting for a foothold at Guantanamo, palm- trees and coral-reefs—in order that he might look for "facts."

There was not a newspaper man left at Key West who did not writhe with envy and anger when he heard of it. When the wire was closed for the night, and they had gathered at Josh Kerry's, Keating was the storm-centre of their indignation.

"What a chance!" they protested. "What a story! It's the chance of a lifetime." They shook their heads mournfully and lashed themselves with pictures of its possibilities.

"And just fancy its being wasted on old Keating," said the Journal man. "Why, everything's likely to happen out there, and whatever does happen, he'll make it read like a Congressional Record. Why, when I heard of it I cabled the office that if the paper would send me I'd not ask for any salary for six months."

"And Keating's kicking because he has to go," growled the Sun man. "Yes, he is, I saw him last night, and he was sore because he'd just moved his wife down here. He said if he'd known this was coming he'd have let her stay in New York. He says he'll lose money on this assignment, having to support himself and his wife in two different places."

Norris, "the star man" of the World, howled with indignation.

"Good Lord!" he said, "is that all he sees in it? Why, there never was such a chance. I tell you, some day soon all of those war-ships will let loose at each other and there will be the best story that ever came over the wire, and if there isn't, it's a regular loaf anyway. It's a picnic, that's what it is, at the expense of the Consolidated Press. Why, he ought to pay them to let him go. Can't you see him, confound him, sitting under a palm-tree in white flannels, with a glass of Jamaica rum in his fist, while we're dodging yellow fever on this coral-reef, and losing our salaries on a crooked roulette-wheel."

"I wonder what Jamaica rum is like as a steady drink," mused the ex- baseball reporter, who had been converted into a war-correspondent by the purchase of a white yachting-cap.

"It won't be long before Keating finds out," said the Journal man.

"Oh, I didn't know that," ventured the new reporter, who had just come South from Boston. "I thought he didn't drink. I never see Keating in here with the rest of the boys."

"You wouldn't," said Norris. "He only comes in here by himself, and he drinks by himself. He's one of those confidential drunkards, You give some men whiskey, and it's like throwing kerosene on a fire, isn't it? It makes them wave their arms about and talk loud and break things, but you give it to another man and it's like throwing kerosene on a cork mat. It just soaks in. That's what Keating is. He's a sort of a cork mat."

"I shouldn't think the C. P. would stand for that," said the Boston man.

"It wouldn't, if it ever interfered with his work, but he's never fallen down on a story yet. And the sort of stuff he writes is machine-made; a man can write C. P. stuff in his sleep."

One of the World men looked up and laughed.

"I wonder if he'll run across Channing out there," he said. The men at the table smiled, a kindly, indulgent smile. The name seemed to act upon their indignation as a shower upon the close air of a summer-day. "That's so," said Norris. "He wrote me last month from Port-au-Prince that he was moving on to Jamaica. He wrote me from that club there at the end of the wharf. He said he was at that moment introducing the President to a new cocktail, and as he had no money to pay his passage to Kingston he was trying to persuade him to send him on there as his Haitian Consul. He said in case he couldn't get appointed Consul, he had an offer to go as cook on a fruit- tramp."

The men around the table laughed. It was the pleased, proud laugh that flutters the family dinner-table when the infant son and heir says something precocious and impudent.

"Who is Channing?" asked the Boston man.

There was a pause, and the correspondents looked at Norris.

"Channing is a sort of a derelict," he said. "He drifted into New York last Christmas from the Omaha Bee. He's been on pretty nearly every paper in the country."

"What's he doing in Haiti?"

"He went there on the Admiral Decatur to write a filibustering story about carrying arms across to Cuba. Then the war broke out and he's been trying to get back to Key West, and now, of course, he'll make for Kingston. He cabled me yesterday, at my expense, to try and get him a job on our paper. If the war hadn't come on he had a plan to beat his way around the world. And he'd have done it, too. I never saw a man who wouldn't help Charlie along, or lend him a dollar." He glanced at the faces about him and winked at the

Boston man. "They all of them look guilty, don't they?" he said.

"Charlie Channing," murmured the baseball reporter, gently, as though he were pronouncing the name of a girl. He raised his glass. "Here's to Charlie Channing," he repeated. Norris set down his empty glass and showed it to the Boston man.

"That's his only enemy," he said. "Write! Heavens, how that man can write, and he'd almost rather do anything else. There isn't a paper in New York that wasn't glad to get him, but they couldn't keep him a week. It was no use talking to him. Talk! I've talked to him until three o'clock in the morning. Why, it was I made him send his first Chinatown story to the International Magazine, and they took it like a flash and wrote him for more, but he blew in the check they sent him and didn't even answer their letter. He said after he'd had the fun of writing a story, he didn't care whether it was published in a Sunday paper or in white vellum, or never published at all. And so long as he knew he wrote it, he didn't care whether anyone else knew it or not. Why, when that English reviewer—what's his name—that friend of Kipling's—passed through New York, he said to a lot of us at the Press Club, 'You've got a young man here on Park Row—an opium-eater, I should say, by the look of him, who if he would work and leave whiskey alone, would make us all sweat.' That's just what he said, and he's the best in England!"

"Charlie's a genius," growled the baseball reporter, defiantly. "I say, he's a genius."

The Boston man shook his head. "My boy," he began, sententiously, "genius is nothing more than hard work, and a man—"

Norris slapped the table with his hand.

"Oh, no, it's not," he jeered, fiercely, "and don't you go off believing it is, neither. I've worked. I've worked twelve hours a day. Keating even has worked eighteen hours a day—all his life—but we never wrote 'The Passing of the Highbinders,' nor the 'Ships that Never Came Home,' nor 'Tales of the Tenderloin,' and we never will. I'm a better news-gatherer than Charlie, I can collect facts and I can put them together well enough, too, so that if a man starts to read my story he'll probably follow it to the bottom of the column, and he may turn over the page, too. But I can't say the things, because I can't see the things that Charlie sees. Why, one night we sent him out on a big railroad-story. It was a beat, we'd got it by accident, and we had it all to ourselves, but Charlie came across a blind beggar on Broadway with a dead dog. The dog had been run over, and the blind beggar couldn't find his way home without him, and was sitting on the curb-stone, weeping over the mongrel. Well, when Charlie came back to the office he said he couldn't find out anything about that railroad deal, but that he'd write them a dog-story. Of course, they were raging crazy, but he sat down just as though it was no concern of his, and, sure enough, he wrote the dog-story. And the next day over five hundred people stopped in at the office on their way downtown and left dimes and dollars to buy that man a new dog. Now, hard work won't do that."

Keating had been taking breakfast in the ward-room of H. M. S. Indefatigable. As an acquaintance the officers had not found him an undoubted acquisition, but he was the representative of seven hundred papers, and when the Indefatigable's ice-machine broke, he had loaned the officers' mess a hundred pounds of it from his own boat.

The cruiser's gig carried Keating to the wharf, the crew tossed their oars and the boatswain touched his cap and asked, mechanically, "Shall I return to the ship, sir?"

Channing, stretched on the beach, with his back to a palm-tree, observed the approach of Keating with cheerful approbation.

"It is gratifying to me," he said, "to see the press treated with such consideration. You came in just like Cleopatra in her barge. If the flag had been flying, and you hadn't steered so badly, I should have thought you were at least an admiral. How many guns does the British Navy give a Consolidated Press reporter when he comes over the side?"

Keating dropped to the sand and, crossing his legs under him, began tossing shells at the water.

"They gave this one a damned good breakfast," he said, "and some very excellent white wine. Of course, the ice-machine was broken, it always is, but then Chablis never should be iced, if it's the real thing."

"Chablis! Ice! Hah!" snorted Channing. "Listen to him! Do you know what I had for breakfast?"

Keating turned away uncomfortably and looked toward the ships in the harbor.

"Well, never mind," said Channing, yawning luxuriously. "The sun is bright, the sea is blue, and the confidences of this old palm are soothing. He's a great old gossip, this palm." He looked up into the rustling fronds and smiled. "He whispers me to sleep," he went on, "or he talks me awake—talks about all sorts of things—things he has seen—cyclones, wrecks, and strange ships and Cuban refugees and Spanish spies and lovers that meet here on moonlight nights. It's always moonlight in Port Antonio, isn't it?"

"You ought to know, you've been here longer than I," said Keating.

"And how do you like it, now that you have got to know it better? Pretty heavenly? eh?"

"Pretty heavenly!" snorted Keating. "Pretty much the other place! What good am I doing? What's the sense of keeping me here? Cervera isn't going to come out, and the people at Washington won't let Sampson go in. Why, those ships have been there a month now, and they'll be there just where they are now when you and I are bald. I'm no use here. All I do is to thrash across there every day and eat up more coal than the whole squadron burns in a month. Why, that tug of mine's costing the C. P. six hundred dollars a day, and I'm not sending them news enough to pay for setting it up. Have you seen 'em yet?"

"Seen what? Your stories?"

"No, the ships!"

"Yes, Scudder took me across once in the Iduna. I haven't got a paper yet, so I couldn't write anything, but—"

"Well, you've seen all there is to it, then; you wouldn't see any more if you went over every day. It's just the same old harbor-mouth, and the same old Morro Castle, and same old ships, drifting up and down; the Brooklyn, full of smoke-stacks, and the New York, with her two bridges, and all the rest of them looking just as they've looked for the last four weeks. There's nothing in that. Why don't they send me to Tampa with the army and Shafter—that's where the story is."

"Oh, I don't know," said Channing, shaking his head. "I thought it was bully!"

"Bully, what was bully?"

"Oh, the picture," said Channing, doubtfully, "and— and what it meant. What struck me about it was that it was so hot, and lazy, and peaceful, that they seemed to be just drifting about, just what you complain of. I don't know what I expected to see; I think I expected they'd be racing around in circles, tearing up the water and throwing broadsides at Morro Castle as fast as fire-crackers.

"But they lay broiling there in the heat just as though they were becalmed. They seemed to be asleep on their anchor-chains. It reminded me of a big bull-dog lying in the sun with his head on his paws and his eyes shut. You think he's asleep, and you try to tiptoe past him, but when you're in reach of his chain—he's at your throat, what? It seemed so funny to think of our being really at war. I mean the United States, and with such an old-established firm as Spain. It seems so presumptuous in a young republic, as though we were strutting around, singing, 'I'm getting a big boy now.' I felt like saying, 'Oh, come off, and stop playing you're a world power, and get back into your red sash and knickerbockers, or you'll get spanked!' It seems as though we must be such a lot of amateurs. But when I went over the side of the New York I felt like kneeling down on her deck and begging every jackey to kick me. I felt about as useless as a fly on a locomotive-engine. Amateurs! Why, they might have been in the business since the days of the ark; all of them might have been descended from bloody pirates; they twisted those eight-inch guns around for us just as though they were bicycles, and the whole ship moved and breathed and thought, too, like a human being, and all the captains of the other war-ships about her were watching for her to give the word. All of them stripped and eager and ready—like a lot of jockeys holding in the big race-horses, and each of them with his eyes on the starter. And I liked the way they all talk about Sampson, and the way the ships move over the stations like parts of one machine, just as he had told them to do.

"Scudder introduced me to him, and he listened while we did the talking, but it was easy to see who was the man in the Conning Tower. Keating—my boy!" Channing cried, sitting upright in his enthusiasm, "he's put a combination-lock on that harbor that can't be picked—and it'll work whether Sampson's asleep in his berth, or fifteen miles away, or killed on the bridge. He doesn't have to worry, he knows his trap will work—he ought to, he set it."

Keating shrugged his shoulders, tolerantly.

"Oh, I see that side of it," he assented. "I see all there is in it for YOU, the sort of stuff you write, Sunday-special stuff, but there's no NEWS in it. I'm not paid to write mail-letters, and I'm not down here to interview palm-trees either."

"Why, you old fraud!" laughed Channing. "You know you're having the time of your life here. You're the pet of Kingston society—you know you are. I only wish I were half as popular. I don't seem to belong, do I? I guess it's my clothes. That English Colonel at Kingston always scowls at me as though he'd like to put me in irons, and whenever I meet our Consul he sees something very peculiar on the horizon-line."

Keating frowned for a moment in silence, and then coughed, consciously.

"Channing," he began, uncomfortably, "you ought to brace up."

"Brace up?" asked Channing.

"Well, it isn't fair to the rest of us," protested Keating, launching into his grievance. "There's only a few of us here, and we—we think you ought to see that and not give the crowd a bad name. All the other correspondents have some regard for—for their position and for the paper, but you loaf around here looking like an old tramp—like any old beach-comber, and it queers the rest of us. Why, those English artillerymen at the Club asked me about you, and when I told them you were a New York correspondent they made all sorts of jokes about American newspapers, and what could I say?"

Channing eyed the other man with keen delight.

"I see, by Jove! I'm sorry," he said. But the next moment he laughed, and then apologized, remorsefully.

"Indeed, I beg your pardon," he begged, "but it struck me as a sort of—I had no idea you fellows were such swells—I knew I was a social outcast, but I didn't know my being a social outcast was hurting anyone else. Tell me some more."

"Well, that's all," said Keating, suspiciously. "The fellows asked me to speak to you about it and to tell you to take a brace. Now, for instance, we have a sort of mess-table at the hotels and we'd like to ask you to belong, but—well—you see how it is—we have the officers to lunch whenever they're on shore, and you're so disreputable"— Keating scowled at Channing, and concluded, impotently, "Why don't you get yourself some decent clothes and—and a new hat?"

Channing removed his hat to his knee and stroked it with affectionate pity.

"It is a shocking bad hat," he said. "Well, go on."

"Oh, it's none of my business," exclaimed Keating, impatiently. "I'm just telling you what they're saying. Now, there's the Cuban refugees, for instance. No one knows what they're doing here, or whether they're real Cubans or Spaniards."

"Well, what of it?"

"Why, the way you go round with them and visit them, it's no wonder they say you're a spy."

Channing stared incredulously, and then threw back his head and laughed with a shout of delight.

"They don't, do they?" he asked.

"Yes, they do, since you think it's so funny. If it hadn't been for us the day you went over to Guantanamo the marines would have had you arrested and court-martialed."

Channing's face clouded with a quick frown, "Oh," he exclaimed, in a hurt voice, "they couldn't have thought that."

"Well, no," Keating admitted grudgingly, "not after the fight, perhaps, but before that, when you were snooping around the camp like a Cuban after rations." Channing recognized the picture with a laugh.

"I do," he said, "I do. But you should have had me court-martialed and shot; it would have made a good story. 'Our reporter shot as a spy, his last words were—' what were my last words, Keating?"

Keating turned upon him with impatience, "But why do you do it?" he demanded. "Why don't you act like the rest of us? Why do you hang out with all those filibusters and runaway Cubans?"

"They have been very kind to me," said Channing, soberly. "They are a very courteous race, and they have ideas of hospitality which make the average New Yorker look like a dog hiding a bone."

"Oh, I suppose you mean that for us," demanded Keating. "That's a slap at me, eh?"

Channing gave a sigh and threw himself back against the trunk of the palm, with his hands clasped behind his head.

"Oh, I wasn't thinking of you at all, Keating," he said. "I don't consider you in the least." He stretched himself and yawned wearily. "I've got troubles of my own." He sat up suddenly and adjusted the objectionable hat to his head.

"Why don't you wire the C. P.," he asked, briskly, "and see if they don't want an extra man? It won't cost you anything to wire, and I need the job, and I haven't the money to cable."

"The Consolidated Press," began Keating, jealously. "Why—well, you know what the Consolidated Press is? They don't want descriptive writers—and I've got all the men I need."

Keating rose and stood hesitating in some embarrassment. "I'll tell you what I could do, Channing," he said, "I could take you on as a stoker, or steward, say. They're always deserting and mutinying; I have to carry a gun on me to make them mind. How would you like that? Forty dollars a month, and eat with the crew?"

For a moment Channing stood in silence, smoothing the sand with the sole of his shoe. When he raised his head his face was flushing.

"Oh, thank you," he said. "I think I'll keep on trying for a paper— I'll try a little longer. I want to see something of this war, of course, and if I'm not too lazy I'd like to write something about it, but—well—I'm much obliged to you, anyway."

"Of course, if it were my money, I'd take you on at once," said Keating, hurriedly.

Channing smiled and nodded. "You're very kind," he answered. "Well, good-by."

A half-hour later, in the smoking-room of the hotel, Keating addressed himself to a group of correspondents.

"There is no doing anything with that man Channing," he said, in a tone of offended pride. "I offered him a good job and he wouldn't take it. Because he got a story in the International Magazine, he's stuck on himself, and he won't hustle for news—he wants to write pipe-dreams. What the public wants just now is news."

"That's it," said one of the group, "and we must give it to them— even if we have to fake it."

Great events followed each other with great rapidity. The army ceased beating time, shook itself together, adjusted its armor and moved, and, to the delight of the flotilla of press-boats at Port Antonio, moved, not as it had at first intended, to the north coast of Cuba, but to Santiago, where its transports were within reach of their megaphones.

"Why, everything's coming our way now!" exclaimed the World manager in ecstasy. "We've got the transports to starboard at Siboney, and the war-ships to port at Santiago, and all we'll need to do is to sit on the deck with a field-glass, and take down the news with both hands."

Channing followed these events with envy. Once or twice, as a special favor, the press-boats carried him across to Siboney and Daiquiri, and he was able to write stories of what he saw there; of the landing of the army, of the wounded after the Guasimas fight, and of the fever-camp at Siboney. His friends on the press-boats sent this work home by mail on the chance that the Sunday editor might take it at space rates. But mail matter moved slowly and the army moved quickly, and events crowded so closely upon each other that Channing's stories, when they reached New York, were ancient history and were unpublished, and, what was of more importance to him, unpaid for. He had no money now, and he had become a beach-comber in the real sense of the word. He slept the warm nights away among the bananas and cocoanuts on the Fruit Company's wharf, and by calling alternately on his Cuban exiles and the different press-boats, he was able to obtain a meal a day without arousing any suspicions in the minds of his hosts that it was his only one.

He was sitting on the stringer of the pier-head one morning, waiting for a press-boat from the "front," when the Three Friends ran in and lowered her dingy, and the "World" manager came ashore, clasping a precious bundle of closely written cable-forms. Channing scrambled to his feet and hailed him.

"Have you heard from the chief about me yet?" he asked. The "World" man frowned and stammered, and then, taking Channing by the arm, hurried with him toward the cable-office.

"Charlie, I think they're crazy up there," he began, "they think they know it all. Here I am on the spot, but they think—"

"You mean they won't have me," said Channing. "But why?" he asked, patiently. "They used to give me all the space I wanted."

"Yes, I know, confound them, and so they should now," said the "World" man, with sympathetic indignation. "But here's their cable; you can see it's not my fault." He read the message aloud. "Channing, no. Not safe, take reliable man from Siboney." He folded the cablegram around a dozen others and stuck it back in his hip-pocket.

"What queered you, Charlie," he explained, importantly, "was that last break of yours, New Year's, when you didn't turn up for a week. It was once too often, and the chief's had it in for you ever since. You remember?"

Channing screwed up his lips in an effort of recollection.

"Yes, I remember," he answered, slowly. "It began on New Year's eve in Perry's drug-store, and I woke up a week later in a hack in Boston. So I didn't have such a run for my money, did I? Not good enough to have to pay for it like this. I tell you," he burst out suddenly, "I feel like hell being left out of this war, with all the rest of the boys working so hard. If it weren't playing it low down on the fellows that have been in it from the start, I'd like to enlist. But they enlisted for glory, and I'd only do it because I can't see the war any other way, and it doesn't seem fair to them. What do you think?"

"Oh, don't do that," protested the World manager. "You stick to your own trade. We'll get you something to do. Have you tried the Consolidated Press yet?"

Channing smiled grimly at the recollection.

"Yes, I tried it first."

"It would be throwing pearls to swine to have you write for them, I know, but they're using so many men now. I should think you could get on their boat."

"No, I saw Keating," Channing explained. "He said I could come along as a stoker, and I guess I'll take him up, it seems—"

"Keating said—what?" exclaimed the "World" man. "Keating? Why, he stands to lose his own job, if he isn't careful. If it wasn't that he's just married, the C. P. boys would have reported him a dozen times."

"Reported him, what for?"

"Why—you know. His old complaint."

"Oh, that," said Channing. "My old complaint?" he added.

"Well, yes, but Keating hasn't been sober for two weeks, and he'd have fallen down on the Guasimas story if those men hadn't pulled him through. They had to, because they're in the syndicate. He ought to go shoot himself; he's only been married three months and he's handling the biggest piece of news the country's had in thirty years, and he can't talk straight. There's a time for everything, I say," growled the "World" man.

"It takes it out of a man, this boat-work," Channing ventured, in extenuation. "It's very hard on him."

"You bet it is," agreed the "World" manager, with enthusiasm. "Sloshing about in those waves, sea-sick mostly, and wet all the time, and with a mutinous crew, and so afraid you'll miss something that you can't write what you have got." Then he added, as an after- thought, "And our cruisers thinking you're a Spanish torpedo-boat and chucking shells at you."

"No wonder Keating drinks," Channing said, gravely. "You make it seem almost necessary."

Many thousand American soldiers had lost themselves in a jungle, and had broken out of it at the foot of San Juan Hill. Not wishing to return into the jungle, they took the hill. On the day they did this Channing had the good fortune to be in Siboney. The "World" man had carried him there and asked him to wait around the waterfront while he went up to the real front, thirteen miles inland. Channing's duty was to signal the press-boat when the first despatch-rider rode in with word that the battle was on. The World man would have liked to ask Channing to act as his despatch-rider, but he did not do so, because the despatch-riders were either Jamaica negroes or newsboys from Park Row—and he remembered that Keating had asked Channing to be his stoker.

Channing tramped through the damp, ill-smelling sand of the beach, sick with self-pity. On the other side of those glaring, inscrutable mountains, a battle, glorious, dramatic, and terrible, was going forward, and he was thirteen miles away. He was at the base, with the supplies, the sick, and the skulkers.

It was cruelly hot. The heat-waves flashed over the sea until the transports in the harbor quivered like pictures on a biograph. From the refuse of company kitchens, from reeking huts, from thousands of empty cans, rose foul, enervating odors, which deadened the senses like a drug. The atmosphere steamed with a heavy, moist humidity. Channing staggered and sank down suddenly on a pile of railroad-ties in front of the commissary's depot. There were some Cubans seated near him, dividing their Government rations, and the sight reminded him that he had had nothing to eat. He walked over to the wide door of the freight-depot, where a white-haired, kindly faced, and perspiring officer was, with his own hands, serving out canned beef to a line of Cubans. The officer's flannel shirt was open at the throat. The shoulder-straps of a colonel were fastened to it by safety-pins. Channing smiled at him uneasily.

"Could I draw on you for some rations?" he asked. "I'm from the Three Friends. I'm not one of their regular accredited correspondents," he added, conscientiously, "I'm just helping them for to-day."

"Haven't you got a correspondent's pass?" asked the officer. He was busily pouring square hardtack down the throat of a saddle-bag a Cuban soldier held open before him.

"No," said Channing, turning away, "I'm just helping."

The officer looked after him, and what he saw caused him to reach under the counter for a tin cup and a bottle of lime-juice.

"Here," he said, "drink this. What's the matter with you—fever? Come in here out of that sun. You can lie down on my cot, if you like."

Channing took the tin cup and swallowed a warm mixture of boiled water and acrid lime-juice.

"Thank you," he said, "but I must keep watch for the first news from the front."

A man riding a Government mule appeared on the bridge of the lower trail, and came toward them at a gallop.

He was followed and surrounded by a hurrying mob of volunteers, hospital stewards, and Cubans.

The Colonel vaulted the counter and ran to meet him.

"This looks like news from the front now," he cried.

The man on the mule was from civil life. His eyes bulged from their sockets and his face was purple. The sweat ran over it and glistened on the cords of his thick neck.

"They're driving us back!" he shrieked.

"Chaffee's killed, an' Roosevelt's killed, an' the whole army's beaten!" He waved his arms wildly toward the glaring, inscrutable mountains. The volunteers and stevedores and Cubans heard him, open- mouthed and with panic-stricken eyes. In the pitiless sunlight he was a hideous and awful spectacle.

"They're driving us into the sea!" he foamed.

"We've got to get out of here, they're just behind me. The army's running for its life. They're running away!"

Channing saw the man dimly, through a cloud that came between him and the yellow sunlight. The man in the saddle swayed, the group about him swayed, like persons on the floor of a vast ball-room. Inside he burned with a mad, fierce hatred for this shrieking figure in the saddle. He raised the tin cup and hurled it so that it hit the man's purple face.

"You lie!" Channing shouted, staggering. "You lie! You're a damned coward. You lie!" He heard his voice repeating this in different places at greater distances. Then the cloud closed about him, shutting out the man in the saddle, and the glaring, inscrutable mountains, and the ground at his feet rose and struck him in the face.

Channing knew he was on a boat because it lifted and sank with him, and he could hear the rush of her engines. When he opened his eyes he was in the wheel-house of the Three Friends, and her captain was at the wheel, smiling down at him. Channing raised himself on his elbow.

"The despatch-rider?" he asked.

"That's all right," said the captain, soothingly. "Don't you worry. He come along same time you fell, and brought you out to us. What ailed you—sunstroke?"

Channing sat up. "I guess so," he said.

When the Three Friends reached Port Antonio, Channing sought out the pile of coffee-bags on which he slept at night and dropped upon them. Before this he had been careful to avoid the place in the daytime, so that no one might guess that it was there that he slept at night, but this day he felt that if he should drop in the gutter he would not care whether anyone saw him there or not. His limbs were hot and heavy and refused to support him, his bones burned like quicklime.

The next morning, with the fever still upon him, he hurried restlessly between the wharves and the cable-office, seeking for news. There was much of it; it was great and trying news, the situation outside of Santiago was grim and critical. The men who had climbed San Juan Hill were clinging to it like sailors shipwrecked on a reef unwilling to remain, but unable to depart. If they attacked the city Cervera promised to send it crashing about their ears. They would enter Santiago only to find it in ruins. If they abandoned the hill, 2,000 killed and wounded would have been sacrificed in vain.

The war-critics of the press-boats and of the Twitchell House saw but two courses left open. Either Sampson must force the harbor and destroy the squadron, and so make it possible for the army to enter the city, or the army must be reinforced with artillery and troops in sufficient numbers to make it independent of Sampson and indifferent to Cervera.

On the night of July 2d, a thousand lies, a thousand rumors, a thousand prophecies rolled through the streets of Port Antonio, were filed at the cable-office, and flashed to the bulletin-boards of New York City.

That morning, so they told, the batteries on Morro Castle had sunk three of Sampson's ships; the batteries on Morro Castle had surrendered to Sampson; General Miles with 8,000 reinforcements had sailed from Charleston; eighty guns had started from Tampa Bay, they would occupy the mountains opposite Santiago and shell the Spanish fleet; the authorities at Washington had at last consented to allow

Sampson to run the forts and mines, and attack the Spanish fleet; the army had not been fed for two days, the Spaniards had cut it off from its base at Siboney; the army would eat its Fourth of July dinner in the Governor's Palace; the army was in full retreat; the army was to attack at daybreak.

When Channing turned in under the fruit-shed on the night of July 2d, there was but one press-boat remaining in the harbor. That was the Consolidated Press boat, and Keating himself was on the wharf, signalling for his dingy. Channing sprang to his feet and ran toward him, calling him by name. The thought that he must for another day remain so near the march of great events and yet not see and feel them for himself, was intolerable. He felt if it would pay his passage to the coast of Cuba, there was no sacrifice to which he would not stoop. Keating watched him approach, but without sign of recognition. His eyes were heavy and bloodshot.

"Keating," Channing begged, as he halted, panting, "won't you take me with you? I'll not be in the way, and I'll stoke or wait on table, or anything you want, if you'll only take me."

Keating's eyes opened and closed, sleepily. He removed an unlit cigar from his mouth and shook the wet end of it at Channing, as though it were an accusing finger.

"I know your game," he murmured, thickly. "You haven't got a boat and you want to steal a ride on mine—for your paper. You can't do it, you see, you can't do it."

One of the crew of the dingy climbed up the gangway of the wharf and took Keating by the elbow. He looked at him and then at Channing and winked. He was apparently accustomed to this complication. "I haven't got a paper, Keating," Channing argued, soothingly. "Who have you got to help you?" he asked. It came to him that there might be on the boat some Philip sober, to whom he could appeal from Philip drunk.

"I haven't got anyone to help me," Keating answered, with dignity. "I don't need anyone to help me." He placed his hand heavily and familiarly on the shoulder of the deck-hand. "You see that man?" he asked. "You see tha' man, do you? Well, tha' man he's too good for me an' you. Tha' man—used to be the best reporter in New York City, an' he was too good to hustle for news, an' now he's—now he can't get a job—see? Nobody'll have him, see? He's got to come and be a stoker."

He stamped his foot with indignation.

"You come an' be a stoker," he commanded. "How long you think I'm going to wait for a stoker? You stoker, come on board and be a stoker."

Channing smiled, guiltily, at his good fortune, He jumped into the bow of the dingy, and Keating fell heavily in the stern.

The captain of the press-boat helped Keating safely to a bunk in the cabin and received his instructions to proceed to Santiago Harbor. Then he joined Channing. "Mr. Keating is feeling bad to-night. That bombardment off Morro," he explained, tactfully, "was too exciting. We always let him sleep going across, and when we get there he's fresh as a daisy. What's this he tells me of your doing stoking?"

"I thought there might be another fight tomorrow, so I said I'd come as a stoker."

The captain grinned.

"Our Sam, that deck-hand, was telling me. He said Mr. Keating put it on you, sort of to spite you—is that so?"

"Oh, I wanted to come," said Channing.

The captain laughed, comprehendingly. "I guess we'll be in a bad way," he said, "when we need you in the engine-room." He settled himself for conversation, with his feet against the rail and his thumbs in his suspenders. The lamps of Port Antonio were sinking into the water, the moonlight was flooding the deck.

"That was quite something of a bombardment Sampson put up against Morro Castle this morning," he began, critically. He spoke of bombardments from the full experience of a man who had seen shells strike off Coney Island from the proving-grounds at Sandy Hook. But Channing heard him, eagerly. He begged the tugboat-captain to tell him what it looked like, and as the captain told him he filled it in and saw it as it really was.

"Perhaps they'll bombard again to-morrow," he hazarded, hopefully.

"We can't tell till we see how they're placed on the station," the captain answered. "If there's any firing we ought to hear it about eight o'clock to-morrow morning. We'll hear 'em before we see 'em."

Channing's conscience began to tweak him. It was time, he thought, that Keating should be aroused and brought up to the reviving air of the sea, but when he reached the foot of the companion-ladder, he found that Keating was already awake and in the act of drawing the cork from a bottle. His irritation against Channing had evaporated and he greeted him with sleepy good-humor.

"Why, it's ol' Charlie Channing," he exclaimed, drowsily. Channing advanced upon him swiftly.

"Here, you've had enough of that!" he commanded. "We'll be off Morro by breakfast-time. You don't want that."

Keating, giggling foolishly, pushed him from him and retreated with the bottle toward his berth. He lurched into it, rolled over with his face to the ship's side, and began breathing heavily.

"You leave me 'lone," he murmured, from the darkness of the bunk. "You mind your own business, you leave me 'lone."

Channing returned to the bow and placed the situation before the captain. That gentleman did not hesitate. He disappeared down the companion-way, and, when an instant later he returned, hurled a bottle over the ship's side.

The next morning when Channing came on deck the land was just in sight, a rampart of dark green mountains rising in heavy masses against the bright, glaring blue of the sky. He strained his eyes for the first sight of the ships, and his ears for the faintest echoes of distant firing, but there was no sound save the swift rush of the waters at the bow. The sea lay smooth and flat before him, the sun flashed upon it; the calm and hush of early morning hung over the whole coast of Cuba.

An hour later the captain came forward and stood at his elbow.

"How's Keating?" Channing asked. "I tried to wake him, but I couldn't."

The captain kept his binoculars to his eyes, and shut his lips grimly. "Mr. Keating's very bad," he said. "He had another bottle hidden somewhere, and all last night—" he broke off with a relieved sigh. "It's lucky for him," he added, lowering the glasses, "that there'll be no fight to-day."

Channing gave a gasp of disappointment. "What do you mean?" he protested.

"You can look for yourself," said the captain, handing him the glasses. "They're at their same old stations. There'll be no bombardment to-day. That's the Iowa, nearest us, the Oregon's to starboard of her, and the next is the Indiana. That little fellow close under the land is the Gloucester."

He glanced up at the mast to see that the press-boat's signal was conspicuous, they were drawing within range.

With the naked eye, Channing could see the monster, mouse-colored war-ships, basking in the sun, solemn and motionless in a great crescent, with its one horn resting off the harbor-mouth. They made great blots on the sparkling, glancing surface of the water. Above each superstructure, their fighting-tops, giant davits, funnels, and gibbet-like yards twisted into the air, fantastic and incomprehensible, but the bulk below seemed to rest solidly on the bottom of the ocean, like an island of lead. The muzzles of their guns peered from the turrets as from ramparts of rock.

Channing gave a sigh of admiration.

"Don't tell me they move," he said. "They're not ships, they're fortresses!"

On the shore there was no sign of human life nor of human habitation. Except for the Spanish flag floating over the streaked walls of Morro, and the tiny blockhouse on every mountain-top, the squadron might have been anchored off a deserted coast. The hills rose from the water's edge like a wall, their peaks green and glaring in the sun, their valleys dark with shadows. Nothing moved upon the white beach at their feet, no smoke rose from their ridges, not even a palm stirred. The great range slept in a blue haze of heat. But only a few miles distant, masked by its frowning front, lay a gayly colored, red-roofed city, besieged by encircling regiments, a broad bay holding a squadron of great war-ships, and gliding cat-like through its choked undergrowth and crouched among the fronds of its motionless palms were the ragged patriots of the Cuban army, silent, watchful, waiting. But the great range gave no sign. It frowned in the sunlight, grim and impenetrable.

"It's Sunday," exclaimed the captain. He pointed with his finger at the decks of the battleships, where hundreds of snow-white figures had gone to quarters. "It's church service," he said, "or it's general inspection."

Channing looked at his watch. It was thirty minutes past nine. "It's church service," he said. "I can see them carrying out the chaplain's reading-desk on the Indiana." The press-boat pushed her way nearer into the circle of battleships until their leaden-hued hulls towered high above her. On the deck of each, the ship's company stood, ranged in motionless ranks. The calm of a Sabbath morning hung about them, the sun fell upon them like a benediction, and so still was the air that those on the press-boat could hear, from the stripped and naked decks, the voices of the men answering the roll-call in rising monotone, "one, two, three, FOUR; one, two, three, FOUR." The white- clad sailors might have been a chorus of surpliced choir-boys.

But, up above them, the battle-flags, slumbering at the mast-heads, stirred restlessly and whimpered in their sleep.

Out through the crack in the wall of mountains, where the sea runs in to meet the waters of Santiago Harbor, and from behind the shield of Morro Castle, a great, gray ship, like a great, gray rat, stuck out her nose and peered about her, and then struck boldly for the open sea. High before her she bore the gold and blood-red flag of Spain, and, like a fugitive leaping from behind his prison-walls, she raced forward for her freedom, to give battle, to meet her death.

A shell from the Iowa shrieked its warning in a shrill crescendo, a flutter of flags painted their message against the sky. "The enemy's ships are coming out," they signalled, and the ranks of white-clad figures which the moment before stood motionless on the decks, broke into thousands of separate beings who flung themselves, panting, down the hatchways, or sprang, cheering, to the fighting-tops.

Heavily, but swiftly, as islands slip into the water when a volcano shakes the ocean-bed, the great battle-ships buried their bows in the sea, their sides ripped apart with flame and smoke, the thunder of their guns roared and beat against the mountains, and, from the shore, the Spanish forts roared back at them, until the air between was split and riven. The Spanish war-ships were already scudding clouds of smoke, pierced with flashes of red flame, and as they fled, fighting, their batteries rattled with unceasing, feverish fury. But the guns of the American ships, straining in pursuit, answered steadily, carefully, with relentless accuracy, with cruel persistence. At regular intervals they boomed above the hurricane of sound, like great bells tolling for the dead.

It seemed to Channing that he had lived through many years; that the strain of the spectacle would leave its mark upon his nerves forever. He had been buffeted and beaten by a storm of all the great emotions; pride of race and country, pity for the dead, agony for the dying, who clung to blistering armor-plates, or sank to suffocation in the sea; the lust of the hunter, when the hunted thing is a fellow-man; the joys of danger and of excitement, when the shells lashed the waves about him, and the triumph of victory, final, overwhelming and complete.

Four of the enemy's squadron had struck their colors, two were on the beach, broken and burning, two had sunk to the bottom of the sea, two were in abject flight. Three battle-ships were hammering them with thirteen-inch guns. The battle was won.

"It's all over," Channing said. His tone questioned his own words.

The captain of the tugboat was staring at the face of his silver watch, as though it were a thing bewitched. He was pale and panting. He looked at Channing, piteously, as though he doubted his own senses, and turned the face of the watch toward him.

"Twenty minutes!" Channing said. "Good God! Twenty minutes!"

He had been to hell and back again in twenty minutes. He had seen an empire, which had begun with Christopher Columbus and which had spread over two continents, wiped off the map in twenty minutes. The captain gave a sudden cry of concern. "Mr. Keating," he gasped. "Oh, Lord, but I forgot Mr. Keating. Where is Mr. Keating?"

"I went below twice," Channing answered. "He's insensible. See what you can do with him, but first—take me to the Iowa. The Consolidated Press will want the 'facts.'"

In the dark cabin the captain found Keating on the floor, where Channing had dragged him, and dripping with the water which Channing had thrown in his face. He was breathing heavily, comfortably. He was not concerned with battles.

With a megaphone, Channing gathered his facts from an officer of the Iowa, who looked like a chimney-sweep, and who was surrounded by a crew of half-naked pirates, with bodies streaked with sweat and powder.

Then he ordered all steam for Port Antonio, and, going forward to the chart-room, seated himself at the captain's desk, and, pushing the captain's charts to the floor, spread out his elbows, and began to write the story of his life.

In the joy of creating it, he was lost to all about him. He did not know that the engines, driven to the breaking-point, were filling the ship with their groans and protests, that the deck beneath his feet was quivering like the floor of a planing-mill, nor that his fever was rising again, and feeding on his veins. The turmoil of leaping engines and of throbbing pulses was confused with the story he was writing, and while his mind was inflamed with pictures of warring battle-ships, his body was swept by the fever, which overran him like an army of tiny mice, touching his hot skin with cold, tingling taps of their scampering feet.

From time to time the captain stopped at the door of the chart-room and observed him in silent admiration. To the man who with difficulty composed a letter to his family, the fact that Channing was writing something to be read by millions of people, and more rapidly than he could have spoken the same words, seemed a superhuman effort. He even hesitated to interrupt it by an offer of food.

But the fever would not let Channing taste of the food when they placed it at his elbow, and even as he pushed it away, his mind was still fixed upon the paragraph before him. He wrote, sprawling across the desk, covering page upon page with giant hieroglyphics, lighting cigarette after cigarette at the end of the last one, but with his thoughts far away, and, as he performed the act, staring uncomprehendingly at the captain's colored calendar pinned on the wall before him. For many months later the Battle of Santiago was associated in his mind with a calendar for the month of July, illuminated by a colored picture of six white kittens in a basket.

At three o'clock Channing ceased writing and stood up, shivering and shaking with a violent chill. He cursed himself for this weakness, and called aloud for the captain.

"I can't stop now," he cried. He seized the rough fist of the captain as a child clings to the hand of his nurse.

"Give me something," he begged. "Medicine, quinine, give me something to keep my head straight until it's finished. Go, quick," he commanded. His teeth were chattering, and his body jerked with sharp, uncontrollable shudders. The captain ran, muttering, to his medicine- chest.

"We've got one drunken man on board," he said to the mate, "and now we've got a crazy one. You mark my words, he'll go off his head at sunset."

But at sunset Channing called to him and addressed him sanely. He held in his hand a mass of papers carefully numbered and arranged, and he gave them up to the captain as though it hurt him to part with them.

"There's the story," he said. "You've got to do the rest. I can't—I- -I'm going to be very ill." He was swaying as he spoke. His eyes burned with the fever, and his eyelids closed of themselves. He looked as though he had been heavily drugged.

"You put that on the wire at Port Antonio," he commanded, faintly; "pay the tolls to Kingston. From there they are to send it by way of Panama, you understand, by the Panama wire."

"Panama!" gasped the captain. "Good Lord, that's two dollars a word." He shook out the pages in his hand until he found the last one. "And there's sixty-eight pages here," he expostulated. "Why the tolls will be five thousand dollars!" Channing dropped feebly to the bench of the chart-room and fell in a heap, shivering and trembling.

"I guess it's worth it," he murmured, drowsily.

The captain was still staring at the last page.

"But—but, look here," he cried, "you've—you've signed Mr. Keating's name to it! 'James R. Keating.' You've signed his name to it!"

Channing raised his head from his folded arms and stared at him dully.

"You don't want to get Keating in trouble, do you?" he asked with patience. "You don't want the C. P. to know why he couldn't write the best story of the war? Do you want him to lose his job? Of course you don't. Well, then, let it go as his story. I won't tell, and see you don't tell, and Keating won't remember."

His head sank back again upon his crossed arms. "It's not a bad story," he murmured.

But the captain shook his head; his loyalty to his employer was still uppermost. "It doesn't seem right!" he protested. "It's a sort of a liberty, isn't it, signing another man's name to it, it's a sort of forgery."

Channing made no answer. His eyes were shut and he was shivering violently, hugging himself in his arms.

A quarter of an hour later, when the captain returned with fresh quinine, Channing sat upright and saluted him.

"Your information, sir," he said, addressing the open door politely, "is of the greatest value. Tell the executive officer to proceed under full steam to Panama. He will first fire a shot across her bows, and then sink her!" He sprang upright and stood for a moment, sustained by the false strength of the fever. "To Panama, you hear me!" he shouted. He beat the floor with his foot. "Faster, faster, faster," he cried. "We've got a great story! We want a clear wire, we want the wire clear from Panama to City Hall. It's the greatest story ever written—full of facts, facts, facts, facts for the Consolidated Press—and Keating wrote it. I tell you, Keating wrote it. I saw him write it. I was a stoker on the same ship."

The mate and crew came running forward and stood gaping stupidly through the doors and windows of the chart-room. Channing welcomed them joyously, and then crumpled up in a heap and pitched forward into the arms of the captain. His head swung weakly from shoulder to shoulder.

"I beg your pardon," he muttered, "I beg your pardon, captain, but your engine-room is too hot. I'm only a stoker and I know my place, sir, but I tell you, your engine-room is too hot. It's a burning hell, sir, it's a hell!"

The captain nodded to the crew and they closed in on him, and bore him, struggling feebly, to a bunk in the cabin below. In the berth opposite, Keating was snoring peacefully.

After the six weeks' siege the Fruit Company's doctor told Channing he was cured, and that he might walk abroad. In this first walk he found that, during his illness, Port Antonio had reverted to her original condition of complete isolation from the world, the press- boats had left her wharves, the correspondents had departed from the veranda of her only hotel, the war was over, and the Peace Commissioners had sailed for Paris. Channing expressed his great gratitude to the people of the hotel and to the Fruit Company's doctor. He made it clear to them that if they ever hoped to be paid those lesser debts than that of gratitude which he still owed them, they must return him to New York and Newspaper Row. It was either that, he said, or, if they preferred, he would remain and work out his indebtedness, checking bunches of bananas at twenty dollars a month. The Fruit Company decided it would be paid more quickly if Channing worked at his own trade, and accordingly sent him North in one of its steamers. She landed him in Boston, and he borrowed five dollars from the chief engineer to pay his way to New York.

It was late in the evening of the same day when he stepped out of the smoking-car into the roar and riot of the Grand Central Station. He had no baggage to detain him, and, as he had no money either, he made his way to an Italian restaurant where he knew they would trust him to pay later for what he ate. It was a place where the newspaper men were accustomed to meet, men who knew him, and who, until he found work, would lend him money to buy a bath, clean clothes, and a hall bedroom.

Norris, the World man, greeted him as he entered the door of the restaurant, and hailed him with a cry of mingled fright and pleasure.

"Why, we didn't know but you were dead," he exclaimed. "The boys said when they left Kingston you weren't expected to live. Did you ever get the money and things we sent you by the Red Cross boat?"

Channing glanced at himself and laughed.

"Do I look it?" he asked. He was wearing the same clothes in which he had slept under the fruit-sheds at Port Antonio. They had been soaked and stained by the night-dews and by the sweat of the fever.

"Well, it's great luck, your turning up here just now," Norris assured him, heartily. "That is, if you're as hungry as the rest of the boys are who have had the fever. You struck it just right; we're giving a big dinner here to-night," he explained, "one of Maria's best. You come in with me. It's a celebration for old Keating, a farewell blow-out."

Channing started and laughed.

"Keating?" he asked. "That's funny," he said. "I haven't seen him since—since before I was ill."

"Yes, old Jimmie Keating. You've got nothing against him, have you?"

Channing shook his head vehemently, and Norris glanced back complacently toward the door of the dining-room, from whence came the sound of intimate revelry.

"You might have had, once," Norris said, laughing; "we were all up against him once. But since he's turned out such a wonder and a war- hero, we're going to recognize it. They're always saying we newspaper men have it in for each other, and so we're just giving him this subscription-dinner to show it's not so. He's going abroad, you know. He sails to-morrow morning."

"No, I didn't know," said Channing.

"Of course not, how could you? Well, the Consolidated Press's sending him and his wife to Paris. He's to cover the Peace negotiations there. It's really a honeymoon-trip at the expense of the C. P. It's their reward for his work, for his Santiago story, and the beat and all that—"

Channing's face expressed his bewilderment.

Norris drew back dramatically.

"Don't tell me," he exclaimed, "that you haven't heard about that!"

Channing laughed a short, frightened laugh, and moved nearer to the street.

"No," he said. "No, I hadn't."

"Yes, but, good Lord! it was the story of the war. You never read such a story! And he got it through by Panama a day ahead of all the other stories! And nobody read them, anyway. Why, Captain Mahan said it was 'naval history,' and the Evening Post had an editorial on it, and said it was 'the only piece of literature the war has produced.' We never thought Keating had it in him, did you? The Consolidated Press people felt so good over it that they've promised, when he comes back from Paris, they'll make him their Washington correspondent. He's their 'star' reporter now. It just shows you that the occasion produces the man. Come on in, and have a drink with him."

Channing pulled his arm away, and threw a frightened look toward the open door of the dining-room. Through the layers of tobacco-smoke he saw Keating seated at the head of a long, crowded table, smiling, clear-eyed, and alert.

"Oh, no, I couldn't," he said, with sudden panic. "I can't drink; doctor won't let me. I wasn't coming in, I was just passing when I saw you. Good-night, I'm much obliged. Good-night."

But the hospitable Norris would not be denied.

"Oh, come in and say 'good-by' to him, anyhow," he insisted. "You needn't stay."

"No, I can't," Channing protested. "I—they'd make me drink or eat and the doctor says I can't. You mustn't tempt me. You say 'good-by' to him for me," he urged. "And Norris—tell him—tell him—that I asked you to say to him, 'It's all right,' that's all, just that, 'It's all right.' He'll understand."

There was the sound of men's feet scraping on the floor, and of chairs being moved from their places.

Norris started away eagerly. "I guess they're drinking his health," he said. "I must go. I'll tell him what you said, 'It's all right.' That's enough, is it? There's nothing more?"

Channing shook his head, and moved away from the only place where he was sure to find food and a welcome that night.

"There's nothing more," he said.

As he stepped from the door and stood irresolutely in the twilight of the street, he heard the voices of the men who had gathered in Keating's honor upraised in a joyous chorus.

"For he's a jolly good fellow," they sang, "for he's a jolly good fellow, which nobody can deny!"

LA LETTRE D'AMOUR

When Bardini, who led the Hungarian Band at the Savoy Restaurant, was promoted to play at the Casino at Trouville, his place was taken by the second violin. The second violin was a boy, and when he greeted his brother Tziganes and the habitues of the restaurant with an apologetic and deprecatory bow, he showed that he was fully conscious of the inadequacy of his years. The maitre d'hotel glided from table to table, busying himself in explanations.

"The boy's name is Edouard; he comes from Budapest," he said. "The season is too late to make it worth the while of the management to engage a new chef d'orchestre. So this boy will play. He plays very good, but he is not like Bardini."

He was not in the least like Bardini. In appearance, Bardini suggested a Roumanian gypsy or a Portuguese sailor; his skin was deeply tanned, his hair was plastered on his low forehead in thick, oily curls, and his body, through much rich living on the scraps that fell from the tables of Girot's and the Casino des Fleurs, was stout and gross. He was the typical leader of an orchestra condemned to entertain a noisy restaurant. His school of music was the school of Maxim's. To his skill with the violin he had added the arts of the head waiter, and he and the cook ran a race for popularity, he pampering to one taste, and the cook, with his sauces, pampering to another. When so commanded, his pride as an artist did not prevent him from breaking off in the middle of Schubert's Serenade to play Daisy Bell, nor was he above breaking it off on his own accord to salute the American patron, as he entered with the Belle of New York, or any one of the Gaiety Girls, hurrying in late for supper, with the Soldiers in the Park. When he walked slowly through the restaurant, pausing at each table, his eyes, even while they ogled the women to whom he played, followed the brother Tzigane—who was passing the plate—and noted which of the patrons gave silver and which gave gold.

Edouard, the second violin, was all that Bardini was not, consequently he was entirely unsuited to lead an orchestra in a restaurant. Indeed, so little did he understand of what was required of him that on the only occasion when Bardini sent him to pass the plate he was so unsophisticated as not to hide the sixpences and shillings under the napkin, and so leave only the half-crowns and gold pieces exposed. And, instead of smiling mockingly at those who gave the sixpences, and waiting for them to give more, he even looked grateful, and at the same time deeply ashamed. He differed from Bardini also in that he was very thin and tall, with the serious, smooth-shaven face of a priest. Except for his fantastic costume, there was nothing about him to recall the poses of the musician: his hair was neither long nor curly; it lay straight across his forehead and flat on either side, and when he played, his eyes neither sought out the admiring auditor nor invited his applause. On the contrary, they looked steadfastly ahead. It was as though they belonged to someone apart, who was listening intently to the music. But in the waits between the numbers the boy's eyes turned from table to table, observing the people in his audience. He knew nearly all of them by sight: the head waiters who brought him their "commands," and his brother-musicians, had often discussed them in his hearing. They represented every city of the world, every part of the social edifice: there were those who came to look at the spectacle, and those who came to be looked at; those who gave a dinner for the sake of the diners, those who dined for the dinner alone. To some the restaurant was a club; others ventured in counting the cost, taking it seriously, even considering that it conferred upon them some social distinction. There were pretty women in paint and spangles, with conscious, half-grown boys just up from Oxford; company- promoters dining and wining possible subscribers or "guinea-pigs" into an acquiescent state; Guardsmen giving a dinner of farewell to brother-officers departing for the Soudan or the Cape; wide-eyed Americans just off the steamer in high dresses, great ladies in low dresses and lofty tiaras, and ladies of the stage, utterly unconscious of the boon they were conferring on the people about them, who, an hour before, had paid ten shillings to look at them from the stalls.

Edouard, as he sat with his violin on his knee, his fingers fretting the silent strings, observed them all without envy and without interest. Had he been able to choose, it would not have been to such a well-dressed mob as this that he would have given his music. For at times a burst of laughter killed a phrase that was sacred to him, and sometimes the murmur of the voices and the clatter of the waiters would drown him out altogether. But the artist in him forced him to play all things well, and for his own comfort he would assure himself that no doubt somewhere in the room someone was listening, someone who thought more of the strange, elusive melodies of the Hungarian folksongs than of the chefs entrees, and that for this unknown one he must be true to himself and true to his work. Covertly, he would seek out some face to which he could make the violin speak—not openly and impertinently, as did Bardini, but secretly and for sympathy, so that only one could understand. It pleased young Edouard to see such a one raise her head as though she had heard her name spoken, and hold it poised to listen, and turn slowly in her chair, so completely engaged that she forgot the man at her elbow, and the food before her was taken away untouched. It delighted him to think that she knew that the music was speaking to her alone. But he would not have had her think that the musician spoke, too—it was the soul of the music, not his soul, that was reaching out to the pretty stranger. When his soul spoke through the music it would not be, so he assured himself, to such chatterers as gathered on the terrace of the Savoy Restaurant.

Mrs. Warriner and her daughter were on their way home, or to one of their homes; this one was up the Hills of Lenox. They had been in Egypt and up the Nile, and for the last two months had been slowly working their way north through Greece and Italy. They were in London, at the Savoy, waiting for their sailing-day, and on the night of their arrival young Corbin was giving them a dinner. For three months Mrs. Warriner and himself had alternated in giving each other dinners in every part of Southern Europe, and the gloom which hung over this one was not due to the fact that the diners had become wearied of one another's society, but that the opportunities still left to them for this exchange of hospitality were almost at an end. That night, for the hundredth time, young Corbin had decided it would have been much better for him if they had come to an end many weeks previous, for the part he played in the trio was a difficult one. It was that of the lover who will not take "no" for an answer. The lover who will take no, and goes on his way disconsolate, may live to love another day, and everyone is content; but the one who will not have no, who will not hear of it, nor consider it, has much to answer for in making life a burden to himself and all around him.

When Corbin joined the Warriners on their trip up the Nile it was considered by all of them, in their ignorance, a happy accident. Other mothers, more worldly than Mrs. Warriner, with daughters less attractive, gave her undeserved credit for having lured into her party one of the young men of Boston who was most to be desired as a son-in-law. But the mind of Mrs. Warriner, so far as Mr. Corbin was concerned, was quite free from any such consideration; so was the mind of the young bachelor; certainly Miss Warriner held no tender thoughts concerning him. The families of the Warriners and the Corbins had been friends ever since the cowpath crossed the Common. Before Corbin entered Harvard Miss Warriner and he had belonged to the same dancing-class. Later she had danced with him at four class-days, and many times between. When he graduated, she had gone abroad with her mother, and he had joined the Somerset Club, and played polo at Pride's Crossing, and talked vaguely of becoming a lawyer, and of re-entering Harvard by the door of the Law School, chiefly, it was supposed, that he might have another year of the football team. He was very young in spirit, very big and athletic, very rich, and without a care or serious thought. Miss Warriner was to him, then, no more than a friend; to her he was a boy, one of many nice, cultivated Harvard boys, who occasionally called upon her and talked football. On the face of things, she was not the sort of girl he should have loved. But for some saving clause in him, he should have loved and married one of the many other girls who had belonged to the same dancing-class, who would have been known as "Mrs. Tom" Corbin, who would have been sought after as a chaperone, and who would have stood up in her cart when he played polo and shouted at him across the field to "ride him off."

Miss Warriner, on the contrary, was much older than he in everything but years, and was conscious of the fact. She was a serious, self- centred young person, and satisfied with her own thoughts, unless her companion gave her better ones. She concerned herself with the character and ideas of her friends. If a young man lacked ideas, the fact that he possessed wealth and good manners could not save him. If these attributes had been pointed out to her as part of his assets she would have been surprised. She was not impressed with her own good looks and fortune—she took them for granted; so why should they count with her in other people?

Miss Warriner made an error of analysis in regard to Mr. Corbin in judging his brain by his topics of conversation. His conversation was limited to the A B C's of life, with which, up to the time of his meeting her, his brain had been fed. When, however, she began to cram it full with all the other letters of the alphabet, it showed itself just as capable of digesting the economic conditions of Egypt as it had

previously succeeded in mastering the chess-like problems of
the game of football.

Young Corbin had not considered the Home Beautiful,
nor Municipal Government, nor How the Other Half Lives
as topics that were worth his while; but when Miss Warriner
showed her interest in them, her doing so made them worth
his while, and he fell upon them greedily. He even went
much further than she had gone, and was not content
merely to theorize and to discuss social questions from the
safe distance of the deck of a dahabiyeh on the Nile, but
proposed to at once put her theories into practice. To this
end he offered her a house in the slums of Boston, rent free,
where she could start her College Settlement. He made out
lists of the men he thought would like to teach there, and
he volunteered to pay the expenses of the experiment until it
failed or succeeded. When her interest changed to the Tombs
of the Rameses, and the succession of the ancient dynasties,
he spent hours studying his Baedeker that he might keep in
step with her; and when she abandoned ancient for modern
Egypt and became deeply charmed with the intricacies of
the dual control and of the Mixed Courts, he interviewed
subalterns, Pashas, and missionaries in a gallant effort to
comprehend the social and political difficulties of the white
men who had occupied the land of the Sphinx, who had
funded her debt, irrigated her deserts, and "made a mummy
fight."

One night, as the dahabiyeh lay moored beneath a group of palms in the moonlight, Miss Warriner gave him praise for offering her the house in the slums for her experiment. He assured her that he was entirely selfish—that he did so because he believed her settlement would be a benefit to the neighborhood, in which he owned some property. When she then accused him of giving sordid reasons for what was his genuine philanthropy he told her flatly that he neither cared for the higher education of the slums nor the increased value of his rents, but for her, and to please her, and that he loved her and would love her always. In answer to this, Miss Warriner told him gently but firmly that she could not love him, but that she liked him and admired him, even though she was disappointed to find that his sudden interest in matters more serious than polo had been assumed to please her. She added that she would always be his friend. This, she thought, ended the matter; it was unfortunate that they should be shipbound on the Nile; but she trusted to his tact and good sense to save them both from embarrassment. She was not prepared, however, to see him come on deck very late the next morning, after, apparently, a long sleep, as keen, as cheerful, and as smiling as he had been before the blow had fallen. It piqued her a little, and partly because of that, and partly because she really was relieved to find him in such a humor, she congratulated him on his most evident happiness.

"Why not?" he asked, suddenly growing sober. "I love you. That is enough to make any man happy, isn't it? You needn't love me, but you can't prevent my going on loving you."

"Well, I am very sorry," she sighed in much perplexity.

"You needn't be," he answered, reassuringly. "I'm more sorry for you than I am for myself. You are going to have a terrible time until you marry me."

They were at Thebes, and he went off that afternoon to the Temple of Luxor with her mother, and made violent use of the sacred altars, the beauty of Cleopatra, the eternity of the scarabea, and the indestructibility of the Pyramids to suggest faintly to Mrs. Warriner how much he loved her daughter. He shook his hand at the crouching sphinxes and said:

"Mrs. Warriner, in forty centuries they have never looked down upon a man as proud as I am, and I am told they have seen Napoleon; but I need help; she won't help me, so you must. It's no use arguing against me. When this Nile dries up I shall have ceased loving your daughter!"

"Did you tell Helen what you have told me? Did you talk to her so?" asked Mrs. Warriner.

"No, not last night," said Corbin; "but I will, in time, after she gets more used to the Idea."

Unfortunately for the peace of Mr. Corbin and all concerned. Miss Warriner did not become reconciled to the idea. On the contrary, she resented it greatly. She had looked at the possibility of something to be carried out later—much later, perhaps not at all. It did not seem possible that before she had really begun to enjoy life it should be subjected to such a change. She saw that it was obviously the thing that should happen. If the match had been arranged by the entire city of Boston it could not have been more obvious. But she argued with him that marriage was a mutual self-sacrifice, and that until she felt ready to make her share of the sacrifice it was impossible for her to consent.

He combated her arguments, which he refused to consider as arguments, and demolished them one by one. But the objection which he destroyed before he went to sleep at night was replaced the next day by another, and his cause never advanced. Each day he found the citadel he was besieging girt in by new and intricate defences. The reason was simple enough: the girl was not in love with him. Her objections, her arguments, her reasons were as absurd as he proved them to be. But they were insurmountable because they were really various disguises of the fact that she did not care for him. They were disguises to herself as well as to him. He was so altogether a good fellow, so earnest, honest, and desperate a lover that the primary fact that she did not want his love did not present itself, and she kept casting about in her mind for excuses and reasons to explain her lack of feeling. He wooed her in every obvious way that would present itself to a boy of deep feeling, of quick mind, and an unlimited letter of credit. He created wants in order to gratify them later. He suggested her need of things which he had already ordered, which, before she had been enticed into expressing a wish for them, were then speeding across the Continent toward her. Every hour brought her some fresh and ingenuous sign of his thought and of his devotion. He treated these tributes as a matter of course; if she failed to observe them and to see his handiwork in them he let them fall to the ground unnoticed.

His love itself was his argument-in-chief; it was its own excuse; it needed no allies; "I love you" was his first and last word. It puzzled her to find that she could not care. When she was alone she asked herself what there was in him of which she disapproved, and she could only answer that there was nothing. She asked herself what other men there were who pleased her more, and she could think of none. On the contrary, she found him entirely charming as a friend— but his love distressed her greatly. It was a foreign language; she could not comprehend it. When he allowed it to appear it completely disguised him in her eyes; it annoyed her so much that at times she considered herself a much ill-used young person.

It was in this way that the matter stood between them when their long journey was ended and they reached London. He was miserable, desperate, and hopeless; the girl was firm in that she would not marry him, and her mother, who respected both the depth of Corbin's feelings and her daughter's reticence, and who had watched the struggle with a troubled heart, was only thankful that they were to part, and that it was at an end. Corbin had no idea where he would go nor what he would do. He recognized that to cross the ocean with them would only subject his love to fresh distress and humiliation, and he had determined to put as much space between him and Miss Warriner as the surface of the globe permitted. The Philippines seemed to offer a picturesque retreat for a broken life. He decided he would go there and enlist and have himself shot. He was uncertain whether he would follow in the steps of his Revolutionary ancestors and join the men who were struggling for their liberty and independence, or his fellow-Americans; but that he would get shot by one side or the other he was determined. And then in days to come she would think, perhaps, of the young man on the other side of the globe, buried in the wet rice-fields, with the palms fanning him through his eternal sleep, and she might be sorry then that she had not listened to his troubled heart. The picture gave him some small comfort, and that night when he ordered dinner for them at the Savoy his manner showed the inspired resolve of one who is soon to mount the scaffold unafraid, and with a rose between his lips.

Edouard, the first violin, saw Miss Warriner when she entered and took her place facing him at one of the tables in the centre of the room. He was sitting with his violin on his knees, touching the strings with his finger-tips. When he saw her he choked the neck of the violin with his hand, as though it had been the hand of a friend which he had grasped in a sudden ecstasy of delight. The effect her appearance had made upon him was so remarkable that he glanced quickly over his shoulder to see if he had betrayed himself by some sign or gesture. But the other musicians were concerned with their own gossip, and he felt free to turn again and from under his half- closed eyelids to observe her covertly.

There was nothing to explain why Miss Warriner, in particular, should have so disturbed him; the English women seated about her were as fair; she showed no great sorrow in her face; her beauty was not of the type which carried observers by assault. And yet not one of the many beautiful women who on one night or another passed before Edouard in the soft light of the red shades had ever stirred him so strangely, had ever depressed him with such a tender melancholy, and filled his soul—the soul of a Hungarian and a musician—with such loneliness and unrest. He knew that, so far as he was concerned, she was as distant as the Venus in the Louvre; she was, for him, a beautiful, unapproachable statue, placed, by some social convention, upon a pedestal.

As he looked at her he felt hotly the degradation of his silly uniform, of the striped sash around his waist, the tawdry braids, and the tasselled boots. He felt as he had often felt before, but now more keenly than ever, the prostitution of his art in this temple of the senses, this home of epicures, where people met to feast their eyes and charm their palates. He could not put his feelings into words, and he knew that if by some upheaval of the social world he should be thrown into her presence he would still be bound, he would not be able to speak or write what she inspired in him. But—and at the thought he breathed quickly, and raised his shoulders with a touch of pride—he could tell her in his own way; after his own fashion he could express what he felt better even than those other men could tell what they feel—these men for whose amusement he performed nightly, to whom it was granted to sit at her side, who spoke the language of her class and of her own people. Edouard was not given to analyzing his emotions; like the music of his Tzigane ancestors, they came to him sweeping every chord in his nature, beating rapidly to the time of the Schardash, or with the fitfulness of the gypsy folksongs sinking his spirits into melancholy. So he did not stop to question why this one face so suddenly inspired him; he only knew that he felt grateful, that he was impatient to pay his tribute of admiration, that he was glad he was an artist who could give his feelings voice.

In the long programme of selected airs he remembered that there was one which would give him this chance to speak, in the playing of which he could put all his skill and all his soul, an air which carried with it infinite sadness and the touch of a caress. The other numbers on the programme had been chosen to please the patrons of a restaurant, this one, La Lettre d'Amour, was included in the list for his own satisfaction. He had put it there to please himself; to-night he would play it to please her—to this unknown girl who had so suddenly awakened and inspired him.

As he waited for this chance to come he watched her, noting her every movement, her troubled smile, her air of being apart and above her surroundings. He noticed, too, the set face of the young man at her side and, with the discernment of one whose own interest is captive, saw the half-concealed longing in his eyes. He felt a quick antipathy to this young man. His assured position at the girl's side accentuated how far he himself was removed from her; he resented also the manner of the young man to the waiters, and he wondered hotly if, in the mind of this favored youth, the musician who played for his entertainment was regarded any more highly than the servant who received his orders. To this feeling of resentment was added one of contempt. For, as he read the tableau at the table below him, the young man was the devotee of the young girl at his side, and if one could judge from her averted eyes, from her silent assent to his questions, from the fact that she withdrew from the talk between him and the older woman, his devotion was not welcome.

This reading of the pantomime pleased Edouard greatly. Nothing could have so crowned the feeling which the beauty of the stranger stirred in him as the thought that another loved her as well as himself, and that the other, who started with all things in his favor, met with none from her.

Edouard assured himself that this was so because he had often heard his people boast that men not of their country could not feel as they could feel. If he had ever considered them at all it was as cold and conscious creatures who taught themselves to cover up what they felt, so that when their emotions strove to assert themselves they were found, through long disuse, to be dumb and inarticulate. Edouard rejoiced that to the men of his race it was given to feel and suffer much. He was sure that beneath the calmness of her beauty this woman before him could feel deeply; he read in her eyes the sympathy of a great soul; she made him think of a Madonna in the church of St. Sophia at Budapest. He saw in her a woman who could love greatly. When he considered how impossible it was for the young man at her side ever to experience the great emotions which alone could reach her, his contempt for him rose almost to pity. His violin, with his power to feel, and with his knowledge of technic added, could send his message as far as sound could carry. He could afford to be generous, and when he rose to play La Lettre d'Amour it was with the elation of a knight entering the lists, with the ardor of a lover singing beneath his lady's window. La Lettre d'Amour is a composition written to a slow measure, and filled with chords of exquisite pathos. It comes hesitatingly, like the confession of a lover who loves so deeply that he halts to find words with which to express his feelings. It moves in broken phrases, each note rising in intensity and growing in beauty. It is not a burst of passionate appeal, but a plea, tender, beseeching, and throbbing with melancholy. As he played, Edouard stepped down from the dais on which the musicians sat, and advanced slowly between the tables. It was late, and the majority of those who had been dining had departed to the theatres. Those who remained were lingering over their coffee, and were smoking; their voices were lowered to a polite monotone; the rush of the waiters had ceased, and the previous chatter had sunk to a subdued murmur. Into this, the quivering sigh of Edouard's violin penetrated like a sunbeam feeling its way into a darkened room, and, at the sound, the voices, one by one, detached themselves from the general chorus, until, lacking support, it ceased altogether. Some were silent, that they might hear the better, others, who preferred their own talk, were silent out of regard for those who desired to listen, and a waiter who was so indiscreet as to clatter a tray of glasses was hushed on the instant. The tribute of attention lent to Edouard an added power; his head lifted on his shoulders with pride; his bow cut deeper and firmer, and with more delicate shading; the notes rose in thrilling, plaintive sadness, and flooded the hot air with melody.

Edouard made his way to within a short distance of the table at which Miss Warriner was seated, and halted there as though he had found his audience. He did not look at her, although she sat directly facing him, but it was evident to all that she was the one to whom his effort was directed, and Corbin, who was seated with his back to Edouard, recognized this and turned in his chair.

The body of the young musician was trembling with the feeling which found its outlet through the violin. He was in ecstasy over his power and its accomplishment. The strings of the violin pulsated to the beating of his heart, and he felt that surely by now the emotion which shook him must have reached the girl who had given it life— and, for one swift second, his eyes sought hers. What he saw was the same beautiful face which had inspired him, but unmoved, cold, and unresponsive. As his eyes followed hers she raised her head and looked, listlessly, around the room, and then turned and glanced up at him with a careless and critical scrutiny. If his music had been the music of an organ in the street, and he the man who raised his hat for coppers, she could not have been less moved. The discovery struck Edouard like a cold blast from an open door. His fingers faltered on the neck of his violin, his bow wavered, drunkenly, across the strings, and he turned away his eyes to shut out the vision of his failure, seeking relief and sympathy. And, in their swift passage, they encountered those of Corbin looking up at him, his eyes aglow with wonder, feeling, and sorrow. They seemed to hold him to account; they begged, they demanded of him not to break the spell, and, in response, the hot blood in the veins of the musician surged back, his pride flared up again, his eyes turned on Corbin's like those of a dog to his master's. Under their spell the music soared, trembling, paused and soared again, thrilling those who heard it with its grief and tenderness.

Edouard's heart leaped with triumph. "The man knows," he whispered to the violin; "he understands us. He knows."

The people, leaning with their elbows on the tables before them, the waiters listening with tolerant smiles, the musicians following Edouard with anxious pride, saw only a young man with his arm thrown heavily across the back of his chair, who was looking up at Edouard with a steady, searching gaze. But Edouard saw in him both a disciple and a master. He saw that this man was lifted up and carried with him, that he understood the message of the music. The notes of the violin sank lower and lower, until they melted into the silence of the room, and the people, freed of the spell the music had put upon them, applauded generously. Edouard placed his violin under his arm, and with his eyes, which had never left Corbin's face, still fastened upon his, bowed low to him, and Corbin raised his head and nodded gravely. It was as though they were the only people in the room. As Edouard retreated his face was shining with triumph, for he knew that the other had understood him, and that the other knew that he knew.

That night until he fell asleep, and all of the day following, the beautiful face of Miss Warriner troubled Edouard, and the thought of her alternately thrilled and depressed him. One moment he mocked at himself for presuming to think that his simple art could reach the depths of such a nature, and the next he stirred himself to hope that he should see her once again, and that he should succeed where he had failed.

The music had moved Corbin so deeply that when he awoke the day following the effect of it still hung upon him. It seemed to him as though all he had been trying to tell Miss Warriner of his love for her, and which he had failed to make her understand in the last three months, had been expressed in the one moment of this song. It was that in it which had so enchanted him. It was as though he had listened to his own deepest and most sacred thoughts, uttered for the first time convincingly, and by a stranger. Why was it, he asked himself, that this unknown youth could translate another's feelings into music, when he himself could not put them into words? He was walking in Piccadilly, deep in this thought, when a question came to him which caused him to turn rapidly into Green Park, where he could consider it undisturbed.

The doubt which had so suddenly presented itself was in some degree the same one which had stirred Edouard. Was it that he was really unable to express his feelings, or was it that Miss Warriner could not understand them? Was it really something lacking in him, or was it not something lacking in her? He flushed at the disloyalty of the thought and put it from him; but, as his memory reached back over the past three months, the question returned again and again with fresh force, and would not be denied. He called himself a fatuous, conceited fool. Because he could not make a woman love him other men could do so. That was really the answer; he was not the man. But the answer did not seem final. What, after all, was the thing his love sought—a woman only, or a woman capable of deep and great feeling? Even if he could not inspire such emotions, even if another could, he would still be content and proud to love a woman capable of such deep feelings. But if she were without them? At the thought, Corbin stared blankly before him as though he had stumbled against a stone wall. What sign had she ever given him that she could care greatly? Was not any form of emotion always distasteful to her? Was not her mind always occupied with abstract questions? Was she not always engaged in her own self-improvement—with schemes, it is true, for bettering the world; but did her heart ever ache once for the individual? What was it, then, he loved? Something he imagined this girl to be, or was he in love with the fact that his own nature had been so mightily stirred? Was it not the joy of caring greatly which had carried him along? And if this was so, was he now to continue to proffer this devotion to one who could not feel, to a statue, to an idol? Were not the very things which rendered her beautiful the offerings which he himself had hung upon her altar? Did the qualities he really loved in her exist? Was he not on the brink of casting his love before one who could neither feel it for him nor for any other man? He stood up, trembling and frightened. Even though the girl had rejected him again and again, he felt a hateful sense of disloyalty. He was ashamed to confess it to himself, and he vowed, hotly, that he must be wrong, that he would not believe. He would still worship her, fight for her, and force her to care for him.

Mrs. Warriner and her daughter were to sail on the morrow, and that night they met Corbin at dinner for the last time. After many days— although self-accused—he felt deeply conscious of his recent lack of faith, and, in the few hours still left him, he determined to atone for the temporary halt in his allegiance. They had never found him more eager, tactful, and considerate than he was that evening. The eyes of Mrs. Warriner softened as she watched him. As one day had succeeded another, her admiration and liking for him had increased, until now she felt as though his cause was hers—as though she was not parting from a friend, but from a son. But the calmness of her daughter was impenetrable; from her manner it was impossible to learn whether the approaching separation was a relief or a regret.

To Edouard the return of the beautiful girl to the restaurant appeared not as an accident, but as a marked favor vouchsafed to him by Fate. He had been given a second chance. He read it as a sign that he should take heart and hope. He felt that fortune was indeed kind. He determined that he would play to her again, and that this time he would not fail.

As the first notes of La Lettre d'Amour brought a pause of silence in the restaurant, Corbin, who was talking at the moment, interrupted himself abruptly, and turned in his chair.

All through the evening he had been conscious of the near presence of the young musician. He had not forgotten how, on the night before, his own feelings had been interpreted in La Lettre d'Amour, and for some time he had been debating in his mind as to whether he would request Edouard to play the air again, or let the evening pass without again submitting himself to so supreme an assault upon his feelings. Now the question had been settled for him, and he found that it had been decided as he secretly desired. It was impossible to believe that Edouard was the same young man who had played the same air on the night previous, for Edouard no longer considered that he was present on sufferance—he invited and challenged the attention of the room; his music commanded it to silence. It dominated all who heard it.

As he again slowly approached the table where Miss Warriner was seated, the eyes of everyone were turned upon him; the pathos, the tenderness of his message seemed to speak to each; the fact that he dared to offer such a wealth of deep feeling to such an audience was in itself enough to engage the attention of all. A group of Guardsmen, their faces flushed with Burgundy and pulling heavily on black cigars, stared at him sleepily, and then sat up, erect and alert, watching him with intent, wide-open eyes; and at tables which had been marked by the laughter of those seated about them there fell a sudden silence. Those who fully understood the value of the music withdrew into themselves, submitting, thankfully, to its spell; others, less susceptible, gathered from the bearing of those about them that something of moment was going forward; but it was recognized by each, from the most severe English matron present down to the youngest "omnibus-boy" among the waiters, that it was a love- story which was being told to them, and that in this public place the deepest, most sacred, and most beautiful of emotions were finding noble utterance.

The music filled Corbin with desperate longing and regret. It was so truly the translation of his own feelings that he was alternately touched with self-pity and inspired to fresh resolve. It seemed to assure him that love such as his could not endure without some return. It emboldened him to make still another and a final appeal. Mrs. Warriner, with all the other people in the room, was watching Edouard, and so, unobserved, and hidden by the flowers upon the table, Corbin leaned toward Miss Warriner and bent his head close to hers. His eyes were burning with feeling; his voice thrilled in unison to the plaint of the violin.

He gave a toss of his head in the direction from whence the music came.

"That is what I have been trying to tell you," he whispered. His voice was hoarse and shaken. "That is how I care, but that man's genius is telling you for me. At last, you must understand." In his eagerness, his words followed each other brokenly and impetuously. "That is love," he whispered. "That is the real voice of love in all its tenderness and might, and—it is love itself. Don't you understand it now?" he demanded.

Miss Warriner raised her head and frowned. She stared at Edouard with a pained expression of perplexity and doubt.

"He shows no lack of feeling," she said, critically, "but his technic is not equal to Ysaye's."

"Good God!" Corbin gasped. He sank away from Miss Warriner and stared at her with incredulous eyes.

"His technic," he repeated, "is not equal to Ysaye's?" He gave a laugh which might have been a sob, and sat up, suddenly, with his head erect and his shoulders squared. He had the shaken look of one who has recovered from a dangerous illness. But when he spoke again it was in the accents of every-day politeness.

At an early hour the following morning, Mrs. Warriner and her daughter left Waterloo Station on the steamer-train for Southampton, and Corbin attended them up to the moment of the train's departure. He concerned himself for their comfort as conscientiously as he had always done throughout the last three months, when he had been their travelling-companion; nothing could have been more friendly, more sympathetic, than his manner. This effort, which Mrs. Warriner was sure cost him much, touched her deeply. But when he shook Miss Warriner's hand and she said, "Good-by, and write to us before you go to the Philippines," Corbin for the first time stammered in some embarrassment.

"Good-by," he said; "I—I am not sure that I shall go."

He dined at the Savoy again that night, in company with some Englishmen. They sat at a table in the corner where they could observe the whole extent of the room, and their talk was eager and their laughter constant and hearty. It was only when the boy who led the orchestra began to walk among the tables, playing an air of peculiar sadness, that Corbin's manner lost its vivacity, and he sank into a sudden silence, with his eyes fixed on the table before him.

"That's odd," said one of his companions. "I say, Corbin, look at that chap! What's he doing?"

Corbin raised his eyes. He saw Edouard standing at the same table at which for the last two nights Miss Warriner had been seated. "What is it?" he asked.

"Why, that violin chap," said the Englishman. "Don't you see? He's been playing to the only vacant table in the room, and to an empty chair."

IN THE FOG

PART I

The Grill is the club most difficult of access in the world. To be placed on its rolls distinguishes the new member as greatly as though he had received a vacant Garter or had been caricatured in "Vanity Fair."

Men who belong to the Grill Club never mention that fact. If you were to ask one of them which clubs he frequents, he will name all save that particular one. He is afraid if he told you he belonged to the Grill, that it would sound like boasting.

The Grill Club dates back to the days when Shakespeare's Theatre stood on the present site of the "Times" office. It has a golden Grill which Charles the Second presented to the Club, and the original manuscript of "Tom and Jerry in London," which was bequeathed to it by Pierce Egan himself. The members, when they write letters at the Club, still use sand to blot the ink.

The Grill enjoys the distinction of having blackballed, without political prejudice, a Prime Minister of each party. At the same sitting at which one of these fell, it elected, on account of his brogue and his bulls, Quiller, Q. C., who was then a penniless barrister.

When Paul Preval, the French artist who came to London by royal command to paint a portrait of the Prince of Wales, was made an honorary member—only foreigners may be honorary members—he said, as he signed his first wine-card, "I would rather see my name on that than on a picture in the Louvre."

At which Quiller remarked, "That is a devil of a compliment, because the only men who can read their names in the Louvre to-day have been dead fifty years."

On the night after the great fog of 1897 there were five members in the Club, four of them busy with supper and one reading in front of the fireplace. There is only one room to the Club, and one long table. At the far end of the room the fire of the grill glows red, and, when the fat falls, blazes into flame, and at the other there is a broad bow-window of diamond panes, which looks down upon the street. The four men at the table were strangers to each other, but as they picked at the grilled bones, and sipped their Scotch and soda, they conversed with such charming animation that a visitor to the Club, which does not tolerate visitors, would have counted them as friends of long acquaintance, certainly not as Englishmen who had met for the first time, and without the form of an introduction. But it is the etiquette and tradition of the Grill that whoever enters it must speak with whomever he finds there. It is to enforce this rule that there is but one long table, and whether there are twenty men at it or two, the waiters, supporting the rule, will place them side by side.

For this reason the four strangers at supper were seated together, with the candles grouped about them, and the long length of the table cutting a white path through the outer gloom.

"I repeat," said the gentleman with the black pearl stud, "that the days for romantic adventure and deeds of foolish daring have passed, and that the fault lies with ourselves. Voyages to the pole I do not catalogue as adventures. That African explorer, young Chetney, who turned up yesterday after he was supposed to have died in Uganda, did nothing adventurous. He made maps and explored the sources of rivers. He was in constant danger, but the presence of danger does not constitute adventure. Were that so, the chemist who studies high explosives, or who investigates deadly poisons, passes through adventures daily. No, 'adventures are for the adventurous.' But one no longer ventures. The spirit of it has died of inertia. We are grown too practical, too just, above all, too sensible. In this room, for instance, members of this Club have, at the sword's point, disputed the proper scanning of one of Pope's couplets. Over so weighty a matter as spilled Burgundy on a gentleman's cuff, ten men fought across this table, each with his rapier in one hand and a candle in the other. All ten were wounded. The question of the spilled Burgundy concerned but two of them. The eight others engaged because they were men of 'spirit.' They were, indeed, the first gentlemen of the day. To-night, were you to spill Burgundy on my cuff, were you even to insult me grossly, these gentlemen would not consider it incumbent upon them to kill each other. They would separate us, and to-morrow morning appear as witnesses against us at Bow Street. We have here to-night, in the persons of Sir Andrew and myself, an illustration of how the ways have changed."

The men around the table turned and glanced toward the gentleman in front of the fireplace. He was an elderly and somewhat portly person, with a kindly, wrinkled countenance, which wore continually a smile of almost childish confidence and good-nature. It was a face which the illustrated prints had made intimately familiar. He held a book from him at arm's-length, as if to adjust his eyesight, and his brows were knit with interest.

"Now, were this the eighteenth century," continued the gentleman with the black pearl, "when Sir Andrew left the Club to-night I would have him bound and gagged and thrown into a sedan chair. The watch would not interfere, the passers-by would take to their heels, my hired bullies and ruffians would convey him to some lonely spot where we would guard him until morning. Nothing would come of it, except added reputation to myself as a gentleman of adventurous spirit, and possibly an essay in the 'Tatler' with stars for names, entitled, let us say, 'The Budget and the Baronet.'"

"But to what end, sir?" inquired the youngest of the members. "And why Sir Andrew, of all persons—why should you select him for this adventure?"

The gentleman with the black pearl shrugged his shoulders.

"It would prevent him speaking in the House to-night. The Navy Increase Bill," he added, gloomily. "It is a Government measure, and Sir Andrew speaks for it. And so great is his influence and so large his following that if he does"—the gentleman laughed ruefully—"if he does, it will go through. Now, had I the spirit of our ancestors," he exclaimed, "I would bring chloroform from the nearest chemist's and drug him in that chair. I would tumble his unconscious form into a hansom-cab, and hold him prisoner until daylight. If I did, I would save the British taxpayer the cost of five more battleships, many millions of pounds."

The gentleman again turned, and surveyed the baronet with freshened interest. The honorary member of the Grill, whose accent already had betrayed him as an American, laughed softly.

"To look at him now," he said, "one would not guess he was deeply concerned with the affairs of state."

The others nodded silently.

"He has not lifted his eyes from that book since we first entered," added the youngest member. "He surely cannot mean to speak to-night."

"Oh, yes, he will speak," muttered the one with the black pearl, moodily. "During these last hours of the session the House sits late, but when the Navy bill comes up on its third reading he will be in his place—and he will pass it."

The fourth member, a stout and florid gentleman of a somewhat sporting appearance, in a short smoking-jacket and black tie, sighed enviously.

"Fancy one of us being as cool as that, if he knew he had to stand up within an hour and rattle off a speech in Parliament. I'd be in a devil of a funk myself. And yet he is as keen over that book he's reading as though he had nothing before him until bedtime."

"Yes, see how eager he is," whispered the youngest member. "He does not lift his eyes even now when he cuts the pages. It is probably an Admiralty Report, or some other weighty work of statistics which bears upon his speech."

The gentleman with the black pearl laughed morosely.

"The weighty work in which the eminent statesman is so deeply engrossed," he said, "is called 'The Great Rand Robbery.' It is a detective novel for sale at all bookstalls."

The American raised his eyebrows in disbelief.

"'The Great Rand Robbery'?" he repeated, incredulously. "What an odd taste!"

"It is not a taste, it is his vice," returned the gentleman with the pearl stud. "It is his one dissipation. He is noted for it. You, as a stranger, could hardly be expected to know of this idiosyncrasy. Mr. Gladstone sought relaxation in the Greek poets, Sir Andrew finds his in Gaboriau. Since I have been a member of Parliament, I have never seen him in the library without a shilling shocker in his hands. He brings them even into the sacred precincts of the House, and from the Government benches reads them concealed inside his hat. Once started on a tale of murder, robbery, and sudden death, nothing can tear him from it, not even the call of the division-bell, nor of hunger, nor the prayers of the party Whip. He gave up his country house because when he journeyed to it in the train he would become so absorbed in his detective-stories that he was invariably carried past his station." The member of Parliament twisted his pearl stud nervously, and bit at the edge of his mustache. "If it only were the first pages of 'The Rand Robbery' that he were reading," he murmured bitterly, "instead of the last! With such another book as that, I swear I could hold him here until morning. There would be no need of chloroform to keep him from the House."

The eyes of all were fastened upon Sir Andrew, and each saw, with fascination, that, with his forefinger, he was now separating the last two pages of the book. The member of Parliament struck the table, softly, with his open palm.

"I would give a hundred pounds," he whispered, "if I could place in his hands at this moment a new story of Sherlock Holmes—a thousand pounds," he added, wildly—"five thousand pounds!"

The American observed the speaker sharply, as though the words bore to him some special application, and then, at an idea which apparently had but just come to him, smiled, in great embarrassment.

Sir Andrew ceased reading, but, as though still under the influence of the book, sat looking, blankly, into the open fire. For a brief space, no one moved until the baronet withdrew his eyes and, with a sudden start of recollection, felt, anxiously, for his watch. He scanned its face eagerly, and scrambled to his feet.

The voice of the American instantly broke the silence in a high, nervous accent.

"And yet Sherlock Holmes himself," he cried, "could not decipher the mystery which to-night baffles the police of London."

At these unexpected words, which carried in them something of the tone of a challenge, the gentlemen about the table started as suddenly as though the American had fired a pistol in the air, and Sir Andrew halted, abruptly, and stood observing him with grave surprise.

The gentleman with the black pearl was the first to recover.

"Yes, yes," he said, eagerly, throwing himself across the table. "A mystery that baffles the police of London. I have heard nothing of it. Tell us at once, pray do—tell us at once."

The American flushed uncomfortably, and picked, uneasily, at the table-cloth.

"No one but the police has heard of it," he murmured, "and they only through me. It is a remarkable crime, to which, unfortunately, I am the only person who can bear witness. Because I am the only witness, I am, in spite of my immunity as a diplomat, detained in London by the authorities of Scotland Yard. My name," he said, inclining his head, politely, "is Sears, Lieutenant Ripley Sears, of the United States Navy, at present Naval Attache to the Court of Russia. Had I not been detained to-day by the police, I would have started this morning for Petersburg."

The gentleman with the black pearl interrupted with so pronounced an exclamation of excitement and delight that the American stammered and ceased speaking.

"Do you hear, Sir Andrew?" cried the member of Parliament, jubilantly. "An American diplomat halted by our police because he is the only witness of a most remarkable crime—THE most remarkable crime, I believe you said, sir," he added, bending eagerly toward the naval officer, "which has occurred in London in many years."

The American moved his head in assent, and glanced at the two other members. They were looking, doubtfully, at him, and the face of each showed that he was greatly perplexed.

Sir Andrew advanced to within the light of the candles and drew a chair toward him.

"The crime must be exceptional, indeed," he said, "to justify the police in interfering with a representative of a friendly power. If I were not forced to leave at once, I should take the liberty of asking you to tell us the details."

The gentleman with the pearl pushed the chair toward Sir Andrew, and motioned him to be seated.

"You cannot leave us now," he exclaimed. "Mr. Sears is just about to tell us of this remarkable crime."

He nodded, vigorously, at the naval officer and the American, after first glancing, doubtfully, toward the servants at the far end of the room, and leaned forward across the table. The others drew their chairs nearer and bent toward him. The baronet glanced, irresolutely, at his watch, and, with an exclamation of annoyance, snapped down the lid. "They can wait," he muttered. He seated himself quickly, and nodded at Lieutenant Sears.

"If you will be so kind as to begin, sir," he said, impatiently.

"Of course," said the American, "you understand that I understand that I am speaking to gentlemen. The confidences of this Club are inviolate. Until the police give the facts to the public press, I must consider you my confederates. You have heard nothing, you know no one connected with this mystery. Even I must remain anonymous."

The gentlemen seated around him nodded gravely.

"Of course," the baronet assented, with eagerness, "of course."

"We will refer to it," said the gentleman with the black pearl, "as 'The Story of the Naval Attaché.'"

"I arrived in London two days ago," said the American, "and I engaged a room at the Bath Hotel. I know very few people in London, and even the members of our embassy were strangers to me. But in Hong Kong I had become great pals with an officer in your navy, who has since retired, and who is now living in a small house in Rutland Gardens, opposite the Knightsbridge Barracks. I telegraphed him that I was in London, and yesterday morning I received a most hearty invitation to dine with him the same evening at his house. He is a bachelor, so we dined alone and talked over all our old days on the Asiatic Station and of the changes which had come to us since we had last met there. As I was leaving the next morning for my post at Petersburg, and had many letters to write, I told him, about ten o'clock, that I must get back to the hotel, and he sent out his servant to call a hansom.

"For the next quarter of an hour, as we sat talking, we could hear the cab-whistle sounding, violently, from the doorstep, but apparently with no result.

"'It cannot be that the cabmen are on strike,' my friend said, as he rose and walked to the window.

"He pulled back the curtains and at once called to me.

"'You have never seen a London fog, have you?' he asked. 'Well, come here. This is one of the best, or, rather, one of the worst, of them.' I joined him at the window, but I could see nothing. Had I not known that the house looked out upon the street I would have believed that I was facing a dead wall. I raised the sash and stretched out my head, but still I could see nothing. Even the light of the street- lamps, opposite, and in the upper windows of the barracks, had been smothered in the yellow mist. The lights of the room in which I stood penetrated the fog only to the distance of a few inches from my eyes.

"Below me the servant was still sounding his whistle, but I could afford to wait no longer, and told my friend that I would try and find the way to my hotel on foot. He objected, but the letters I had to write were for the Navy Department, and, besides, I had always heard that to be out in a London fog was the most wonderful experience, and I was curious to investigate one for myself.

"My friend went with me to his front door, and laid down a course for me to follow. I was first to walk straight across the street to the brick wall of the Knightsbridge Barracks. I was then to feel my way along the wall until I came to a row of houses set back from the sidewalk. They would bring me to a cross street. On the other side of this street was a row of shops which I was to follow until they joined the iron railings of Hyde Park. I was to keep to the railings until I reached the gates at Hyde Park Corner, where I was to lay a diagonal course across Piccadilly, and tack in toward the railings of Green Park. At the end of these railings, going east, I would find the Walsingham, and my own hotel.

"To a sailor the course did not seem difficult, so I bade my friend good-night and walked forward until my feet touched the paving. I continued upon it until I reached the curbing of the sidewalk. A few steps further, and my hands struck the wall of the barracks. I turned in the direction from which I had just come, and saw a square of faint light cut in the yellow fog. I shouted, 'All right,' and the voice of my friend answered, 'Good luck to you.' The light from his open door disappeared with a bang, and I was left alone in a dripping, yellow darkness. I have been in the Navy for ten years, but I have never known such a fog as that of last night, not even among the icebergs of Behring Sea. There one at least could see the light of the binnacle, but last night I could not even distinguish the hand by which I guided myself along the barrack-wall. At sea a fog is a natural phenomenon. It is as familiar as the rainbow which follows a storm, it is as proper that a fog should spread upon the waters as that steam shall rise from a kettle. But a fog which springs from the paved streets, that rolls between solid house-fronts, that forces cabs to move at half speed, that drowns policemen and extinguishes the electric lights of the music-hall, that to me is incomprehensible. It is as out of place as a tidal wave on Broadway.

"As I felt my way along the wall, I encountered other men who were coming from the opposite direction, and each time when we hailed each other I stepped away from the wall to make room for them to pass. But the third time I did this, when I reached out my hand, the wall had disappeared, and the further I moved to find it the further I seemed to be sinking into space. I had the unpleasant conviction that at any moment I might step over a precipice. Since I had set out, I had heard no traffic in the street, and now, although I listened some minutes, I could only distinguish the occasional footfalls of pedestrians. Several times I called aloud, and once a jocular gentleman answered me, but only to ask me where I thought he was, and then even he was swallowed up in the silence. Just above me I could make out a jet of gas which I guessed came from a street-lamp, and I moved over to that, and, while I tried to recover my bearings, kept my hand on the iron post. Except for this nicker of gas, no larger than the tip of my finger, I could distinguish nothing about me. For the rest, the mist hung between me and the world like a damp and heavy blanket.

"I could hear voices, but I could not tell from whence they came, and the scrape of a foot, moving cautiously, or a muffled cry as someone stumbled, were the only sounds that reached me.

"I decided that until someone took me in I had best remain where I was, and it must have been for ten minutes that I waited by the lamp, straining my ears and hailing distant footfalls. In a house near me some people were dancing to the music of a Hungarian band. I even fancied I could hear the windows shake to the rhythm of their feet, but I could not make out from which part of the compass the sounds came. And sometimes, as the music rose, it seemed close at my hand, and, again, to be floating high in the air above my head. Although I was surrounded by thousands of householders, I was as completely lost as though I had been set down by night in the Sahara Desert. There seemed to be no reason in waiting longer for an escort, so I again set out, and at once bumped against a low, iron fence. At first I believed this to be an area railing, but, on following it, I found that it stretched for a long distance, and that it was pierced at regular intervals with gates. I was standing, uncertainly, with my hand on one of these, when a square of light suddenly opened in the night, and in it I saw, as you see a picture thrown by a biograph in a darkened theatre, a young gentleman in evening dress, and, back of him, the lights of a hall. I guessed, from its elevation and distance from the sidewalk, that this light must come from the door of a house set back from the street, and I determined to approach it and ask the young man to tell me where I was. But, in fumbling with the lock of the gate, I instinctively bent my head, and when I raised it again the door had partly closed, leaving only a narrow shaft of light. Whether the young man had re-entered the house, or had left it I could not tell, but I hastened to open the gate, and as I stepped forward I found myself upon an asphalt walk. At the same instant there was the sound of quick steps upon the path, and someone rushed past me. I called to him, but he made no reply, and I heard the gate click and the footsteps hurrying away upon the sidewalk.

"Under other circumstances the young man's rudeness, and his recklessness in dashing so hurriedly through the mist, would have struck me as peculiar, but everything was so distorted by the fog that at the moment I did not consider it. The door was still as he had left it, partly open. I went up the path, and, after much fumbling, found the knob of the door-bell and gave it a sharp pull. The bell answered me from a great depth and distance, but no movement followed from inside the house, and, although I pulled the bell again and again, I could hear nothing save the dripping of the mist about me. I was anxious to be on my way, but unless I knew

231

where I was going there was little chance of my making any speed, and I was determined that until I learned my bearings I would not venture back into the fog. So I pushed the door open and stepped into the house.

"I found myself in a long and narrow hall, upon which doors opened from either side. At the end of the hall was a staircase with a balustrade which ended in a sweeping curve. The balustrade was covered with heavy, Persian rugs, and the walls of the hall were also hung with them. The door on my left was closed, but the one nearer me on the right was open, and, as I stepped opposite to it, I saw that it was a sort of reception or waiting-room, and that it was empty. The door below it was also open, and, with the idea that I would surely find someone there, I walked on up the hall. I was in evening dress, and I felt I did not look like a burglar, so I had no great fear that, should I encounter one of the inmates of the house, he would shoot me on sight. The second door in the hall opened into a dining-room. This was also empty. One person had been dining at the table, but the cloth had not been cleared away, and a flickering candle showed half-filled wineglasses and the ashes of cigarettes. The greater part of the room was in complete darkness.

"By this time I had grown conscious of the fact that I was wandering about in a strange house, and that, apparently, I was alone in it. The silence of the place began to try my nerves, and in a sudden, unexplainable panic I started for the open street. But as I turned, I saw a man sitting on a bench, which the curve of the balustrade had hidden from me. His eyes were shut, and he was sleeping soundly.

"The moment before I had been bewildered because I could see no one, but at sight of this man I was much more bewildered.

"He was a very large man, a giant in height, with long, yellow hair, which hung below his shoulders. He was dressed in a red silk shirt, that was belted at the waist and hung outside black velvet trousers, which, in turn, were stuffed into high, black boots. I recognized the costume at once as that of a Russian servant, but what a Russian servant in his native livery could be doing in a private house in Knightsbridge was incomprehensible.

"I advanced and touched the man on the shoulder, and, after an effort, he awoke, and, on seeing me, sprang to his feet and began bowing rapidly, and making deprecatory gestures. I had picked up enough Russian in Petersburg to make out that the man was apologizing for having fallen asleep, and I also was able to explain to him that I desired to see his master.

"He nodded vigorously, and said, 'Will the Excellency come this way? The Princess is here.'

"I distinctly made out the word 'princess,' and I was a good deal embarrassed. I had thought it would be easy enough to explain my intrusion to a man, but how a woman would look at it was another matter, and as I followed him down the hall I was somewhat puzzled.

"As we advanced, he noticed that the front door was standing open, and with an exclamation of surprise, hastened toward it and closed it. Then he rapped twice on the door of what was apparently the drawing-room. There was no reply to his knock, and he tapped again, and then, timidly, and cringing subserviently, opened the door and stepped inside. He withdrew himself at once and stared stupidly at me, shaking his head.

"'She is not there,' he said. He stood for a moment, gazing blankly through the open door, and then hastened toward the dining-room. The solitary candle which still burned there seemed to assure him that the room also was empty. He came back and bowed me toward the drawing-room. 'She is above,' he said; 'I will inform the Princess of the Excellency's presence.'

"Before I could stop him, he had turned and was running up the staircase, leaving me alone at the open door of the drawing-room. I decided that the adventure had gone quite far enough, and if I had been able to explain to the Russian that I had lost my way in the fog, and only wanted to get back into the street again, I would have left the house on the instant.

"Of course, when I first rang the bell of the house I had no other expectation than that it would be answered by a parlor-maid who would direct me on my way. I certainly could not then foresee that I would disturb a Russian princess in her boudoir, or that I might be thrown out by her athletic bodyguard. Still, I thought I ought not now to leave the house without making some apology, and, if the worst should come, I could show my card. They could hardly believe that a member of an Embassy had any designs upon the hat-rack.

"The room in which I stood was dimly lighted, but I could see that, like the hall, it was hung with heavy, Persian rugs. The corners were filled with palms, and there was the unmistakable odor in the air of Russian cigarettes, and strange, dry scents that carried me back to the bazaars of Vladivostock. Near the front windows was a grand piano, and at the other end of the room a heavily carved screen of some black wood, picked out with ivory. The screen was overhung with a canopy of silken draperies, and formed a sort of alcove. In front of the alcove was spread the white skin of a polar bear, and set on that was one of those low, Turkish coffee-tables. It held a lighted spirit-lamp and two gold coffee-cups. I had heard no movement from above stairs, and it must have been fully three minutes that I stood waiting, noting these details of the room and wondering at the delay, and at the strange silence.

"And then, suddenly, as my eye grew more used to the half-light, I saw, projecting from behind the screen, as though it were stretched along the back of a divan, the hand of a man and the lower part of his arm. I was as startled as though I had come across a footprint on a deserted island. Evidently, the man had been sitting there since I had come into the room, even since I had entered the house, and he had heard the servant knocking upon the door. Why he had not declared himself I could not understand, but I supposed that, possibly, he was a guest, with no reason to interest himself in the Princess's other visitors, or, perhaps, for some reason, he did not wish to be observed. I could see nothing of him except his hand, but I had an unpleasant feeling that he had been peering at me through the carving in the screen, and that he still was doing so. I moved my feet noisily on the floor and said, tentatively, 'I beg your pardon.'

"There was no reply, and the hand did not stir. Apparently, the man was bent upon ignoring me, but, as all I wished was to apologize for my intrusion and to leave the house, I walked up to the alcove and peered around it. Inside the screen was a divan piled with cushions, and on the end of it nearer me the man was sitting. He was a young Englishman with light-yellow hair and a deeply bronzed face. He was seated with his arms stretched out along the back of the divan, and with his head resting against a cushion. His attitude was one of complete ease. But his mouth had fallen open, and his eyes were set with an expression of utter horror. At the first glance, I saw that he was quite dead.

"For a flash of time I was too startled to act, but in the same flash I was convinced that the man had met his death from no accident, that he had not died through any ordinary failure of the laws of nature. The expression on his face was much too terrible to be misinterpreted. It spoke as eloquently as words. It told me that before the end had come he had watched his death approach and threaten him.

"I was so sure he had been murdered that I instinctively looked on the floor for the weapon, and, at the same moment, out of concern for my own safety, quickly behind me; but the silence of the house continued unbroken.

"I have seen a great number of dead men; I was on the Asiatic Station during the Japanese-Chinese war. I was in Port Arthur after the massacre. So a dead man, for the single reason that he is dead, does not repel me, and, though I knew that there was no hope that this man was alive, still, for decency's sake, I felt his pulse, and, while I kept my ears alert for any sound from the floors above me, I pulled open his shirt and placed my hand upon his heart. My fingers instantly touched upon the opening of a wound, and as I withdrew them I found them wet with blood. He was in evening dress, and in the wide bosom of his shirt I found a narrow slit, so narrow that in the dim light it was scarcely discernible. The wound was no wider than the smallest blade of a pocket-knife, but when I stripped the shirt away from the chest and left it bare, I found that the weapon, narrow as it was, had been long enough to reach his heart. There is no need to tell you how I felt as I stood by the body of this boy, for he was hardly older than a boy, or of the thoughts that came into my head. I was bitterly sorry for this stranger, bitterly indignant at his murderer, and, at the same time, selfishly concerned for my own safety and for the notoriety which I saw was sure to follow. My instinct was to leave the body where it lay, and to hide myself in the fog, but I also felt that since a succession of accidents had made me the only witness to a crime, my duty was to make myself a good witness and to assist to establish the facts of this murder.

"That it might, possibly, be a suicide, and not a murder, did not disturb me for a moment. The fact that the weapon had disappeared, and the expression on the boy's face were enough to convince, at least me, that he had had no hand in his own death. I judged it, therefore, of the first importance to discover who was in the house, or, if they had escaped from it, who had been in the house before I entered it. I had seen one man leave it; but all I could tell of him was that he was a young man, that he was in evening dress, and that he had fled in such haste that he had not stopped to close the door behind him.

"The Russian servant I had found apparently asleep, and, unless he acted a part with supreme skill, he was a stupid and ignorant boor, and as innocent of the murder as myself. There was still the Russian princess whom he had expected to find, or had pretended to expect to find, in the same room with the murdered man. I judged that she must now be either upstairs with the servant, or that she had, without his knowledge, already fled from the house. When I recalled his apparently genuine surprise at not finding her in the drawing-room, this latter supposition seemed the more probable. Nevertheless, I decided that it was my duty to make a search, and after a second hurried look for the weapon among the cushions of the divan, and upon the floor, I cautiously crossed the hall and entered the dining-room.

"The single candle was still flickering in the draught, and showed only the white cloth. The rest of the room was draped in shadows. I picked up the candle, and, lifting it high above my head, moved around the corner of the table. Either my nerves were on such a stretch that no shock could strain them further, or my mind was inoculated to horrors, for I did not cry out at what I saw nor retreat from it. Immediately at my feet was the body of a beautiful woman, lying at full length upon the floor, her arms flung out on either side of her, and her white face and shoulders gleaming, dully, in the unsteady light of the candle. Around her throat was a great chain of diamonds, and the light played upon these and made them flash and blaze in tiny flames. But the woman who wore them was dead, and I was so certain as to how she had died that, without an instant's hesitation, I dropped on my knees beside her and placed my hands above her heart. My fingers again touched the thin slit of a wound. I had no doubt in my mind but that this was the Russian princess, and when I lowered the candle to her face I was assured that this was so. Her features showed the finest lines of both the Slav and the Jewess; the eyes were black, the hair blue-black and wonderfully heavy, and her skin, even in death, was rich in color. She was a surpassingly beautiful woman.

"I rose and tried to light another candle with the one I held, but I found that my hand was so unsteady that I could not keep the wicks together. It was my intention to again search for this strange dagger which had been used to kill both the English boy and the beautiful princess, but before I could light the second candle I heard footsteps descending the stairs, and the Russian servant appeared in the doorway.

"My face was in darkness, or I am sure that, at the sight of it, he would have taken alarm, for at that moment I was not sure but that this man himself was the murderer. His own face was plainly visible to me in the light from the hall, and I could see that it wore an expression of dull bewilderment. I stepped quickly toward him and took a firm hold upon his wrist.

"'She is not there,' he said. 'The Princess has gone. They have all gone.'

"'Who have gone?' I demanded. 'Who else has been here? '

"'The two Englishmen,' he said.

"'What two Englishmen?' I demanded. 'What are their names?'

"The man now saw by my manner that some question of great moment hung upon his answer, and he began to protest that he did not know the names of the visitors and that until that evening he had never seen them.

"I guessed that it was my tone which frightened him, so I took my hand off his wrist and spoke less eagerly.

"'How long have they been here?' I asked, 'and when did they go?'

"He pointed behind him toward the drawing-room.

"'One sat there with the Princess,' he said; 'the other came after I had placed the coffee in the drawing-room. The two Englishmen talked together, and the Princess returned here to the table. She sat there in that chair, and I brought her cognac and cigarettes. Then I sat outside upon the bench. It was a feast-day, and I had been drinking. Pardon, Excellency, but I fell asleep. When I woke, your Excellency was standing by me, but the Princess and the two Englishmen had gone. That is all I know.'

"I believed that the man was telling me the truth. His fright had passed, and he was now apparently puzzled, but not alarmed.

"'You must remember the names of the Englishmen,' I urged. 'Try to think. When you announced them to the Princess what name did you give?'

"At this question he exclaimed, with pleasure, and, beckoning to me, ran hurriedly down the hall and into the drawing-room. In the corner furthest from the screen was the piano, and on it was a silver tray. He picked this up and, smiling with pride at his own intelligence, pointed at two cards that lay upon it. I took them up and read the names engraved upon them."

The American paused abruptly, and glanced at the faces about him. "I read the names," he repeated. He spoke with great reluctance.

"Continue!" cried the baronet, sharply.

"I read the names," said the American with evident distaste, "and the family name of each was the same. They were the names of two brothers. One is well known to you. It is that of the African explorer of whom this gentleman was just speaking. I mean the Earl of Chetney. The other was the name of his brother. Lord Arthur Chetney."

The men at the table fell back as though a trapdoor had fallen open at their feet.

"Lord Chetney?" they exclaimed, in chorus. They glanced at each other and back to the American, with every expression of concern and disbelief.

"It is impossible!" cried the Baronet. "Why, my dear sir, young Chetney only arrived from Africa yesterday. It was so stated in the evening papers."

The jaw of the American set in a resolute square, and he pressed his lips together.

"You are perfectly right, sir," he said, "Lord Chetney did arrive in London yesterday morning, and yesterday night I found his dead body."

The youngest member present was the first to recover. He seemed much less concerned over the identity of the murdered man than at the interruption of the narrative.

"Oh, please let him go on!" he cried. "What happened then? You say you found two visiting-cards. How do you know which card was that of the murdered man?"

The American, before he answered, waited until the chorus of exclamations had ceased. Then he continued as though he had not been interrupted.

"The instant I read the names upon the cards," he said, "I ran to the screen and, kneeling beside the dead man, began a search through his pockets. My hand at once fell upon a card-case, and I found on all the cards it contained the title of the Earl of Chetney. His watch and cigarette-case also bore his name. These evidences, and the fact of his bronzed skin, and that his cheek-bones were worn with fever, convinced me that the dead man was the African explorer, and the boy who had fled past me in the night was Arthur, his younger brother.

"I was so intent upon my search that I had forgotten the servant, and I was still on my knees when I heard a cry behind me. I turned, and saw the man gazing down at the body in abject horror.

"Before I could rise, he gave another cry of terror, and, flinging himself into the hall, raced toward the door to the street. I leaped after him, shouting to him to halt, but before I could reach the hall he had torn open the door, and I saw him spring out into the yellow fog. I cleared the steps in a jump and ran down the garden-walk but just as the gate clicked in front of me. I had it open on the instant, and, following the sound of the man's footsteps, I raced after him across the open street. He, also, could hear me, and he instantly stopped running, and there was absolute silence. He was so near that I almost fancied I could hear him panting, and I held my own breath to listen. But I could distinguish nothing but the dripping of the mist about us, and from far off the music of the Hungarian band, which I had heard when I first lost myself.

"All I could see was the square of light from the door I had left open behind me, and a lamp in the hall beyond it flickering in the draught. But even as I watched it, the flame of the lamp was blown violently to and fro, and the door, caught in the same current of air, closed slowly. I knew if it shut I could not again enter the house, and I rushed madly toward it. I believe I even shouted out, as though it were something human which I could compel to obey me, and then I caught my foot against the curb and smashed into the sidewalk. When I rose to my feet I was dizzy and half stunned, and though I thought then that I was moving toward the door, I know now that I probably turned directly from it; for, as I groped about in the night, calling frantically for the police, my fingers touched nothing but the dripping fog, and the iron railings for which I sought seemed to have melted away. For many minutes I beat the mist with my arms like one at blind man's buff, turning sharply in circles, cursing aloud at my stupidity and crying continually for help. At last a voice answered me from the fog, and I found myself held in the circle of a policeman's lantern.

"That is the end of my adventure. What I have to tell you now is what I learned from the police.

"At the station-house to which the man guided me I related what you have just heard. I told them that the house they must at once find was one set back from the street within a radius of two hundred yards from the Knightsbridge Barracks, that within fifty yards of it someone was giving a dance to the music of a Hungarian band, and that the railings before it were as high as a man's waist and filed to a point. With that to work upon, twenty men were at once ordered out into the fog to search for the house, and Inspector Lyle himself was despatched to the home of Lord Edam, Chetney's father, with a warrant for Lord Arthur's arrest. I was thanked and dismissed on my own recognizance.

"This morning, Inspector Lyle called on me, and from him I learned the police theory of the scene I have just described.

"Apparently, I had wandered very far in the fog, for up to noon to- day the house had not been found, nor had they been able to arrest Lord Arthur. He did not return to his father's house last night, and there is no trace of him; but from what the police knew of the past lives of the people I found in that lost house, they have evolved a theory, and their theory is that the murders were committed by Lord Arthur.

"The infatuation of his elder brother, Lord Chetney, for a Russian princess, so Inspector Lyle tells me, is well known to everyone. About two years ago the Princess Zichy, as she calls herself, and he were constantly together, and Chetney informed his friends that they were about to be married. The woman was notorious in two continents, and when Lord Edam heard of his son's infatuation he appealed to the police for her record.

"It is through his having applied to them that they know so much concerning her and her relations with the Chetneys. From the police Lord Edam learned that Madame Zichy had once been a spy in the employ of the Russian Third

246

Section, but that lately she had been repudiated by her own government and was living by her wits, by blackmail, and by her beauty. Lord Edam laid this record before his son, but Chetney either knew it already or the woman persuaded him not to believe in it, and the father and son parted in great anger. Two days later the marquis altered his will, leaving all of his money to the younger brother, Arthur.

"The title and some of the landed property he could not keep from Chetney, but he swore if his son saw the woman again that the will should stand as it was, and he would be left without a penny.

"This was about eighteen months ago, when, apparently, Chetney tired of the Princess, and suddenly went off to shoot and explore in Central Africa. No word came from him, except that twice he was reported as having died of fever in the jungle, and finally two traders reached the coast who said they had seen his body. This was accepted by all as conclusive, and young Arthur was recognized as the heir to the Edam millions. On the strength of this supposition he at once began to borrow enormous sums from the money-lenders. This is of great importance, as the police believe it was these debts which drove him to the murder of his brother. Yesterday, as you know, Lord Chetney suddenly returned from the grave, and it was the fact that for two years he had been considered as dead which lent such importance to his return and which gave rise to those columns of detail concerning him which appeared in all the afternoon papers. But, obviously, during his absence he had not tired of the Princess Zichy, for we know that a few hours after he reached London he sought her out. His brother, who had also learned of his reappearance through the papers, probably suspected which would be the house he would first visit, and followed him there, arriving, so the Russian servant tells us, while the two were at coffee in the drawing-room. The Princess, then, we also learn from the servant, withdrew to the dining-room, leaving the brothers together. What happened one can only guess.

"Lord Arthur knew now that when it was discovered he was no longer the heir, the moneylenders would come down upon him. The police believe that he at once sought out his brother to beg for money to cover the post-obits, but that, considering the sum he needed was several hundreds of thousands of pounds, Chetney refused to give it him. No one knew that Arthur had gone to seek out his brother. They were alone. It is possible, then, that in a passion of disappointment, and crazed with the disgrace which he saw before him, young Arthur made himself the heir beyond further question. The death of his brother would have availed nothing if the woman remained alive. It is then possible that he crossed the hall, and, with the same weapon which made him Lord Edam's heir, destroyed the solitary witness to the murder. The only other person who could have seen it was sleeping in a drunken stupor, to which fact undoubtedly he owed his life. And yet," concluded the Naval Attache, leaning forward and marking each word with his finger, "Lord Arthur blundered fatally. In his haste he left the door of the house open, so giving access to the first passer-by, and he forgot that when he entered it he had handed his card to the servant. That piece of paper may yet send him to the gallows. In the meantime, he has disappeared completely, and somewhere, in one of the millions of streets of this great capital, in a locked and empty house, lies the body of his brother, and of the woman his brother loved, undiscovered, unburied; and with their murder unavenged."

In the discussion which followed the conclusion of the story of the Naval Attache, the gentleman with the pearl took no part. Instead, he arose, and, beckoning a servant to a far corner of the room, whispered earnestly to him until a sudden movement on the part of Sir Andrew caused him to return hurriedly to the table.

"There are several points in Mr. Sears's story I want explained," he cried. "Be seated, Sir Andrew," he begged. "Let us have the opinion of an expert. I do not care what the police think, I want to know what you think."

But Sir Andrew rose reluctantly from his chair.

"I should like nothing better than to discuss this," he said. "But it is most important that I proceed to the House.

I should have been there some time ago." He turned toward the servant and directed him to call a hansom.

The gentleman with the pearl stud looked appealingly at the Naval Attache. "There are surely many details that you have not told us," he urged. "Some you have forgotten."

The Baronet interrupted quickly.

"I trust not," he said, "for I could not possibly stop to hear them."

"The story is finished," declared the Naval Attache; "until Lord Arthur is arrested or the bodies are found there is nothing more to tell of either Chetney or the Princess Zichy."

"Of Lord Chetney, perhaps not," interrupted the sporting-looking gentleman with the black tie, "but there'll always be something to tell of the Princess Zichy. I know enough stories about her to fill a book. She was a most remarkable woman." The speaker dropped the end of his cigar into his coffee-cup and, taking his case from his pocket, selected a fresh one. As he did so he laughed and held up the case that the others might see it. It was an ordinary cigar-case of well-worn pig-skin, with a silver clasp.

"The only time I ever met her," he said, "she tried to rob me of this."

The Baronet regarded him closely.

"She tried to rob you?" he repeated.

"Tried to rob me of this," continued the gentleman in the black tie, "and of the Czarina's diamonds." His tone was one of mingled admiration and injury.

"The Czarina's diamonds!" exclaimed the Baronet. He glanced quickly and suspiciously at the speaker, and then at the others about the table. But their faces gave evidence of no other emotion than that of ordinary interest.

"Yes, the Czarina's diamonds," repeated the man with the black tie. "It was a necklace of diamonds. I was told to take them to the Russian Ambassador in Paris, who was to deliver them at Moscow. I am a Queen's Messenger," he added.

"Oh, I see," exclaimed Sir Andrew, in a tone of relief. "And you say that this same Princess Zichy, one of the victims of this double murder, endeavored to rob you of—of—that cigar-case."

"And the Czarina's diamonds," answered the Queen's Messenger, imperturbably. "It's not much of a story, but it gives you an idea of the woman's character. The robbery took place between Paris and Marseilles."

The Baronet interrupted him with an abrupt movement. "No, no," he cried, shaking his head in protest. "Do not tempt me. I really cannot listen. I must be at the House in ten minutes."

"I am sorry," said the Queen's Messenger. He turned to those seated about him. "I wonder if the other gentlemen—"

251

he inquired, tentatively. There was a chorus of polite murmurs, and the Queen's Messenger, bowing his head in acknowledgment, took a preparatory sip from his glass. At the same moment the servant to whom the man with the black pearl had spoken, slipped a piece of paper into his hand. He glanced at it, frowned, and threw it under the table.

The servant bowed to the Baronet.

"Your hansom is waiting, Sir Andrew," he said.

"The necklace was worth twenty thousand pounds," began the Queen's Messenger, "It was a present from the Queen of England to celebrate— " The Baronet gave an exclamation of angry annoyance.

"Upon my word, this is most provoking," he interrupted. "I really ought not to stay. But I certainly mean to hear this." He turned irritably to the servant. "Tell the hansom to wait," he commanded, and, with an air of a boy who is playing truant, slipped guiltily into his chair.

The gentleman with the black pearl smiled blandly, and rapped upon the table.

"Order, gentlemen," he said. "Order for the story of the Queen's Messenger and the Czarina's diamonds."

PART II

"The necklace was a present from the Queen of England to the Czarina of Russia," began the Queen's Messenger. "It was to celebrate the occasion of the Czar's coronation. Our Foreign Office knew that the Russian Ambassador in Paris was to proceed to Moscow for that ceremony, and I was directed to go to Paris and turn over the necklace to him. But when I reached Paris I found he had not expected me for a week later and was taking a few days' vacation at Nice. His people asked me to leave the necklace with them at the Embassy, but I had been charged to get a receipt for it from the Ambassador himself, so I started at once for Nice. The fact that Monte Carlo is not two thousand miles from Nice may have had something to do with making me carry out my instructions so carefully.

"Now, how the Princess Zichy came to find out about the necklace I don't know, but I can guess. As you have just heard, she was at one time a spy in the service of the Russian Government. And after they dismissed her she kept up her acquaintance with many of the Russian agents in London. It is probable that through one of them she learned that the necklace was to be sent to Moscow, and which one of the Queen's Messengers had been detailed to take it there. Still, I doubt if even that knowledge would have helped her if she had not also known something which I supposed no one else in the world knew but myself and one other man. And, curiously enough, the other man was a Queen's Messenger, too, and a friend of mine. You must know that up to the time of this robbery I had always concealed my despatches in a manner peculiarly my own. I got the idea from that play called 'A Scrap of Paper.' In it a man wants to hide a certain compromising document. He knows that all his rooms will be secretly searched for it, so he puts it in a torn envelope and sticks it up where anyone can see it on his mantle-shelf. The result is that the woman who is ransacking the house to find it looks in all the unlikely places, but passes over the scrap of paper that is just under her nose. Sometimes the papers and packages they give us to carry about Europe are of very great value, and sometimes they are special makes of cigarettes, and orders to court-dressmakers. Sometimes we know what we are carrying and sometimes we do not. If it is a large sum of money or a treaty, they generally tell us. But, as a rule, we have no knowledge of what the package contains; so to be on the safe side, we naturally take just as great care of it as though we knew it held the terms of an ultimatum or the crown-jewels. As a rule, my confreres carry the official packages in a despatch-box, which is just as obvious as a lady's jewel-bag in the hands of her maid. Everyone knows they are carrying something of value. They put a premium on dishonesty. Well, after I saw the 'Scrap-of-Paper' play, I determined to put the government valuables in the most unlikely place that anyone would look for them. So I used to hide the documents they gave me inside my riding-boots, and small articles, such as money or jewels, I carried in an old cigar-case. After I took to using my case for that purpose I bought a new one, exactly like it, for my cigars. But, to avoid mistakes, I had my initials placed on both sides of the new one, and the moment I touched the case, even in the dark, I could tell which it was by the raised initials.

"No one knew of this except the Queen's Messenger of whom I spoke. We once left Paris together on the Orient Express. I was going to Constantinople and he was to stop off at Vienna. On the journey I told him of my peculiar way of hiding things and showed him my cigar- case. If I recollect rightly, on that trip it held the grand cross of St. Michael and St. George, which the Queen was sending to our Ambassador. The Messenger was very much entertained at my scheme, and some months later when he met the Princess he told her about it as an amusing story. Of course, he had no idea she was a Russian spy. He didn't know anything at all about her, except that she was a very attractive woman. It was indiscreet, but he could not possibly have guessed that she could ever make any use of what he told her.

"Later, after the robbery, I remembered that I had informed this young chap of my secret hiding-place, and when I saw him again I questioned him about it. He was greatly distressed, and said he had never seen the importance of the secret. He remembered he had told several people of it, and among others the Princess Zichy. In that way I found out that it was she who had robbed me, and I know that from the moment I left London she was following me, and that she knew then that the diamonds were concealed in my cigar-case.

"My train for Nice left Paris at ten in the morning. When I travel at night I generally tell the chef de gare that I am a Queen's Messenger, and he gives me a compartment to myself, but in the daytime I take whatever offers. On this morning I had found an empty compartment, and I had tipped the guard to keep everyone else out, not from any fear of losing the diamonds, but because I wanted to smoke. He had locked the door, and as the last bell had rung I supposed I was to travel alone, so I began to arrange my traps and make myself comfortable. The diamonds in the cigar-case were in the inside pocket of my waistcoat, and as they made a bulky package, I took them out, intending to put them in my hand-bag. It is a small satchel like a bookmaker's, or those hand-bags that couriers carry. I wear it slung from a strap across my shoulders, and, no matter whether I am sitting or walking, it never leaves me.

"I took the cigar-case which held the necklace from my inside pocket and the case which held the cigars out of the satchel, and while I was searching through it for a box of matches I laid the two cases beside me on the seat.

"At that moment the train started, but at the same instant there was a rattle at the lock of the compartment, and a couple of porters lifted and shoved a woman through the door, and hurled her rugs and umbrellas in after her.

"Instinctively I reached for the diamonds. I shoved them quickly into the satchel and, pushing them far down to the bottom of the bag, snapped the spring-lock. Then I put the cigars in the pocket of my coat, but with the thought that now that I had a woman as a travelling companion I would probably not be allowed to enjoy them.

"One of her pieces of luggage had fallen at my feet, and a roll of rugs had landed at my side. I thought if I hid the fact that the lady was not welcome, and at once endeavored to be civil, she might permit me to smoke. So I picked her hand-bag off the floor and asked her where I might place it.

"As I spoke I looked at her for the first time, and saw that she was a most remarkably handsome woman.

"She smiled charmingly and begged me not to disturb myself. Then she arranged her own things about her, and, opening her dressing-bag, took out a gold cigarette-case.

"'Do you object to smoke?' she asked.

"I laughed and assured her I had been in great terror lest she might object to it herself.

"'If you like cigarettes,' she said, 'will you try some of these? They are rolled especially for my husband in Russia, and they are supposed to be very good.'

"I thanked her, and took one from her case, and I found it so much better than my own that I continued to smoke her cigarettes throughout the rest of the journey. I must say that we got on very well. I judged from the coronet on her cigarette-case, and from her manner, which was quite as well bred as that of any woman I ever met, that she was someone of importance, and though she seemed almost too good-looking to be respectable, I determined that she was some grande dame who was so assured of her position that she could afford to be unconventional. At first she read her novel, and then she made some comment on the scenery, and finally we began to discuss the current politics of the Continent. She talked of all the cities in Europe, and seemed to know everyone worth knowing. But she volunteered nothing about herself except that she frequently made use of the expression, 'When my husband was stationed at Vienna,' or 'When my husband was promoted to Rome.' Once she said to me, 'I have often seen you at Monte Carlo. I saw you when you won the pigeon- championship.' I told her that I was not a pigeon-shot, and she gave a little start of surprise. 'Oh, I beg your pardon,' she said; 'I thought you were Morton Hamilton, the English champion.' As a matter of fact, I do look like Hamilton, but I know now that her object was to make me think that she had no idea as to who I really was. She needn't have acted at all, for I certainly had no suspicions of her, and was only too pleased to have so charming a companion.

"The one thing that should have made me suspicious was the fact that at every station she made some trivial excuse to get me out of the compartment. She pretended that her maid was travelling back of us in one of the second-class carriages, and kept saying she could not imagine why the woman did not come to look after her, and if the maid did not turn up at the next stop, would I be so very kind as to get out and bring her whatever it was she pretended she wanted.

"I had taken my dressing-case from the rack to get out a novel, and had left it on the seat opposite to mine, and at the end of the compartment farthest from her. And once when I came back from buying her a cup of chocolate, or from some other fool-errand, I found her standing at my end of the compartment with both hands on the dressing-bag. She looked at me without so much as winking an eye, and shoved the case carefully into a corner. 'Your bag slipped off on the floor,' she said. 'If you've got any bottles in it, you had better look and see that they're not broken.'

"And I give you my word, I was such an ass that I did open the case and looked all through it. She must have thought I WAS a Juggins. I get hot all over whenever I remember it. But, in spite of my dulness, and her cleverness, she couldn't gain anything by sending me away, because what she wanted was in the hand-bag, and every time she sent me away the hand-bag went with me.

"After the incident of the dressing-case her manner changed. Either in my absence she had had time to look through it, or, when I was examining it for broken bottles, she had seen everything it held.

"From that moment she must have been certain that the cigar-case, in which she knew I carried the diamonds, was in the bag that was fastened to my body, and from that time on she probably was plotting how to get it from me.

"Her anxiety became most apparent. She dropped the great-lady manner, and her charming condescension went with it. She ceased talking, and, when I spoke, answered me irritably, or at random. No doubt her mind was entirely occupied with her plan. The end of our journey was drawing rapidly nearer, and her time for action was being cut down with the speed of the express-train. Even I, unsuspicious as I was, noticed that something was very wrong with her. I really believe that before we reached Marseilles if I had not, through my own stupidity, given her the chance she wanted, she might have stuck a knife in me and rolled me out on the rails. But as it was, I only thought that the long journey had tired her. I suggested that it was a very trying trip, and asked her if she would allow me to offer her some of my cognac.

"She thanked me and said, 'No,' and then suddenly her eyes lighted, and she exclaimed, 'Yes, thank you, if you will be so kind.'

"My flask was in the hand-bag, and I placed it on my lap and, with my thumb, slipped back the catch. As I keep my tickets and railroad- guide in the bag, I am so constantly opening it that I never bother to lock it, and the fact that it is strapped to me has always been sufficient protection. But I can appreciate now what a satisfaction, and what a torment, too, it must have been to that woman when she saw that the bag opened without a key.

"While we were crossing the mountains I had felt rather chilly and had been wearing a light racing-coat. But after the lamps were lighted the compartment became very hot and stuffy, and I found the coat uncomfortable. So I stood up, and after first slipping the strap of the bag over my head, I placed the bag in the seat next me and pulled off the racing-coat. I don't blame myself for being careless; the bag was still within reach of my hand, and nothing would have happened if at that exact moment the train had not stopped at Arles. It was the combination of my removing the bag and our entering the station at the same instant which gave the Princess Zichy the chance she wanted to rob me.

"I needn't say that she was clever enough to take it. The train ran into the station at full speed and came to a sudden stop. I had just thrown my coat into the rack, and had reached out my hand for the bag. In another instant I would have had the strap around my shoulder. But at that moment the Princess threw open the door of the compartment and beckoned wildly at the people on the platform. 'Natalie!' she called, 'Natalie! here I am. Come here! This way!' She turned upon me in the greatest excitement. 'My maid!' she cried. 'She is looking for me. She passed the window without seeing me. Go, please, and bring her back.' She continued pointing out of the door and beckoning me with her other hand. There certainly was something about that woman's tone which made one jump. When she was giving orders you had no chance to think of anything else. So I rushed out on my errand of mercy, and then rushed back again to ask what the maid looked like.

"'In black,' she answered, rising and blocking the door of the compartment. 'All in black, with a bonnet!'

"The train waited three minutes at Arles, and in that time I suppose I must have rushed up to over twenty women and asked, 'Are you Natalie?' The only reason I wasn't punched with an umbrella or handed over to the police was that they probably thought I was crazy.

"When I jumped back into the compartment the Princess was seated where I had left her, but her eyes were burning with happiness. She placed her hand on my arm almost affectionately, and said, in a hysterical way, 'You are very kind to me. I am so sorry to have troubled you.'

"I protested that every woman on the platform was dressed in black.

"'Indeed, I am so sorry,' she said, laughing; and she continued to laugh until she began to breathe so quickly that I thought she was going to faint.

"I can see now that the last part of that journey must have been a terrible half-hour for her. She had the cigar-case safe enough, but she knew that she herself was not safe. She understood if I were to open my bag, even at the last minute, and miss the case, I would know positively that she had taken it. I had placed the diamonds in the bag at the very moment she entered the compartment, and no one but our two selves had occupied it since. She knew that when we reached Marseilles she would either be twenty thousand pounds richer than when she left Paris, or that she would go to jail. That was the situation as she must have read it, and I don't envy her her state of mind during that last half-hour. It must have been hell.

"I saw that something was wrong, and, in my innocence, I even wondered if possibly my cognac had not been a little too strong. For she suddenly developed into a most brilliant conversationalist, and applauded and laughed at everything I said, and fired off questions at me like a machine-gun, so that I had no time to think of anything but of what she was saying. Whenever I stirred, she stopped her chattering and leaned toward me, and watched me like a cat over a mouse-hole. I wondered how I could have considered her an agreeable travelling-companion. I thought I would have preferred to be locked in with a lunatic. I don't like to think how she would have acted if I had made a move to examine the bag, but as I had it safely strapped around me again, I did not open it, and I reached Marseilles alive. As we drew into the station she shook hands with me and grinned at me like a Cheshire cat.

"'I cannot tell you,' she said, 'how much I have to thank you for.' What do you think of that for impudence?

"I offered to put her in a carriage, but she said she must find Natalie, and that she hoped we would meet again at the hotel. So I drove off by myself, wondering who she was, and whether Natalie was not her keeper.

"I had to wait several hours for the train to Nice; and as I wanted to stroll around the city I thought I had better put the diamonds in the safe of the hotel. As soon as I reached my room I locked the door, placed the hand-bag on the table, and opened it. I felt among the things at the top of it, but failed to touch the cigar-case. I shoved my hand in deeper, and stirred the things about, but still I did not reach it. A cold wave swept down my spine, and a sort of emptiness came to the pit of my stomach. Then I turned red-hot, and the sweat sprung out all over me. I wet my lips with my tongue, and said to myself, 'Don't be an ass. Pull yourself together, pull yourself together. Take the things out, one at a time. It's there, of course, it's there. Don't be an ass.'

"So I put a brake on my nerves and began very carefully to pick out the things, one by one, but, after another second, I could not stand it, and I rushed across the room and threw out everything on the bed. But the diamonds were not among them. I pulled the things about and tore them open and shuffled and rearranged and sorted them, but it was no use. The cigar-case was gone. I threw everything in the dressing-case out on the floor, although I knew it was useless to look for it there. I knew that I had put it in the bag. I sat down and tried to think. I remembered I had put it in the satchel at Paris just as that woman had entered the compartment, and I had been alone with her ever since, so it was she who had robbed me. But how? It had never left my shoulder. And then I remembered that it had—that I had taken it off when I had changed my coat and for the few moments that I was searching for Natalie. I remembered that the woman had sent me on that goose-chase, and that at every other station she had tried to get rid of me on some fool-errand.

"I gave a roar like a mad bull, and I jumped down the stairs, six steps at a time.

"I demanded at the office if a distinguished lady of title, possibly a Russian, had just entered the hotel.

"As I expected, she had not. I sprang into a cab and inquired at two other hotels, and then I saw the folly of trying to catch her without outside help, and I ordered the fellow to gallop to the office of the Chief of Police. I told my story, and the ass in charge asked me to calm myself, and wanted to take notes. I told him this was no time for taking notes, but for doing something. He got wrathy at that, and I demanded to be taken at once to his Chief. The Chief, he said, was very busy, and could not see me. So I showed him my silver greyhound. In eleven years I had never used it but once before. I stated, in pretty vigorous language, that I was a Queen's Messenger, and that if the Chief of Police did not see me instantly he would lose his official head. At that the fellow jumped off his high horse and ran with me to his Chief—a smart young chap, a colonel in the army, and a very intelligent man.

"I explained that I had been robbed, in a French railway-carriage, of a diamond-necklace belonging to the Queen of England, which her Majesty was sending as a present to the Czarina of Russia. I pointed out to him that if he succeeded in capturing the thief he would be made for life, and would receive the gratitude of three great powers.

"He wasn't the sort that thinks second thoughts are best. He saw Russian and French decorations sprouting all over his chest, and he hit a bell, and pressed buttons, and yelled out orders like the captain of a penny-steamer in a fog. He sent her description to all the city-gates, and ordered all cabmen and railway-porters to search all trains leaving

Marseilles. He ordered all passengers on outgoing vessels to be examined, and telegraphed the proprietors of every hotel and pension to send him a complete list of their guests within the hour. While I was standing there he must have given at least a hundred orders, and sent out enough commissaires, sergeants de ville, gendarmes, bicycle-police, and plain-clothes Johnnies to have captured the entire German army. When they had gone he assured me that the woman was as good as arrested already. Indeed, officially, she was arrested; for she had no more chance of escape from Marseilles than from the Chateau D'If.

"He told me to return to my hotel and possess my soul in peace. Within an hour he assured me he would acquaint me with her arrest.

"I thanked him, and complimented him on his energy, and left him. But I didn't share in his confidence. I felt that she was a very clever woman, and a match for any and all of us. It was all very well for him to be jubilant. He had not lost the diamonds, and had everything to gain if he found them; while I, even if he did recover the necklace, would only be where I was before I lost them, and if he did not recover it I was a ruined man. It was an awful facer for me. I had always prided myself on my record. In eleven years I had never mislaid an envelope, nor missed taking the first train. And now I had failed in the most important mission that had ever been intrusted to me. And it wasn't a thing that could be hushed up, either. It was too conspicuous, too spectacular. It was sure to invite the widest notoriety. I saw myself ridiculed all over the Continent, and perhaps dismissed, even suspected of having taken the thing myself.

"I was walking in front of a lighted cafe, and I felt so sick and miserable that I stopped for a pick-me-up. Then I considered that if I took one drink I would probably, in my present state of mind, not want to stop under twenty, and I decided I had better leave it alone. But my nerves were jumping like a frightened rabbit, and I felt I must have something to quiet them, or I would go crazy. I reached for my cigarette-case, but a cigarette seemed hardly adequate, so I put it back again and took out this cigar-case, in which I keep only the strongest and blackest cigars. I opened it and stuck in my fingers, but, instead of a cigar, they touched on a thin leather envelope. My heart stood perfectly still. I did not dare to look, but I dug my finger-nails into the leather, and I felt layers of thin paper, then a layer of cotton, and then they scratched on the facets of the Czarina's diamonds!

"I stumbled as though I had been hit in the face, and fell back into one of the chairs on the sidewalk. I tore off the wrappings and spread out the diamonds on the cafe-table; I could not believe they were real. I twisted the necklace between my fingers and crushed it between my palms and tossed it up in the air. I believe I almost kissed it. The women in the cafe stood up on the chairs to see better, and laughed and screamed, and the people crowded so close around me that the waiters had to form a body-guard. The proprietor thought there was a fight, and called for the police. I was so happy I didn't care. I laughed, too, and gave the proprietor a five-pound note, and told him to stand everyone a drink. Then I tumbled into a fiacre and galloped off to my friend the Chief of Police. I felt very sorry for him. He had been so happy at the chance I gave him, and he was sure to be disappointed when he learned I had sent him off on a false alarm.

"But now that I had found the necklace, I did not want him to find the woman. Indeed, I was most anxious that she should get clear away, for, if she were caught, the truth would come out, and I was likely to get a sharp reprimand, and sure to be laughed at.

"I could see now how it had happened. In my haste to hide the diamonds when the woman was hustled into the carriage, I had shoved the cigars into the satchel, and the diamonds into the pocket of my coat. Now that I had the diamonds safe again, it seemed a very natural mistake. But I doubted if the Foreign Office would think so. I was afraid it might not appreciate the beautiful simplicity of my secret hiding-place. So, when I reached the police-station, and found that the woman was still at large, I was more than relieved.

"As I expected, the Chief was extremely chagrined when he learned of my mistake, and that there was nothing for him to do. But I was feeling so happy myself that I hated to have anyone else miserable, so I suggested that this attempt to steal the Czarina's necklace might be only the first of a series of such attempts by an unscrupulous gang, and that I might still be in danger.

"I winked at the Chief, and the Chief smiled at me, and we went to Nice together in a saloon-car with a guard of twelve carabineers and twelve plain-clothes men, and the Chief and I drank champagne all the way. We marched together up to the hotel where the Russian Ambassador was stopping, closely surrounded by our escort of carabineers, and delivered the necklace with the most profound ceremony. The old Ambassador was immensely impressed, and when we hinted that already I had been made the object of an attack by robbers, he assured us that his Imperial Majesty would not prove ungrateful.

"I wrote a swinging personal letter about the invaluable services of the Chief to the French Minister of Foreign Affairs, and they gave him enough Russian and French medals to satisfy even a French soldier. So, though he never caught the woman, he received his just reward."

The Queen's Messenger paused and surveyed the faces of those about him in some embarrassment.

"But the worst of it is," he added, "that the story must have got about; for, while the Princess obtained nothing from me but a cigar- case and five excellent cigars, a few weeks after the coronation the Czar sent me a gold cigar-case with his monogram in diamonds. And I don't know yet whether that was a coincidence, or whether the Czar wanted me to know that he knew that I had been carrying the Czarina's diamonds in my pig-skin cigar-case. What do you fellows think?"

PART III

Sir Andrew rose, with disapproval written in every lineament.

"I thought your story would bear upon the murder," he said. "Had I imagined it would have nothing whatsoever to do with it, I would not have remained." He pushed back his chair and bowed, stiffly. "I wish you good night," he said.

There was a chorus of remonstrance, and, under cover of this and the Baronet's answering protests, a servant, for the second time, slipped a piece of paper into the hand of the gentleman with the pearl stud. He read the lines written upon it and tore it into tiny fragments.

The youngest member, who had remained an interested but silent listener to the tale of the Queen's Messenger, raised his hand, commandingly.

"Sir Andrew," he cried, "in justice to Lord Arthur Chetney, I must ask you to be seated. He has been accused in our hearing of a most serious crime, and I insist that you remain until you have heard me clear his character."

"You!" cried the Baronet.

"Yes," answered the young man, briskly. "I would have spoken sooner," he explained, "but that I thought this gentleman"—he inclined his head toward the Queen's Messenger—"was about to contribute some facts of which I was ignorant. He, however, has told us nothing, and so

I will take up the tale at the point where Lieutenant Sears laid it down and give you those details of which Lieutenant Sears is ignorant. It seems strange to you that I should be able to add the sequel to this story. But the coincidence is easily explained. I am the junior member of the law firm of Chudleigh & Chudleigh. We have been solicitors for the Chetneys for the last two hundred years. Nothing, no matter how unimportant, which concerns Lord Edam and his two sons is unknown to us, and naturally we are acquainted with every detail of the terrible catastrophe of last night."

The Baronet, bewildered but eager, sank back into his chair.

"Will you be long, sir?" he demanded.

"I shall endeavor to be brief," said the young solicitor; "and," he added, in a tone which gave his words almost the weight of a threat, "I promise to be interesting."

"There is no need to promise that," said Sir Andrew, "I find it much too interesting as it is." He glanced ruefully at the clock and turned his eyes quickly from it.

"Tell the driver of that hansom," he called to the servant, "that I take him by the hour."

"For the last three days," began young Mr. Chudleigh, "as you have probably read in the daily papers, the Marquis of Edam has been at the point of death, and his physicians have never left his house. Every hour he seemed to grow weaker; but although his bodily strength is apparently leaving him forever, his mind has remained clear and active. Late yesterday evening, word was received at our office that he wished my father to come at once to Chetney House and to bring with him certain papers. What these papers were is not essential; I mention them only to explain how it was that last night I happened to be at Lord Edam's bedside. I accompanied my father to Chetney House, but at the time we reached there Lord Edam was sleeping, and his physicians refused to have him awakened. My father urged that he should be allowed to receive Lord Edam's instructions concerning the documents, but the physicians would not disturb him, and we all gathered in the library to wait until he should awake of his own accord. It was about one o'clock in the morning, while we were still there, that Inspector Lyle and the officers from Scotland Yard came to arrest Lord Arthur on the charge of murdering his brother. You can imagine our dismay and distress. Like everyone else, I had learned from the afternoon papers that Lord Chetney was not dead, but that he had returned to England, and, on arriving at Chetney House, I had been told that Lord Arthur had gone to the Bath Hotel to look for his brother and to inform him that if he wished to see their father alive he must come to him at once. Although it was now past one o'clock, Arthur had not returned. None of us knew where Madame Zichy lived, so we could not go to recover Lord Chetney's body. We spent a most miserable night, hastening to the window whenever a cab came into the square, in the hope that it was Arthur returning, and endeavoring to explain away the facts that pointed to him as the murderer. I am a friend of Arthur's, I was with him at Harrow and at Oxford, and I refused to believe for an instant that he was capable of such a crime; but as a lawyer I could not help but see that the circumstantial evidence was strongly against him.

"Toward early morning, Lord Edam awoke, and in so much better a state of health that he refused to make the changes in the papers which he had intended, declaring that he was no nearer death than ourselves. Under other circumstances, this happy change in him would have relieved us greatly, but none of us could think of anything save the death of his elder son and of the charge which hung over Arthur.

"As long as Inspector Lyle remained in the house, my father decided that I, as one of the legal advisers of the family, should also remain there. But there was little for either of us to do. Arthur did not return, and nothing occurred until late this morning, when Lyle received word that the Russian servant had been arrested. He at once drove to Scotland Yard to question him. He came back to us in an hour, and informed me that the servant had refused to tell anything of what had happened the night before, or of himself, or of the Princess Zichy. He would not even give them the address of her house.

"'He is in abject terror,' Lyle said. 'I assured him that he was not suspected of the crime, but he would tell me nothing.'

"There were no other developments until two o'clock this afternoon, when word was brought to us that Arthur had been found, and that he was lying in the accident-ward of St. George's Hospital. Lyle and I drove there together, and found him propped up in bed with his head bound in a bandage. He had been brought to the hospital the night before by the driver of a hansom that had run over him in the fog. The cab-horse had kicked him on the head, and he had been carried in unconscious. There was nothing on him to tell who he was, and it was not until he came to his senses this afternoon that the hospital authorities had been able to send word to his people. Lyle at once informed him that he was under arrest, and with what he was charged, and though the Inspector warned him to say nothing which might be used against him, I, as his solicitor, instructed him to speak freely and to tell us all he knew of the occurrences of last night. It was evident to anyone that the fact of his brother's death was of much greater concern to him than that he was accused of his murder.

"'That,' Arthur said, contemptuously, 'that is damned nonsense. It is monstrous and cruel. We parted better friends than we have been in years. I will tell you all that happened—not to clear myself, but to help you to find out the truth.' His story is as follows: Yesterday afternoon, owing to his constant attendance on his father, he did not look at the evening papers, and it was not until after dinner, when the butler brought him one and told him of its contents, that he learned that his brother was alive and at the Bath Hotel. He drove there at once, but was told that about eight o'clock his brother had gone out, but without giving any clew to his destination. As Chetney had not at once come to see his father, Arthur decided that he was still angry with him, and his mind, turning naturally to the cause of their quarrel, determined him to look for Chetney at the home of the Princess Zichy.

"Her house had been pointed out to him, and though he had never visited it, he had passed it many times and knew its exact location. He accordingly drove in that direction, as far as the fog would permit the hansom to go, and walked the rest of the way, reaching the house about nine o'clock. He rang, and was admitted by the Russian servant. The man took his card into the drawing-room, and at once his brother ran out and welcomed him. He was followed by the Princess Zichy, who also received Arthur most cordially.

"'You brothers will have much to talk about,' she said. 'I am going to the dining-room. When you have finished, let me know.'

"As soon as she had left them, Arthur told his brother that their father was not expected to outlive the night, and that he must come to him at once.

"'This is not the moment to remember your quarrel,' Arthur said to him; 'you have come back from the dead only in time to make your peace with him before he dies.'

"Arthur says that at this Chetney was greatly moved.

"'You entirely misunderstand me, Arthur,' he returned. 'I did not know the governor was ill, or I would have gone to him the instant I arrived. My only reason for not doing so was because I thought he was still angry with me. I shall return with you immediately, as soon as I have said good-by to the Princess. It is a final good-by. After to- night I shall never see her again.'

"'Do you mean that?' Arthur cried.

"'Yes,' Chetney answered. 'When I returned to London I had no intention of seeking her again, and I am here only through a mistake.' He then told Arthur that he had separated from the Princess even before he went to Central Africa, and that, moreover, while at Cairo on his way south, he had learned certain facts concerning her life there during the previous season, which made it impossible for him to ever wish to see her again. Their separation was final and complete.

"'She deceived me cruelly,' he said; 'I cannot tell you how cruelly. During the two years when I was trying to obtain my father's consent to our marriage she was in love with a Russian diplomat. During all that time he was secretly visiting her here in London, and her trip to Cairo was only an excuse to meet him there.'

"'Yet you are here with her to-night,' Arthur protested, 'only a few hours after your return.'

"'That is easily explained,' Chetney answered. 'As I finished dinner to-night at the hotel, I received a note from her from this address. In it she said she had just learned of my arrival, and begged me to come to her at once. She wrote that she was in great and present trouble, dying of an incurable illness, and without friends or money. She begged me, for the sake of old times, to come to her assistance. During the last two years in the jungle all my former feeling for Zichy has utterly passed away, but no one could have dismissed the appeal she made in that letter. So I came here, and found her, as you have seen her, quite as beautiful as she ever was, in very good health, and, from the look of the house, in no need of money.

"'I asked her what she meant by writing me that she was dying in a garret, and she laughed, and said she had done so because she was afraid, unless I thought she needed help, I would not try to see her. That was where we were when you arrived. And now,' Chetney added, 'I will say good-by to her, and you had better return home. No, you can trust me, I shall follow you at once. She has no influence over me now, but I believe, in spite of the way she has used me, that she is, after her queer fashion, still fond of me, and when she learns that this good-by is final there may be a scene, and it is not fair to her that you should be here. So, go home at once, and tell the governor that I am following you in ten minutes.'

"'That,' said Arthur, 'is the way we parted. I never left him on more friendly terms. I was happy to see him alive again, I was happy to think he had returned in time to make up his quarrel with my father, and I was happy that at last he was shut of that woman. I was never better pleased with him in my life.' He turned to Inspector Lyle, who was sitting at the foot of the bed, taking notes of all he told us.

"'Why, in the name of common-sense,' he cried, 'should I have chosen that moment, of all others, to send my brother back to the grave?' For a moment the Inspector did not answer him. I do not know if any of you gentlemen are acquainted with Inspector Lyle, but if you are not, I can assure you that he is a very remarkable man. Our firm often applies to him for aid, and he has never failed us; my father has the greatest possible respect for him. Where he has the advantage over the ordinary police-official is in the fact that he possesses imagination. He imagines himself to be the criminal, imagines how he would act under the same circumstances, and he imagines to such purpose that he generally finds the man he wants. I have often told Lyle that if he had not been a detective he would have made a great success as a poet or a playwright.

"When Arthur turned on him, Lyle hesitated for a moment, and then told him exactly what was the case against him,

"'Ever since your brother was reported as having died in Africa,' he said, 'your lordship has been collecting money on post-obits. Lord Chetney's arrival, last night, turned them into waste-paper. You were suddenly in debt for thousands of pounds—for much more than you could ever possibly pay. No one knew that you and your brother had met at Madame Zichy's. But you knew that your father was not expected to outlive the night, and that if your brother were dead also, you would be saved from complete ruin, and that you would become the Marquis of Edam.'

"'Oh, that is how you have worked it out, is it?' Arthur cried. 'And for me to become Lord Edam was it necessary that the woman should die, too?'

"'They will say,' Lyle answered, 'that she was a witness to the murder—that she would have told.'

"'Then why did I not kill the servant as well?' Arthur said.

"'He was asleep, and saw nothing.'

"'And you believe that?' Arthur demanded.

"'It is not a question of what I believe,' Lyle said, gravely. 'It is a question for your peers.'

"'The man is insolent!' Arthur cried. 'The thing is monstrous! Horrible!'

"Before we could stop him, he sprang out of his cot and began pulling on his clothes. When the nurses tried to hold him down, he fought with them.

"'Do you think you can keep me here,' he shouted, 'when they are plotting to hang me? I am going with you to that house!' he cried at Lyle. 'When you find those bodies I shall be beside you. It is my right. He is my brother. He has been murdered, and I can tell you who murdered him. That woman murdered him.'

'She first ruined his life, and now she has killed him. For the last five years she has been plotting to make herself his wife, and last night, when he told her he had discovered the truth about the Russian, and that she would never see him again, she flew into a passion and stabbed him, and then in terror of the gallows, killed herself. She murdered him, I tell you, and I promise you that we will find the knife she used near her—perhaps still in her hand. What will you say to that?'

"Lyle turned his head away and stared down at the floor. 'I might say,' he answered, 'that you placed it there.'

"Arthur gave a cry of anger and sprang at him, and then pitched forward into his arms. The blood was running from the cut under the bandage, and he had fainted. Lyle carried him back to the bed again, and we left him with the police and the doctors, and drove at once to the address he had given us. We found the house not three minutes' walk from St. George's Hospital. It stands in Trevor Terrace, that little row of houses set back from Knightsbridge, with one end in Hill Street.

"As we left the hospital, Lyle had said to me, 'You must not blame me for treating him as I did. All is fair in this work, and if by angering that boy I could have made him commit himself, I was right in trying to do so; though, I assure you, no one would be better pleased than myself if I could prove his theory to be correct. But we cannot tell. Everything depends upon what we see for ourselves within the next few minutes.'

"When we reached the house, Lyle broke open the fastenings of one of the windows on the ground-floor, and, hidden by the trees in the garden, we scrambled in. We found ourselves in the reception-room, which was the first room on the right of the hall. The gas was still burning behind the colored glass and red, silk shades, and when the daylight streamed in after us it gave the hall a hideously dissipated look, like the foyer of a theatre at a matinee, or the entrance to an all-day gambling-hall. The house was oppressively silent, and, because we knew why it was so silent, we spoke in whispers. When Lyle turned the handle of the drawing-room door, I felt as though someone had put his hand upon my throat. But I followed, close at his shoulder, and saw,

in the subdued light of many-tinted lamps, the body of
Chetney at the foot of the divan, just as Lieutenant Sears
had described it. In the drawing-room we found the body of
the Princess Zichy, her arms thrown out, and the blood from
her heart frozen in a tiny line across her bare shoulder. But
neither of us, although we searched the floor on our hands
and knees, could find the weapon which had killed her.

"'For Arthur's sake,' I said, 'I would have given a
thousand pounds if we had found the knife in her hand, as
he said we would.'

"'That we have not found it there,' Lyle answered, 'is to
my mind the strongest proof that he is telling the truth, that
he left the house before the murder took place. He is not a
fool, and had he stabbed his brother and this woman, he
would have seen that by placing the knife near her he could
help to make it appear as if she had killed Chetney and then
committed suicide. Besides, Lord Arthur insisted that the
evidence in his behalf would be our finding the knife here.
He would not have urged that if he knew we would NOT
find it, if he knew he himself had carried it away. This is no
suicide. A suicide does not rise and hide the weapon with
which he kills himself, and then lie down again. No, this
has been a double murder, and we must look outside of the
house for the murderer.'

"While he was speaking, Lyle and I had been searching
every corner, studying the details of each room. I was so

afraid that, without telling me, he would make some deductions prejudicial to Arthur, that I never left his side. I was determined to see everything that he saw, and, if possible, to prevent his interpreting it in the wrong way. He finally finished his examination, and we sat down together in the drawing-room, and he took out his note-book and read aloud all that Mr. Sears had told him of the murder and what we had just learned from Arthur. We compared the two accounts, word for word, and weighed statement with statement, but I could not determine, from anything Lyle said, which of the two versions he had decided to believe.

"'We are trying to build a house of blocks,' he exclaimed, 'with half of the blocks missing. We have been considering two theories,' he went on: 'one that Lord Arthur is responsible for both murders, and the other that the dead woman in there is responsible for one of them, and has committed suicide; but, until the Russian servant is ready to talk, I shall refuse to believe in the guilt of either.'

"'What can you prove by him?' I asked. 'He was drunk and asleep. He saw nothing.'

"Lyle hesitated, and then, as though he had made up his mind to be quite frank with me, spoke freely.

"'I do not know that he was either drunk or asleep,' he answered. 'Lieutenant Sears describes him as a stupid boor. I am not satisfied that he is not a clever actor. What was his position in this house? What was his real duty here? Suppose it was not to guard this woman, but to watch her. Let us imagine that it was not the woman he served, but a master, and see where that leads us. For this house has a master, a mysterious, absentee landlord, who lives in St. Petersburg, the unknown Russian who came between Chetney and Zichy, and because of whom Chetney left her. He is the man who bought this house for Madame Zichy, who sent these rugs and curtains from St. Petersburg to furnish it for her after his own tastes, and, I believe, it was he also who placed the Russian servant here, ostensibly to serve the Princess, but in reality to spy upon her. At Scotland Yard we do not know who this gentleman is; the Russian police confess to equal ignorance concerning him. When Lord Chetney went to Africa, Madame Zichy lived in St. Petersburg; but there her receptions and dinners were so crowded with members of the nobility and of the army and diplomats, that, among so many visitors, the police could not learn which was the one for whom she most greatly cared.'

"Lyle pointed at the modern French paintings and the heavy, silk rugs which hung upon the walls.

"'The unknown is a man of taste and of some fortune,' he said, 'not the sort of man to send a stupid peasant to guard the woman he loves. So I am not content to believe, with Mr. Sears, that the servant is a boor. I believe him, instead, to be a very clever ruffian. I believe him to be the protector of his master's honor, or, let us say, of his master's property, whether that property be silver plate or the woman his master loves. Last night, after Lord Arthur had gone away, the servant was left alone in this house with Lord Chetney and Madame Zichy. From where he sat in the hall, he could hear Lord Chetney bidding her farewell; for, if my idea of him is correct, he understands English quite as well as you or I. Let us imagine that he heard her entreating Chetney not to leave her, reminding him of his former wish to marry her, and let us suppose that he hears Chetney denounce her, and tell her that at Cairo he has learned of this Russian admirer—the servant's master. He hears the woman declare that she has had no admirer but himself, that this unknown Russian was, and is, nothing to her, that there is no man she loves but him, and that she cannot live, knowing that he is alive, without his love. Suppose Chetney believed her, suppose his former infatuation for her returned, and that, in a moment of weakness, he forgave her and took her in his arms. That is the moment the Russian master has feared. It is to guard against it that he has placed his watch-dog over the Princess, and how do we know but that, when the moment came, the watch-dog served his master, as he saw his duty, and killed them both? What do you think?' Lyle demanded. 'Would not that explain both murders?'

"I was only too willing to hear any theory which pointed to anyone else as the criminal than Arthur, but Lyle's explanation was too utterly fantastic. I told him that he certainly showed imagination, but that he could not hang a man for what he imagined he had done.

"'No,' Lyle answered, 'but I can frighten him by telling him what I think he has done, and now when I again question the Russian servant I will make it quite clear to him that I believe he is the murderer. I think that will open his mouth. A man will at least talk to defend himself. Come,' he said, 'we must return at once to Scotland Yard and see him. There is nothing more to do here.'

"He arose, and I followed him into the hall, and in another minute we would have been on our way to Scotland Yard. But just as he opened the street-door a postman halted at the gate of the garden, and began fumbling with the latch.

"Lyle stopped, with an exclamation of chagrin.

"'How stupid of me!' he exclaimed. He turned quickly and pointed to a narrow slit cut in the brass plate of the front door. 'The house has a private letter-box,' he said, 'and I had not thought to look in it! If we had gone out as we came in, by the window, I would never have seen it. The moment I entered the house I should have thought of securing the letters which came this morning. I have been grossly careless.' He stepped back into the hall and pulled at the lid of the letter-box, which hung on the inside of the door, but it was tightly locked. At the same moment the postman came up the steps holding a letter. Without a word, Lyle took it from his hand and began to examine it. It was addressed to the Princess Zichy, and on the back of the envelope was the name of a West End dressmaker.

"'That is of no use to me,' Lyle said. He took out his card and showed it to the postman. 'I am Inspector Lyle from Scotland Yard,' he said. 'The people in this house are under arrest. Everything it contains is now in my keeping. Did you deliver any other letters here this morning?'

"The man looked frightened, but answered, promptly, that he was now upon his third round. He had made one postal delivery at seven that morning and another at eleven.

"'How many letters did you leave here?' Lyle asked.

"'About six altogether,' the man answered.

"'Did you put them through the door into the letter-box?'

"The postman said, 'Yes, I always slip them into the box, and ring and go away. The servants collect them from the inside.'

"'Have you noticed if any of the letters you leave here bear a Russian postage-stamp?' Lyle asked.

"'The man answered, 'Oh, yes, sir, a great many.'

"'From the same person, would you say?'

"'The writing seems to be the same,' the man answered. 'They come regularly about once a week—one of those I delivered this morning had a Russian postmark.'

"'That will do,' said Lyle, eagerly. 'Thank you, thank you very much.'

"He ran back into the hall, and, pulling out his penknife, began to pick at the lock of the letter-box.

"'I have been supremely careless,' he said, in great excitement. 'Twice before when people I wanted had flown from a house I have been able to follow them by putting a guard over their mailbox. These letters, which arrive regularly every week from Russia in the same handwriting, they can come but from one person. At least, we shall now know the name of the master of this house. Undoubtedly, it is one of his letters that the man placed here this morning. We may make a most important discovery.'

"As he was talking he was picking at the lock with his knife, but he was so impatient to reach the letters that he pressed too heavily on the blade and it broke in his hand. I took a step backward and drove my heel into the lock, and burst it open. The lid flew back, and we pressed forward, and each ran his hand down into the letter-box. For a moment we were both too startled to move. The box was empty.

"I do not know how long we stood, staring stupidly at each other, but it was Lyle who was the first to recover. He seized me by the arm and pointed excitedly into the empty box.

"'Do you appreciate what that means?' he cried. 'It means that someone has been here ahead of us. Someone

290

has entered this house not three hours before we came, since eleven o'clock this morning.'

"'It was the Russian servant!' I exclaimed.

"'The Russian servant has been under arrest at Scotland Yard,' Lyle cried. 'He could not have taken the letters. Lord Arthur has been in his cot at the hospital. That is his alibi. There is someone else, someone we do not suspect. and that someone is the murderer. He came back here either to obtain those letters because he knew they would convict him, or to remove something he had left here at the time of the murder, something incriminating—the weapon, perhaps, or some personal article; a cigarette-case, a handkerchief with his name upon it, or a pair of gloves. Whatever it was, it must have been damning evidence against him to have made him take so desperate a chance.'

"'How do we know,' I whispered, 'that he is not hidden here now?'

"'No, I'll swear he is not,' Lyle answered. 'I may have bungled in some things, but I have searched this house thoroughly. Nevertheless,' he added, 'we must go over it again, from the cellar to the roof. We have the real clew now, and we must forget the others and work only it.' As he spoke he began again to search the drawing- room, turning over even the books on the tables and the music on the piano.

"'Whoever the man is,' he said, over his shoulder, 'we know that he has a key to the front door and a key to the letter-box. That shows us he is either an inmate of the house or that he comes here when he wishes. The Russian says that he was the only servant in the house. Certainly, we have found no evidence to show that any other servant slept here. There could be but one other person who would possess a key to the house and the letter-box—and he lives in St. Petersburg. At the time of the murder he was two thousand miles away.' Lyle interrupted himself, suddenly, with a sharp cry, and turned upon me, with his eyes flashing. 'But was he?' he cried. 'Was he? How do we know that last night he was not in London, in this very house when Zichy and Chetney met?'

"He stood, staring at me without seeing me, muttering, and arguing with himself.

"'Don't speak to me,' he cried, as I ventured to interrupt him. 'I can see it now. It is all plain. It was not the servant, but his master, the Russian himself, and it was he who came back for the letters! He came back for them because he knew they would convict him. We must find them. We must have those letters. If we find the one with the Russian postmark, we shall have found the murderer.' He spoke like a madman, and as he spoke he ran around the room, with one hand held out in front of him as you have seen a mind-reader at a theatre seeking for something hidden in the stalls. He pulled the old letters from the writing-desk, and ran them over as swiftly as a gambler deals out cards; he dropped on his knees before the fireplace and dragged out the dead coals with his bare fingers, and then, with a low, worried cry, like a hound on a scent, he ran back to the waste-paper basket and, lifting the papers from it, shook them out upon the floor. Instantly, he gave a shout of triumph, and, separating a number of torn pieces from the others, held them up before me.

"'Look!' he cried. 'Do you see? Here are five letters, torn across in two places. The Russian did not stop to read them, for, as you see, he has left them still sealed. I have been wrong. He did not return for the letters. He could not have known their value. He must have returned for some other reason, and, as he was leaving, saw the letter-box, and, taking out the letters, held them together—so—and tore them twice across, and then, as the fire had gone out, tossed them into this basket. Look!' he cried, 'here in the upper corner of this piece is a Russian stamp. This is his own letter—unopened!'

"We examined the Russian stamp and found it had been cancelled in St. Petersburg four days ago. The back of the envelope bore the postmark of the branch-station in upper Sloane Street, and was dated this morning. The envelope was of official, blue paper, and we had no difficulty in finding the other two parts of it. We drew the torn pieces of the letter from them and joined them together, side by side. There were but two lines of writing, and this was the message: 'I leave Petersburg on the night-train, and I shall see you at Trevor Terrace, after dinner, Monday evening.'

"'That was last night!' Lyle cried. 'He arrived twelve hours ahead of his letter—but it came in time—it came in time to hang him!'"

The Baronet struck the table with his hand.

"The name!" he demanded. "How was it signed? What was the man's name?"

The young Solicitor rose to his feet and, leaning forward, stretched out his arm. "There was no name," he cried. "The letter was signed with only two initials. But engraved at the top of the sheet was the man's address. That address was 'THE AMERICAN EMBASSY, ST. PETERSBURG, BUREAU OF THE NAVAL ATTACHE,' and the initials," he shouted, his voice rising into an exultant and bitter cry, "were those of the gentleman who sits opposite who told us that he was the first to find the murdered bodies, the Naval Attache to Russia, Lieutenant Sears!"

A strained and awful hush followed the Solicitor's words, which seemed to vibrate like a twanging bowstring that had just hurled its bolt. Sir Andrew, pale and staring, drew away, with an exclamation of repulsion. His eyes were fastened upon the Naval Attache with fascinated horror. But the American emitted a sigh of great content, and sank, comfortably, into the arms of his chair. He clapped his hands, softly, together.

"Capital!" he murmured. "I give you my word I never guessed what you were driving at. You fooled ME, I'll be hanged if you didn't—you certainly fooled me."

The man with the pearl stud leaned forward, with a nervous gesture. "Hush! be careful!" he whispered. But at that instant, for the third time, a servant, hastening through the room, handed him a piece of paper which he scanned eagerly. The message on the paper read, "The light over the Commons is out. The House has risen."

The man with the black pearl gave a mighty shout, and tossed the paper from him upon the table.

"Hurrah!" he cried. "The House is up! We've won!" He caught up his glass, and slapped the Naval Attache, violently, upon the shoulder. He nodded joyously at him, at the Solicitor, and at the Queen's Messenger. "Gentlemen, to you!" he cried; "my thanks and my congratulations!" He drank deep from the glass, and breathed forth a long sigh of satisfaction and relief.

"But I say," protested the Queen's Messenger, shaking his finger, violently, at the Solicitor, "that story won't do. You didn't play fair—and—and you talked so fast I couldn't make out what it was all about. I'll bet you that evidence wouldn't hold in a court of law— you couldn't hang a cat on such evidence. Your story is condemned tommy-rot. Now, my story might have happened, my story bore the mark- -"

In the joy of creation, the story-tellers had forgotten their audience, until a sudden exclamation from Sir Andrew caused them to turn, guiltily, toward him. His face was knit with lines of anger, doubt, and amazement.

"What does this mean?" he cried. "Is this a jest, or are you mad? If you know this man is a murderer, why is he at large? Is this a game you have been playing? Explain yourselves at once. What does it mean?"

The American, with first a glance at the others, rose and bowed, courteously.

"I am not a murderer, Sir Andrew, believe me," he said; "you need not be alarmed. As a matter of fact, at this moment I am much more afraid of you than you could possibly be of me. I beg you, please to be indulgent. I assure you, we meant no disrespect. We have been matching stories, that is all, pretending that we are people we are not, endeavoring to entertain you with better detective-tales than, for instance, the last one you read, 'The Great Rand Robbery.'"

The Baronet brushed his hand, nervously, across his forehead.

"Do you mean to tell me," he exclaimed, "that none of this has happened? That Lord Chetney is not dead, that his Solicitor did not find a letter of yours, written from your post in Petersburg, and that just now, when he charged you with murder, he was in jest?"

"I am really very sorry," said the American, "but you see, sir, he could not have found a letter written by me in St. Petersburg because I have never been in Petersburg. Until this week, I have never been outside of my own country. I am not a naval officer. I am a writer of short stories. And to-night, when this gentleman told me that you were fond of detective-stories, I thought it would be amusing to tell you one of my own—one I had just mapped out this afternoon."

"But Lord Chetney IS a real person," interrupted the Baronet, "and he did go to Africa two years ago, and he was supposed to have died there, and his brother, Lord Arthur, has been the heir. And yesterday Chetney did return. I read it in the papers."

"So did I," assented the American, soothingly; "and it struck me as being a very good plot for a story. I mean his unexpected return from the dead, and the probable disappointment of the younger brother. So I decided that the younger brother had better murder the older one. The Princess Zichy I invented out of a clear sky. The fog I did not have to invent. Since last night I know all that there is to know about a London fog. I was lost in one for three hours."

The Baronet turned, grimly, upon the Queen's Messenger.

"But this gentleman," he protested, "he is not a writer of short stories; he is a member of the Foreign Office. I have often seen him in Whitehall, and, according to him, the Princess Zichy is not an invention. He says she is very well known, that she tried to rob him."

The servant of the Foreign Office looked, unhappily, at the Cabinet Minister, and puffed, nervously, on his cigar.

"It's true, Sir Andrew, that I am a Queen's Messenger," he said, appealingly, "and a Russian woman once did try to rob a Queen's Messenger in a railway carriage—only it did not happen to me, but to a pal of mine. The only Russian princess I ever knew called herself Zabrisky. You may have seen her. She used to do a dive from the roof of the Aquarium."

Sir Andrew, with a snort of indignation, fronted the young Solicitor.

"And I suppose yours was a cock-and-bull story, too," he said. "Of course, it must have been, since Lord Chetney is not dead. But don't tell me," he protested, "that you are not Chudleigh's son either."

"I'm sorry," said the youngest member, smiling, in some embarrassment, "but my name is not Chudleigh. I assure you, though, that I know the family very well, and that I am on very good terms with them."

"You should be!" exclaimed the Baronet; "and, judging from the liberties you take with the Chetneys, you had better be on very good terms with them, too."

The young man leaned back and glanced toward the servants at the far end of the room.

"It has been so long since I have been in the Club," he said, "that I doubt if even the waiters remember me. Perhaps Joseph may," he added. "Joseph!" he called, and at the word a servant stepped briskly forward.

The young man pointed to the stuffed head of a great lion which was suspended above the fireplace.

"Joseph," he said, "I want you to tell these gentlemen who shot that lion. Who presented it to the Grill?"

Joseph, unused to acting as master of ceremonies to members of the Club, shifted, nervously, from one foot to the other.

"Why, you—you did," he stammered.

"Of course I did!" exclaimed the young man. "I mean, what is the name of the man who shot it? Tell the gentlemen who I am. They wouldn't believe me."

"Who you are, my lord?" said Joseph. "You are Lord Edam's son, the Earl of Chetney."

"You must admit," said Lord Chetney, when the noise had died away, "that I couldn't remain dead while my little brother was accused of murder. I had to do something. Family pride demanded it. Now, Arthur, as the younger brother, can't afford to be squeamish, but, personally, I should hate to have a brother of mine hanged for murder."

"You certainly showed no scruples against hanging me," said the American, "but, in the face of your evidence, I admit my guilt, and I sentence myself to pay the full penalty of the law as we are made to pay it in my own country. The order of this court is," he announced, "that Joseph shall bring me a wine-card, and that I sign it for five bottles of the Club's best champagne."

"Oh, no!" protested the man with the pearl stud, "it is not for YOU to sign it. In my opinion, it is Sir Andrew who should pay the costs. It is time you knew," he said, turning to that gentleman, "that, unconsciously, you have been the victim of what I may call a patriotic conspiracy. These stories have had a more serious purpose than merely to amuse. They have been told with the worthy object of detaining you from the House of Commons. I must explain to you that, all through this evening, I have had a servant waiting in Trafalgar Square with instructions to bring me word as soon as the light over the House of Commons had ceased to burn. The light is now out, and the object for which we plotted is attained."

The Baronet glanced, keenly, at the man with the black pearl, and then, quickly, at his watch. The smile disappeared from his lips, and his face was set in stern and forbidding lines.

"And may I know," he asked, icily, "what was the object of your plot?"

"A most worthy one," the other retorted. "Our object was to keep you from advocating the expenditure of many millions of the people's money upon more battle-ships. In a word, we have been working together to prevent you from passing the Navy Increase Bill."

Sir Andrew's face bloomed with brilliant color. His body shook with suppressed emotion.

"My dear sir!" he cried, "you should spend more time at the House and less at your Club. The Navy Bill was brought up on its third reading at eight o'clock this evening. I spoke for three hours in its favor. My only reason for wishing to return again to the House to-night was to sup on the terrace with my old friend, Admiral Simons; for my work at the House was completed five hours ago, when the Navy Increase Bill was passed by an overwhelming majority."

The Baronet rose and bowed. "I have to thank you, sir," he said, "for a most interesting evening."

The American shoved the wine-card which Joseph had given him toward the gentleman with the black pearl.

"You sign it," he said.

www.ingramcontent.com/pod-product-compliance
Lightning Source LLC
Chambersburg PA
CBHW020432030726
47495CB00006B/1767